BRIDGE DAUGHTER

JIM NELSON

This is a work of fiction. Any similarity between the characters and situations within its pages and places or persons, living or dead, is unintentional and coincidental.

ISBN 1533006598
ISBN-13 978-1533006592

Nariko

So wise so young they say,
do never live long

ONE

ON THE MORNING of her thirteenth birthday, Hanna Driscoll decided it was time to learn if she was a woman.

She eased out of bed and tiptoed to her bedroom door. She gingerly opened it to avoid making it creak. The house was silent, no noise from the kitchen, meaning her parents were still in bed. She closed the door as gingerly as she had cracked it open. Time to move quickly now.

Hanna swept an arm between the bed's mattress and box spring. She located by feel a slender pink cardboard box. Then she tiptoed across the carpeted hallway to the bathroom, box in hand. There she peed, feeling a bit queasy. The room tilted as she sat on the toilet, then righted itself. She washed her face and drank warm water, which she'd learned helped reduce the sick feeling in her head and stomach. She drank more, then gargled out the remaining sticky saltiness in her mouth. She returned to her room with the pink cardboard box and softly closed the door once more, checking that it was latched.

A stack of books stood on Hanna's bed stand, along with a squat reading lamp and a lavender alarm clock. All of the books regarded flowers and floristry and flower arranging. Her bookshelf held more books on the subject, as well as a dictionary and a children's encyclopedia set, along with other books her mother assigned in her homeschooling. One of her books was not on the bed stand or the shelf. She'd stashed it between the mattress and the box spring, the same place she'd hidden the slender pink cardboard box.

It was a children's book. Rather, it was a book written for children but stocked in the bookstore's Parenting section: *Mother & Baby* by Margaret Millard, M.D., Ph.D.

Mother & Baby was below Hanna's reading level, written in simple language and illustrated with chalk-colored drawings of a family similar to Hanna's own. The book's family had a five-year-old son, whereas Hanna was the only daughter. And the pregnant mother was Hanna's mother's age, not thirteen years old, like Hanna's friends Alondra and Cheryl. This did not concern Hanna, who knew girls of all ages could become pregnant, thirteen and up.

Mother & Baby had enlightened Hanna on many points of reproduction, as Hanna's parents had not discussed sex with her at all, either informally or in their homeschooling. Yes, *Mother & Baby* confirmed, a man is necessary to make a woman pregnant. Men possessed different equipment for that very reason. With each page showing the mother's tummy growing, a calendar in the bottom corner counted the advancing weeks. Six months after conception, the mother gave birth to a baby girl.

During the pregnancy, the father and son helped out around the house as best they could, especially later, when the mother's belly was engorged. The father's and son's attempts were inevitably comedic, such as when they burned dinner, or when they couldn't figure out how to operate the washing machine. The mother, practically bursting out of her maternity dress in the fifth month of pregnancy, had to show them which buttons to press. Then they all laughed.

In between these family moments, Hanna gleaned the information of the most concern to her. For one, the mother in the book stopped menstruating when she conceived. Hanna knew something about menstruation. Her mother subscribed to a number of women's magazines. Hanna would steal peeks at their columns and articles, curious what lay ahead for her in womanhood. She gleaned that most girls began menstruating at age eleven or twelve. Hanna was almost thirteen—no, she *was* thirteen, as of that morning—and, be it God or Nature, she was not menstruating.

The book was also clear that pregnancy started with lying in bed with a man. Whatever procedure the father and mother actually performed in bed, she was positive she'd not done it. She'd not even held a boy's hand. How could she, with her parents hovering over her every moment?

If she wasn't pregnant, how then could she explain the queasiness every morning? At that moment, looking through the children's book, the thick, salty taste had returned to her mouth, even though she'd gargled it out minutes earlier. Worse, she recently started growing hot and flushed at odd times of the day. Sometimes her stomach tied itself in a knot and she would lose her appetite, even if she had been famished minutes earlier. At that moment, re-reading *Mother & Baby* for the *n*th time, she lacked any hunger pangs, even though she'd eaten only a dollop of casserole the night before. The thought of orange juice for breakfast made her slightly ill. Lately, orange juice tasted like sour milk.

In *Mother & Baby*, the mother had a husband. So how did Hanna's friend Alondra get pregnant? She was thirteen when she began showing. Or her friend Cheryl Vannberg, who was about to turn fourteen and so big she looked as if the baby might pop out at any moment? Neither had a husband, not even a boyfriend—unless they were keeping secrets.

Hanna set aside *Mother & Baby*. Did she want to have a baby? People seemed to think having a baby was a gift. Hanna watched adults shower their affection and support on Cheryl when she became pregnant, but Hanna didn't crave those things. When she thought about growing up, she thought of college and studying flowers and maybe even becoming a scientist. She never saw a baby in her future. But pregnancy would explain so much, such as why she wasn't menstruating yet.

Inside the pink cardboard box was an instruction sheet folded in a tight paper wad. It said to urinate on the stick and wait ten minutes. Hanna had peed on the stick in the bathroom, but now the ten minutes were taking an eternity. The possibilities had consumed her for weeks, a dozen medical reasons she imagined for not menstruating, and her curiosity grew excruciating as she waited for the test results.

She'd stolen the kit from the pharmacy where her mother picked up prescriptions and analgesics. Hanna was not the sort of girl to shoplift, but she saw no other option. She couldn't imagine asking her mother for help on this matter. Her mother turned off the television when the late-night comedians began using bawdy language and double entendres. Why would she give a straight answer to Hanna's questions, let alone purchase a pregnancy test for her?

The instructions said much more than to urinate on the stick and wait. Hanna found the finely printed sheet numbingly detailed and lawyerly about each step of the process. She was to unwrap the tube with care and to avoid touching the felt stick protruding from its end. If she touched the felt stick, she was to discard the tainted test and wash her hands thoroughly in warm soapy water to remove the chemicals from her skin. When she urinated, she was to let the initial liquid flow, then dip the felt stick into the stream, to prevent contamination. The instructions also included a long list of drugs and medications that, if consumed forty-eight hours prior to administering the test, would corrupt the results. Hanna even held her breath while peeing on the stick, worried bacteria in her mouth might somehow affect the chemicals soaked into the felt strip. The process seemed so complicated and the question so simple, she wondered if she could expect to receive a straight answer at all.

Hanna's appetite returned, and she looked forward to eating.

The ten minutes were not quite up, but the tube's window was already displaying colored lines. Hanna searched the instruction sheet to decode the results. One red line on the right indicated a negative result, no pregnancy. One purple line on the left indicated a positive result. Hanna held the plastic tube under the bed stand light for an accurate look.

Twin purple lines were distinctly visible across the white felt stick. One line on the right, one on the left. Purple lines, positive.

She checked the instruction sheet once again. It said one line, not two. But they were purple, so yes, she was pregnant? She reread the "Test Results" section, careful to consider each step and warning. Nothing seemed amiss.

Then she spotted something she'd previously overlooked, a faint asterisk no larger than a pinhead. Hanna's eyes dropped to the bottom of the sheet:

> *Two purple lines indicate pons viviparous*
> *hemotrophism. Contact your legal guardian or*
> *medical professional.*

Pons viviparous hemotrophism sounded like a rare disease: incurable, perhaps painful, most likely fatal. She went to the slender bookcase on the opposite wall of her bedroom and took down her dictionary, one compiled for grade schoolers. It offered no definition for *viviparous*, but Hanna wondered if the word *vivid* was related. *Hemotrophism* was also missing, but Hanna took some comfort from the entry for *hemo–*, defined as "of or relating to blood." For *pons,* she found nothing.

She waited five more minutes, hoping one of the lines would fade off and the other would color-shift to red. The twin purple pillars remained fast. Perhaps this was the good news she craved. The test might indicate her first menstruation was on its way. That would explain the lightheaded queasiness, she told herself, the sticky saltiness in her mouth every morning, and her random lack of appetite. Her period might even arrive today, her thirteenth birthday, a trumpet fanfare of her first step toward womanhood.

The illustration on the last page of *Mother & Baby* depicted the mother lying in a hospital bed cradling her newborn girl. Around the bed stood her husband and son and a gray-haired doctor holding a stethoscope. Printed at the bottom of the page in cursive script:

> *With their beautiful bridge daughter now a part*
> *of their family, Sam & Laurie & Timmy have*
> *years of joy to look forward to until the finality.*

The back cover advised the reader to purchase the next book in the series, *Mother & Bridge Daughter*.

Hanna, relieved and delighted, returned the plastic tube to its cardboard box. She slipped it and the book back under the mattress. Before this morning, she'd planned to ask her mother for a trip to the bookstore so she could secretly search for *Mother & Bridge Daughter*. Now with the gift of the matching purple lines—*vivid blood* on the way—she happily told herself she did not need it, that she had all the answers she wanted. She went to her closet and dressed, eager to sit down to her mother's Saturday morning pancake breakfast, only to discover she'd lost her appetite once again.

TWO

AFTER BREAKFAST, Hanna and her mother drove to a downtown family-run bakery that specialized in decorated sheet cakes. Inside, rows of iced cakes stood under glass like exquisitely wrapped gifts waiting to be opened. The bakery made their own doughnuts too. Their fried richness, mixed with the aroma of chocolate and vanilla, made the bakery heavenly for Hanna, now finally hungry.

Some customers eyed the cake and bread displays. Others stood off to the side with numbered tickets, waiting to be called to the order window. Hanna's mother tugged one free from the ticket dispenser. The electronic wall display read *46*, but her ticket read *60*. She retreated to the rear standing counters where customers ate and sipped coffee, Hanna close behind her.

"We should have come earlier," her mother said. "We hit the lunch rush." The bakery also sold soup and made-to-order sandwiches.

Hanna stood close to her mother, back upright and her chin level with the ground. She kept her hands at the small of her back and her ankles together. Her public posture was as her mother had taught her since she was young. The other girls here wandered freely about the store and talked among themselves or with the boys. A few pressed their faces to the display glass to ogle the racks of cupcakes organized by color, a tempting sugary rainbow. Hanna remained mute and upright behind her mother, as she'd been raised.

Then Hanna noticed Cheryl Vannberg on the other side of the bakery. Cheryl was thirteen, Hanna's age. Like Hanna, Cheryl stood behind her mother, back erect and chin level, her posture even more exemplary than Hanna's own. Cheryl's thick blond hair cascaded in waves down past her shoulders. She always wore clothes Hanna never saw other girls their age wear: designer blouses and brand-name tops, skirts that flared at the knees, and dresses with jazzy or delicate prints. At the bakery, Cheryl wore a dark blue maternity dress hemmed just above her knees with satin embroidery along the neckline. Cheryl's belly made the dress bulge. Cheryl rested her hands on top of the bulge, occasionally massaging it while her mother transacted business at the counter.

Hanna knew why everyone thought Cheryl was so charming. Be it God or Nature, Cheryl enjoyed the gift of a dainty, exquisite face and high-boned, sun-kissed cheeks. Her mother allowed Cheryl to use lip-gloss and eyeliner, and they often went together to department stores for makeovers. In the center of Cheryl's face was a perfectly proportioned nose that danced like a bee when she laughed. Her smile revealed smooth, straight teeth, and Cheryl always smiled. Both were thirteen, but it felt like Cheryl was twenty-one and glamorous and on the covers of magazines.

Although Hanna didn't go to school, every weekday, Hanna's mother taught her math and reading and penmanship at the kitchen table. Cheryl was similarly excused from school, but she and her mother took day trips to the department stores in Union Square and spent weekends at Napa Valley spas and boutiques. Cheryl had been to Disneyland three times, whereas Hanna had only seen the park on television. It was all just so unfair.

Hanna chanced to peer down at herself. A plain brown sweater balding at the elbows. A pair of blue jeans she'd worn since she was eleven. Sneakers curled at the toes, thanks to runs through the dryer after rainy days. Plain clipped fingernails; nothing as elegant as Cheryl's nails, all ten of them manicured and polished turquoise to accent her blond mane. Even Hanna's mousy auburn hair made her self-conscious. Hanna's father still took her to his barber, an elderly man named Ray who stocked men's magazines in the waiting area and knew only one cut for girls.

"Did you get my invitation?" Cheryl said, face glowing. "We mailed them on Monday."

Hanna, lost in thought, did not notice Cheryl's approach until she was before her. "I don't know," Hanna said softly.

"I'm sure you'll receive it soon," Cheryl said. "We're having a bridge party!"

"I don't know how to play bridge," Hanna said, still gathering herself.

Hanna's mother was not particularly tall, but she stood over the two thirteen year olds like a totem pole. "I received your mother's invitation yesterday," Hanna's mother said to Cheryl. "I don't believe Hanna will be able to attend."

"It's not a *bridge* party," Cheryl said to Hanna. She laughed imperiously, her petite nose dancing. "We're not playing *cards*."

"I know what a bridge party is," Hanna's mother said. "Hanna will not be able to make it. Thank you for the invitation. Say hello to your mother for me."

"All right," Cheryl said, shrugging. She rejoined her mother on the other side of the bakery and said something to her. They exited smiling and shaking their heads.

When they were gone, Hanna asked, "Why didn't you tell me?"

"You're not going to their little...*bridge* party."

"Why not?" Hanna said.

Hanna's mother turned her back to Hanna. She peered up at the electronic display over the cash register. It read *58*, meaning their number would be called soon.

"Does Cheryl have a boyfriend?" Hanna asked softly. Her

mother appeared not to hear her, or else was ignoring the question.

"I want to go to Cheryl's bridge party," Hanna said firmly under her breath.

Hanna's mother twisted her neck to peer down at Hanna behind her. "Do you know what a bridge party is for?"

"Yes," Hanna lied.

Hanna's mother studied Hanna's face, trying to read her. Finally, she looked straight ahead. "Let me think about it." Their number was called.

Hanna had a vague idea about bridge parties. She'd heard the term many times. She knew it didn't involve cards; that was a nervous slip on her part. She also knew a bridge party was for adults and not children. In particular, it was not for the bridge daughter, at least in the sense that the bridge daughter did not participate in it.

Family television shows often featured episodes about bridge parties. Hanna never understood the fuss. The bridge daughter would sit off to the side staring into the camera, pregnant and mute, as she always did in these TV shows. Family and neighbors arrived at the house with food, flowers, and wine. Every so often, the bridge daughter would rise from her isolated chair and go about the party gathering dirty plates and discarded wrapping paper. If the party went late, the bridge daughter would be sent to her bedroom while the revelry continued.

Often in these television shows, some major dramatic moment would occur. The family doctor, Scotch-and-soda in hand, would let slip he'd diagnosed the father with cancer. Or the eldest sister would announce she'd been accepted to a prestigious university like Harvard or Stanford. The bridge daughter never spoke, of course. On television, everything important happened to other people, never the bridge daughter.

Hanna never quite understood why they were called "bridge parties." The bridge daughter had little to do in these TV shows.

She stood to one side while the rest of the family went through their weekly crises and upheavals. The bridge daughter served dinner and cleaned the house and answered the door when the bell rang. On shows set in the costumed past, she darned socks and tended the sheep pen and threw logs on the fire when the flames drew low. Even that afternoon at the bakery, a few bridge daughters were helping their mothers with the day's errands. Mute and deferential, clad in neutral-color dresses and soft-soled shoes, they were easily overlooked, but not by Hanna.

On the drive home, Hanna asked her mother, "Is Cheryl a bridge daughter?"

Hanna's mother considered her answer. "Bridge daughters are supposed to stay home and take care of the family, not get their hair done and go to Napa for spa weekends."

"Like Erica," Hanna said. Erica Grimond was the eldest daughter of the family across the street. They'd moved into the neighborhood a month earlier.

"That's right," her mother said. "Erica's a bridge daughter."

"Will she have a bridge party?" Hanna asked.

"I doubt the Grimonds will invite us to it," Hanna's mother said. "They're traditional people. They'll only invite their family."

Hanna thought some more. "Is that why you don't want me going to Cheryl's bridge party?" she asked. "Because we're not their family?"

They reached a stoplight. Hanna's mother set the car's left turn signal blinking, *click-click-click*. "What Cheryl Vannberg's mother is doing isn't right. It's not fair to Cheryl."

"But—"

"You are not going to the party," her mother said. "That's final."

Hanna pushed back in the seat, frustrated. She considered pleading. It had worked before. She had begged her way to attending Cheryl's extravagant birthday parties. She could try it again for her bridge party. Cheryl's parties were more spectacular than any of the humdrum birthday parties that Hanna's parents had arranged for her. They were worth the indignity.

One year, Cheryl's mother rented a pony. All the children got ride tickets in their goodie bags. The pony was saddled and muzzled and tethered to a metal pole. It walked a circular path of hay all afternoon with bouncy children on its back. Cheryl's mother had contacted the city for permission to put the pony ride in the street before their house, a quiet road that dead-ended half a block away.

When it was Hanna's turn, a man in black denim and a floppy cowboy hat lifted her by the armpits and set her in the saddle. Hanna wove her fingers into the pony's fine, soft mane, silky as down. She patted and rubbed the side of its neck. The pony demonstrated no appreciation of her caresses and merely plodded along its hay-lined track.

Hanna wondered how the cowboy treated the pony at the stable. Was it allowed to run free in a field or was it locked in a pen? Was this the only life it knew, muzzled and saddled and restricted by blinders? She suspected she could cut the tether and the pony would continue walking the monotonous circle, unaware it could bolt and be free.

After the ride, she dug out the remaining pony tickets from her goodie bag. She could trade them for more candy or bubble-gum-flavored lip-gloss. But those tickets meant more circles for the pony, so Hanna stuffed them to the bottom of her bag. No one could use them. She wished she could buy the entire roll of tickets and set the pony free, but Hanna knew the animal would merely sidle up to its owner and wait for the next command.

Hanna's mother pulled the car up the inclined driveway of their house. She would get the sheet cake from the trunk and Hanna would take the bags of groceries that were in the back seat.

Bags in hand, Hanna chanced to look across the street at the Grimond house. The Driscolls and the Grimonds lived in stock suburban one-stories with oval front yards and attached garages. Unlike the Driscolls' mauve exterior, the Grimond house was painted flat white with gray trim with a double-door entrance on their front stoop. Their first week of residence, Mr. Grimond installed oversized brass knockers on both of them, although Hanna had never seen anyone prefer them to the doorbell.

A wide picture window faced the street. When the drapes were open, as they were now, Hanna could see straight into the living room. As Hanna's eyes adjusted, she realized someone was standing in the picture window. Grocery bags in each hand, Hanna took one step down the driveway to get a better look, then took another. She wondered who of the Grimond family it may be. They had three children: twin sons and their bridge daughter Erica. Realizing it had to be one of the children, Hanna did her best to wave, the full bags weighing down her attempt.

Clock-clock-clock. The silhouette in the window rapped the glass three times.

Hanna took one more step down the driveway to the sidewalk. Head cocked, she tried to wave again, bags in each hand. She wondered if it was Erica. She'd never talked with her, or even met her. Erica seemed penned-up in the Grimonds' house all day, every day.

Clock-clock-clock, the silhouette knocked harder this time. The figure raised a shadowy open hand by way of greeting. Or beckoning.

Then, startled, the figure at the window wheeled about to face Mrs. Grimond, who was marching across the room. Now Hanna could identify the silhouette. It *was* Erica, the Grimonds' bridge daughter. Mrs. Grimond pulled Erica from the window, scolding her, although Hanna couldn't hear a word. Then Mrs. Grimond stared disapprovingly across the street at Hanna. With two sharp tugs of the curtain cord, she drew the drapes closed.

Hanna's mother called from the front door to hurry inside. Hanna shouted she was coming and waddled up the driveway, the grocery bags weighing her down with each unsteady step.

THREE

THE DOORBELL RANG at ten after twelve. Hanna yelled *I got it!* and rushed to the front door. Without hesitating, she flung it open and ran into the waiting arms of Uncle Rick.

"Hey, squirt," Uncle Rick said into her hair, hugging her back. His grin stretched his full auburn beard wide. "Happy birthday."

"Happy birthday," Aunt Azami said as well.

Hanna's mother appeared at the doorway in a half-apron with her hands buried in a kitchen towel. "Ritchie," she greeted Uncle Rick. She was the only one who could call him that. To Aunt Azami, she offered a "Hello."

Uncle Rick was wide and beefy, bearded and hairy-armed, a grinning teddy bear of a man. Aunt Azami was his physical opposite. Thin and composed of straight lines, with little womanly figure to speak of, Azami had fine dark hair cut evenly around her head. Her bangs framed the black rectangular glasses on her narrow face. Hanna thought her glasses were very, very cool. She wished she needed corrective lenses just so she could wear the same ones. Aunt Azami never wore makeup, which Hanna also secretly admired.

Uncle Rick presented Hanna with a scuffed-up plastic bucket. He gripped it the way a bricklayer would carry a bucket of grout.

"Let's see what I got this time." He considered the mismatched assortment of flowers standing in the bucket's water. "Freesia, white roses, a couple of sunflowers, daffs, some carnations—"

"Well, don't get any water on my floors," Hanna's mother warned.

Hanna couldn't believe the assortment he'd brought. The bucket was packed so tight the flowers seemed to be craning for air. It was like he brought her a starter's kit for a sidewalk florist shop. Her mind began formulating bouquets and arrangements she could assemble with this raw material.

"Tell you what," he said to Hanna, "this is dripping, so let's leave it here." He set the bucket on the porch beside the front door, in the shade.

"Thank you so much," Hanna said and hugged him again. She knelt before the bucket and began selecting the best of the lot for her first arrangement.

"What's going on, Dee?" Uncle Rick said to Hanna's mother. He leaned in and kissed her on the cheek. "Sorry we're late."

"Someone slept in," Aunt Azami said. Uncle Rick grinned sheepishly through his beard.

They followed Hanna's mother inside. Hanna took her time on the porch, choosing blossoms with an eye for color and shape. When she'd selected eight or nine of the best from the bucket, she joined them in the kitchen.

Uncle Rick already had a can of beer open. He stood off to the side and watched the women at work. Hanna's mother was at the sink, flattening and rounding meat patties for the hamburgers. Hanna's father was still at the hardware store. When he returned, he would light the backyard grill and cook them up.

Aunt Azami produced a wood bowl with a fastened lid from a muslin tote bag. She opened it to reveal a dark, leafy green salad with roasted sesame seeds and strange star-shaped vegetables with pinkish centers. She also produced from the tote a glass jar of loose tealeaves. "I thought we could make a pot after lunch."

"We have coffee," Hanna's mother said.

"Tea might be nice as well," Aunt Azami said.

"I don't have a kettle."

"I brought a tea ball. I can make it on the stove."

Hanna's mother, busy pressing patties, forced a small smile.

The tension wasn't thick, there was never anything vindictive between Azami and Hanna's mother, but the tension was present whenever they visited. Hanna so wished it could be mended, but she didn't even know what was broken. Her mother just seemed to dislike Aunt Azami, and Hanna couldn't fathom why.

Uncle Rick wandered into the adjacent room, where everyone would be eating soon. "Hey, Dee," he called through the doorway, "where'd you get these blooms?"

Uncle Rick was evaluating the vase of tulips Hanna's mother had placed on the dining room table. He rubbed their petals between his thumb and forefinger the way a tailor would evaluate a bolt of bargain polyester.

"Did you go to that shopping mall florist again?" he called to her.

"Don't start, Ritchie," Hanna's mother called back. "I like them."

"Bah," he said. "Greenhouse tu's picked early."

"I wouldn't have bought them if I thought you would bring me tulips," she called back. "But you never do."

"Greenhouse tu's, a fern sprig, a little dry gyp," he said, evaluating the bouquet's elements in the industry parlance Hanna so loved to hear.

Uncle Rick returned to the kitchen. "Tell you what," he confided to Hanna, pretending to be covert, "you put together your arrangement and we'll ditch this tulip crap. Deal?"

"Watch the language," Hanna's mother singsonged while smacking a patty.

From the bucket, Hanna had selected three brilliant red freesia, a white rose with an elegant petal display, and a clutch of carnations of varying pastels. She took the morning paper's auto section and spread it open on the kitchen table. She asked permission to use her mother's good scissors, which was refused, so she fetched the hand shears from the garage. While Uncle Rick and her mother verbally jabbed at each other, Hanna's deft little hands stripped the flowers' green leaves and snipped the stems so each was a different height; the carnations the shortest and the white rose the tallest. She cut the stems at a diagonal to maximize the amount of water they could draw in.

Then Hanna fetched from her room a slender ceramic vase and a bag of colored glass marbles. Her mother kept a box of powdered water conditioner under the kitchen sink. She filled the vase halfway with cold water, added two shakes of the powder, and swirled it until dissolved. Then she added marbles until there were three layers of them in the boot of the vase. She inserted the flowers one at a time, making the silken ivory rose the centerpiece and the surrounding colorful flowers its complement. So devoted to her work, she failed to notice the women had retired to the couches in the living room. Hanna's father was late.

"Perfect-o," Uncle Rick said behind her. He'd opened the highest cabinet in the kitchen, the small boxy one over the refrigerator. Standing on his tiptoes to reach in, he rooted around with one hand while the other gripped his can of beer.

"Did I do it right?" she said to him.

"That arrangement's a pro job if I ever saw one."

His hand emerged from the cabinet holding a bottle of bourbon. Hanna's parents kept their liquor collection up there. They only brought it out for guests they intended to impress, which did not include Uncle Rick. Putting a finger over his lips for silence, he unscrewed the whiskey's top and poured a generous amount into the can of beer. Then he capped the bottle and returned it to its place.

"Next time you're in the city, you should come by the Mart," he said.

Uncle Rick worked at the San Francisco Flower Mart, loading and unloading pallets five days a week, from five thirty in the morning to two in the afternoon. The bucket of flowers he brought Hanna would normally run well over three hundred dollars, but the picks were at the end of their bloom and doomed for fertilizer, so he could take them away at no cost.

Aunt Azami entered the kitchen. "That's beautiful," she said of the arrangement. She procured from the refrigerator the bottle of Chardonnay they'd brought from the city. She eyed Uncle Rick's can of beer. "Only one more after this," she warned.

He tipped the can of beer at her to acknowledge who was the boss. Hanna knew he wouldn't stop until he'd finished at least four more, and most of the remaining whiskey as well.

Hanna's stomach knotted again. Pressure swelled around her eyes. The walls seemed to be squeezing in on her, like a tin submarine descending the ocean's depths.

Uncle Rick picked up Hanna's arrangement and admired it. "Let's move those junk tulips out of the way and get this on the table."

Hanna was falling, falling away from the flowers, falling away from him.

"Squirt?" It was Uncle Rick's voice. "Squirt—"

Darkness washed up and over Hanna, and then there was nothing at all.

"—maybe she's dehydrated—" Hanna heard a woman say.

"—been so excited about the party—" Her mother's voice, Hanna thought.

"—make room, give her some air—" Definitely Uncle Rick.

Hanna lay on the kitchen linoleum with her legs stretched out. Someone had pillowed her head with a couch cushion. Uncle Rick and Aunt Azami leaned over her, their faces filling Hanna's field of vision. A gentle soothing hand massaged her forehead. Hanna peered up and saw, upside-down, her mother kneeling on the floor tending to her. Worry-lines had made her mother's stern face even more granite-like.

"What happened?" Hanna said.

"Passed out, squirt," Uncle Rick said. "You okay?"

Hanna took a deep breath. The salty stickiness had returned to her mouth. "I'm thirsty."

"Let's see if she can sit up," Hanna's mother said.

The three of them helped her up. Uncle Rick drew a glass of water from the kitchen tap. She drank it greedily, offering him a breathless *Thank you* when she finally withdrew the glass from her lips.

"Should we take her to the emergency room?" he asked.

"I don't think so," Hanna's mother said. She took Hanna's free hand and rubbed it. "She just needs to lie down and close her eyes."

"I want cake," Hanna said automatically.

Uncle Rick laughed. "Later," Hanna's mother said.

The knotting in her stomach had returned. She pushed on her belly, just under her navel. Something hard and tender was under the skin. She'd noticed it for about a week, but now it was throbbing, making its presence known to Hanna.

"I know what happened." Hanna whispered to her mother that she didn't want Uncle Rick to hear. A bit confused, she asked her brother to step outside. Uncle Rick shrugged, said "No problem," and left the kitchen.

Hanna waited until she heard the sliding glass door shut, meaning Uncle Rick was in the backyard. She wanted Aunt Azami to hear this too. It was exciting, like procuring the final approval stamp on a club membership application.

She said to the women, "It's finally happening." She needed a moment to recall the terminology. "*Pons viviparous hemotrophism.*" She looked to them for approval or a hug.

Aunt Azami straightened up. She gave Hanna's mother a concerned look.

"Hanna," her mother said flatly, "where did you hear that term?"

"Some of Cheryl Vannberg's friends told me," she lied. She knew they'd started their periods, so it wouldn't hurt to use them as references. "It's okay. I know what it means." Excited, she related what the dictionary had suggested to her.

"Oh, Hanna," her mother said softly.

Hanna climbed to her feet and stood before her. "What's wrong?"

"You and I need to talk," her mother said.

"What did I do? Is something my fault?"

Aunt Azami said, "I'll leave you two," and she went outside.

Hanna's mother sighed. "Let's talk in your room."

Walking past the dining room, Hanna saw through the sliding glass door Aunt Azami talking to Uncle Rick in the backyard. Both were smoking cigarettes. While Aunt Azami talked, Uncle Rick peered back at Hanna. He held up a gentle hand, palm out, indicating peace, or perhaps his concern. Hanna flushed red. She didn't appreciate Azami sharing her news with Uncle Rick without her permission, not one bit.

In Hanna's bedroom, her mother sat on the made bed. She patted the spread for Hanna to join her. Hanna wondered if she should risk showing the urine test to her mother, to prove she had *pons viviparous hemotrophism* and was not just making it up. Did she think Hanna was pretending to have it, like a child behind the wheel of a parked car pretending she was driving?

"Why do you think you have *hemotrophism*?" Hanna's mother said.

"I know what it means," Hanna said. "I'm not a little child."

"It's not menstruation," Hanna's mother said. "Where did you hear that term?"

Hanna, not accustomed to lying to her mother, bent her head and confessed everything: *Mother & Baby*, stealing the pregnancy test from Cullers' Pharmacy, her queasiness and the salty-sticky taste in her mouth, the knots in her stomach. They got up from the bed and Hanna produced the contraband from under the mattress. She laid it all out across the spread: the book, the cardboard box, the instruction sheet, and the tube itself with its two purple lines. Hanna located the footnote on the instruction sheet and pointed it out to her mother. "See? *Viviparous hemotrophism*. Vivid blood."

From outside came the squeaking of car brakes. Hanna's father was home with the charcoal and lighter fluid.

Hanna's mother considered the situation for a moment. Finally, she said, "My first thought is to ask Ritchie and Azami to go home. I know they drove all the way out from the city, but I think we need to discuss this now rather than later."

"And ruin the party?" Hanna said.

"What would you have me do?"

"I want to know what's going on." If her mother had explained all this long before, her party wouldn't be in jeopardy. "Tell me and then we can have the party."

"Hanna, I don't think you're going to want to have any party after we've talked."

There was a knock on the bedroom door. Hanna's mother called "Yes?" and the door opened. Aunt Azami was in the hall. Uncle Rick stood behind her, can of beer in hand, peering over Azami's head with a concerned, quizzical expression.

"We're going to go," Aunt Azami said. "We can come back another time—"

"No!" Hanna said. "It's my birthday."

Down the hallway, the front door opened. Hanna's father called out that he was home. *Let's get the grill started; it's party time!* Uncle Rick hurried down the hall to intercept him.

Hanna realized her right cheek was wet with moisture. It was trailing down from the corner of her eye. She checked and felt moisture on her left cheek too. She wasn't sad; she was scared. Aunt Azami would've told her a long time ago about *pons viviparous hemotrophism*. If Aunt Azami and Uncle Rick had raised her in the city, she would've learned the truth ages ago.

"Will you stay with me, Aunt Azami?" Her voice was as wet as her cheeks.

"I don't think—" she said. "You and your mother should talk."

"Please?"

Hanna's mother motioned her inside. "If you don't mind,"

Hanna's mother said to Azami, as though embarrassed about putting her out. Aunt Azami carefully shut the door and came beside the bed.

"Hanna," her mother said, *"pons viviparous hemotrophism* means you're a bridge daughter."

"No I'm not," she said. On television, bridge daughters were mute and obedient. They prepared and served meals to their family. They answered the door and folded laundry. Bridge daughters sat off to the side, blank and expressionless, staring into the camera, while the rest of the family told jokes and the studio audience laughed on cue. Bridge daughters were like Erica across the street. Plain girls who wore old-fashioned, characterless dresses. Weird girls who rarely left the house.

"When women are pregnant," Hanna's mother said, "they give birth to bridge daughters." She pushed a damp strand of Hanna's bangs out of her eyes. "Little girls like you."

"And little boys," Hanna said.

"No, women only have bridge daughters," her mother said.

"But where did Dad come from? And Uncle Rick?"

Aunt Azami took the chair from Hanna's writing desk and pulled it close to the bed. She placed a reassuring hand on Hanna's leg.

Hanna's mother said softly and firmly, "Grandma Driscoll had a bridge daughter, and that bridge daughter produced your father. I came from a bridge daughter too. Aunt Azami, Ritchie, all of us came from bridge daughters."

Hanna stretched the cuff of her sweater sleeve over her fingers. She wiped the wetness off her face with the makeshift mitten. "You mean my grandmother is a bridge daughter?"

"No, Grandma Driscoll is your grandmother."

"But that doesn't make any sense."

Hanna's mother leaned close. "You're carrying my child right now, Hanna. Right here." She touched Hanna's belly, just below her navel. "You were born pregnant. The baby inside you has been growing for thirteen years. In about a year, you'll give birth to her. Or him."

Hanna looked back and forth at the women as though they were insane. "I'm having a baby?"

"*My* baby," her mother said.

"You're a bridge," Aunt Azami said. "You carry your mother's child until it's born. Until you give birth."

Hanna felt the room tilt, but differently than her recent queasy spells. "I'm going to have my own sister?"

"Not a sister," Hanna's mother said. "She will look exactly like you. She will be a perfect duplicate. A twin."

"If it's a girl," Aunt Azami added. "If it's a boy, it will look *mostly* like you."

"A baby?" Hanna sputtered, still digesting everything being said. It was too much at once, brute force pelting her from all sides. How did she not see this coming?

But, of course, she had seen this coming. On those family television shows, the bridge daughter would not return after a bridge party episode. The next week, she was missing, her disappearance never explained. Usually, the actress playing the bridge daughter would find a new role on a different television show. Maybe she'd appear on a celebrity game show stumping guests, or host an awards ceremony in a fabulous, stunning gown. But on the show, the plain-Jane bridge daughter simply vanished. The episode after the bridge party would open with the joyous family returning home from the hospital with an infant in swaddling. No one on the television show mentioned the bridge daughter again.

Hanna turned to Aunt Azami. "What happens to me after the baby?" She faced her mother. "What happens?"

Hanna's mother chose her next words with care. "You'll pass away."

"Pass away?" Hanna felt her cheeks growing hot again. "You mean I die?"

Aunt Azami squeezed Hanna's leg. "The finality," she said.

FOUR

HANNA GOT TO CHOOSE what went on her hamburger: American cheese, ketchup, lettuce, no pickles, no mayonnaise. The birthday cake was her father's favorite flavor: yellow vanilla cake with white vanilla frosting. The flowers on the birthday table were her mother's greenhouse tulips orbited by hard nubs of baby's breath, the "cheap gyp" her uncle had referred to in his industry lingo. It was Hanna's birthday, but it wasn't really her birthday party. It never was, not once in thirteen years. They sang the birthday song for Hanna, and it made her smile, but the smile caused the dried tears in the corners of her eyes to crack, reminding her of the hard truth she'd learned in her bedroom just two hours earlier.

Hanna had insisted the birthday party would continue. Her mother had finally conceded and instructed her to wash her face. She dared to ask if she could use some of her mother's blush to hide her crying from Uncle Rick, but her mother would not permit such a thing.

After the cake, Hanna sat on the floor opening presents while the adults took their after-meal drinks on the couches. Her parents drank coffee with plenty of milk, while Aunt Azami drank her nourishing tea and Uncle Rick had another beer. Her parents' present was a gift certificate for a florist shop, the one in the strip mall where her mother had purchased the tulips. The certificate was for ten dollars, more money than Hanna ever had at her disposal at any one time.

"I don't know if that's so useful now," Hanna's mother said, "considering all the flowers your uncle brought today."

"I wish they were going to last longer," Uncle Rick said. "Enjoy them while you can, squirt."

Hanna considered the certificate for a moment. "I'll use this to buy a new vase," she declared. "I'm tired of my old one."

Aunt Azami offered Hanna a gift wrapped in paper of colorful geometric patterns. It was a hardcover book bound in warm yellow cloth; *The Symphony of Flowers* by Charlotte Dunhill Woolsey. The book smelled musty and was cotton-dry to the touch. The spine was so well worn, the book practically fell open in her hands. As Hanna carefully turned the desiccated pages, the typeface and language appeared antiquated. Hanna wondered if it was beyond her reading level but told herself she would at least try. Then she reached the center of the book.

"Careful with those color plates," Aunt Azami warned. "Some of them are loose."

Although the rest of the book was faded black-and-white text, the center of the book featured a dozen hand-tinted illustrations of blooms in their habitat. Birds-of-paradise, chrysanthemums, four popular rose varieties, and tulips not grown in greenhouses. Each was illustrated with intense care and an eye for detail. So exquisite, they seemed to capture velvety folds of each blossom that even a modern camera would miss.

"That looks expensive," Hanna's mother said cautiously.

While turning pages, a flat wad of paper fell from the book and into Hanna's lap. It had been tucked in between the last page and the marbled end paper. It was one of Aunt Azami's origami, a crane folded from mauve paper. Hanna held it so her parents could see.

"What a considerate gift from Aunt Azami," her mother said.

"What do you say?"

"Thank you, Aunt Azami."

Hanna's mother went to the kitchen for more coffee. Her father sat forward and asked Hanna to show him the crane. "You really have a knack for these things," he said to Azami. "You learn this in school?"

"My grandmother," she said.

Azami was born in Sacramento and raised in Modesto, a farming town in California's Central Valley. Azami's parents grew cherry tomatoes and, later, wine grapes for E & J Gallo. Hanna met Azami's father once, when they'd all gone to Modesto for Azami's mother's funeral. For the services, Azami's father wore a crisp cowboy hat, pressed denim, and hand-tooled boots polished to a high sheen. He did not seem particularly Japanese to Hanna, but neither did Azami. At a young age, Hanna learned to think of them not as Japanese but as family, even if Uncle Rick and Aunt Azami weren't actually married.

"I want to learn how to make them," Hanna said.

"I'll teach you," Aunt Azami said. "I even brought some origami paper with me."

The men went out to the backyard to clean off the barbecue and talk about whatever men talk about when they're alone. Hanna's mother never returned with her coffee. The garbage disposal began grinding its teeth on scraps and the sink tap shushed on and off, meaning her mother was cleaning up.

Aunt Azami produced from her muslin tote a sheaf of origami paper, each sheet perfectly square, blank white on one side and varying bright colors on the other. Fanned, the ream made a paper rainbow. She joined Hanna on the floor, crossing her legs, and instructed Hanna to pick a color she liked. Hanna took a creamy chocolate-colored sheet. The colored side was treated, slick to the touch and shiny, while the blank white side felt like writing paper.

"With origami, it's always important to keep in mind the shiny side of the paper," Aunt Azami said. "If you do this upside-down, you won't see the nice color when you're finished."

And they began, Aunt Azami making a fold on a sheet and Hanna mimicking the fold on her own. The first folds were big, sometimes folding the sheet in half. The later folds became more precise and detailed, creating sharp lines at exact angles. Hanna followed Aunt Azami's instructions to the letter but could not fathom how this mishmash of folds and creases was going to form a crane.

"In Japan, a crane is called a *tsuru*," Aunt Azami said. She spelled the word for Hanna.

"*Tsuru*," Hanna repeated and spelled it aloud.

"My grandmother taught me how to make *tsuru* when I was your age. I practiced them over and over again so I could get them just right. Now they're easy."

Aunt Azami corrected Hanna's fold, showing her how to make the tip of the point sharp. Hanna watched Aunt Azami make the final three folds. Like a stage magician, the crane did not appear until the last moment. Then, even more magical, Aunt Azami took the paper crane by its wings and gently pulled. As the wings extended, the neck and tail stretched out, as though the crane was preparing for flight. Hanna's eyes lit up. She so wanted to make her *tsuru* come to life just as Aunt Azami's had.

It did not happen. Her folds were not quite right and the neck and tail did not move when she pulled the wings. The beak was misshapen and the tail seemed too large for the rest of the body. Hanna said, "I'll never get it right."

"No, you will. You just have to practice. Here." Aunt Azami took two more sheets of origami paper from the ream. "Let's do it again."

They made another *tsuru* together, Aunt Azami leading the way fold by fold. Hanna's fingers felt fat and clumsy with the paper, and the second one came out worse than the first. Aunt Azami offered two more sheets and they went at it again. This time, Hanna's third attempt, the neck and tail stretched for flight when she pulled, albeit not as majestically as Aunt Azami's *tsuru* did every time.

"Take these." Aunt Azami offered the remainder of the origami paper to Hanna. "Take them, take them," she said over Hanna's protests. "There's an origami store in Japantown. They're easy for me to get. I'll bring more the next time we come out."

Hanna, cross-legged on the floor with Aunt Azami, considered the half-dozen paper cranes around her. She felt she was a giant sitting in a pond among a flock of tiny cranes. Aunt Azami could make dozens of these in no time flat. Hanna wanted that skill too. She wanted to make *tsuru* as though she was folding a napkin for dinnertime. She could even incorporate them into her arrangements. With Uncle Rick's blooms and Aunt Azami's *tsuru*, she could arrange bouquets that would outshine any florist's plasticky greenhouse flowers.

"Do you know about the thousand cranes?" Aunt Azami asked. Hanna shook her head. "There's a legend," Azami said, "if you make a thousand paper cranes in a year, you get one wish."

"A thousand?" Just making three seemed like so much work. "What can you wish for?"

"Anything you want," Aunt Azami said. "Do you know the story of Sadako Sasaki?"

"No," Hanna said.

"Sadako was a bridge daughter."

That's why I never read about her, Hanna thought.

"Sadako was born in Hiroshima right before America dropped the atomic bomb," Aunt Azami said softly. "She developed cancer when she was eleven. She wanted to reach her finality and give birth to her mother's child. So, for a year, she folded *tsuru*."

"And she lived?"

"No," Aunt Azami said. "She died before she could finish the thousand cranes."

"Do you think she would've lived if she did finish them?"

"Oh, Hanna—"

"Then how?" Hanna insisted under her breath.

Hanna's mother entered the room, interrupting. "So, what are you two up to? Making origami?"

Aunt Azami rose from the floor. "Hanna picked up on it quickly. I suspect you're going to have paper cranes all over your house soon enough."

"As long as you pick them up and put them away," her mother said. She smiled weakly. "I hope it was a good birthday, Hanna. I know it was a lot to take in today."

"Did you make a wish when you blew out the candles?" Aunt Azami asked.

"Don't tell us," her mother said. "Otherwise, it won't come true."

I wished I'd never have my finality, Hanna thought as she glared up from the floor, and she had no intention of telling her mother about it.

FIVE

DR. MAYHEW PRESSED the stethoscope's cold metal button against Hanna's chest. "Deep breaths."

Hanna performed the requested breathing while staring at her mother, who was sitting across the examination room in a padded chair. She watched on with what seemed to be distant interest, fingers drumming her purse now and then.

Dr. Mayhew pressed the metal button on several locations across Hanna's back while she breathed. "Everything sounds fine." She wrapped the blood pressure cuff about Hanna's upper right arm and began pumping the bulb. "Any changes since I last saw you? Pain, pressure, discomfort?"

"Sometimes I feel sick. Especially when I wake up."

"She fainted on her birthday," Hanna's mother said.

Dr. Mayhew quit pumping the bulb. "Bump yourself?" She felt around the back of Hanna's head.

"My brother caught her in time," Hanna's mother said.

Dr. Mayhew listened with the stethoscope while letting the cuff's pressure drop. She noted the result on Hanna's chart. "When you say 'sick,' what do you mean?"

"Like I'm going to..." Uncomfortable with the word, Hanna waved her hand under her chin, illustrating her stomach expelling its contents.

"I see," Dr. Mayhew said. "Go ahead and lie down."

The paper on the examination table crunched as she reclined. Dr. Mayhew began probing Hanna's midsection with three stiff fingers.

"Don't let her lie down after meals," she said to Hanna's mother. "That makes the nausea worse. A vitamin B_6 supplement can help if it's particularly bad. I would just make sure she's drinking enough water every day."

"I'm sure she'll be fine," Hanna's mother said.

At the moment, Hanna felt slightly nauseous from Dr. Mayhew's iron fingers. They jabbed so deeply Hanna thought they might reach her spine.

"Hanna, we're going to do something different today." Dr. Mayhew went to the end of the table and retracted two metal arms from the underside of the table. She flipped pedals at their ends, creating stirrups. "Put your feet here and here," she said, meaning the stirrups. "I need to look inside you. There will be some discomfort."

Hanna, wide-eyed, looked to her mother for help, but her mother merely nodded. "Just do what the doctor says."

Hanna's nausea was replaced with a kind of disgust she'd never felt before, a terrible anticipation of violation. With her privates spread open by a gleaming metal device, Dr. Mayhew stared up into Hanna's body with the aid of a penlight, then reached inside Hanna with two gloved fingers. She ran them around the way the dentist ran his fingers along the inside of her gums to check for cavities. Finally, Dr. Mayhew snapped the gloves off her hands and told Hanna to get dressed. Again, Hanna tasted the sticky saltiness in her mouth, feeling vaguely ill at what had just transpired.

Dr. Mayhew wrote an order on a pad of paper, tore it off, and handed it to Hanna's mother. "On your way out, stop by the blood draw on the second floor."

More tests? Hanna thought. Every visit to Dr. Mayhew's ended with fresh blood drawn with a spiny needle. Dr. Mayhew would call Hanna's parents later that week with the results, results never shared with Hanna.

"Hanna," Dr. Mayhew said, washing up, "why don't you sit outside for a moment while your mother and I talk." After drying her hands, she offered Hanna a lollipop from a glass jar. This was the routine conclusion of every visit to Dr. Mayhew's office, Hanna sitting in the hall sucking on a pea-sized sugar-free lollipop while the doctor discussed the examination with Hanna's mother.

Hanna tied her last shoe, accepted the candy with a soft "Thank you," and then said, "This is for you." She placed a paper crane on the counter beside the sink. On the underside of the crane, Hanna had written the number *16*. Dr. Mayhew noted the crane with a questioning smile, saying "Thank you" as Hanna went to the examination room door.

Hand on the doorknob, Hanna turned around. "Why can't I hear?" she said.

"Hanna," her mother said, "just give us a moment."

"I want to hear too," Hanna insisted.

"We'll talk about it in the car," Hanna's mother said. Hanna knew there would be nothing discussed in the car other than the preparations for dinner that night.

Hanna considered her options. She could put up a fit in the examination room. What would her mother do? Her parents had never physically punished her. Would she take away her allowance? Ignorance no longer seemed worth twenty-five cents a week.

Hanna returned to the examination table. She used the stepping stool to climb up and onto the wrinkled paper. "I know about *pons viviparous hemotrophism*," she said to the doctor.

Dr. Mayhew suppressed an amused smile. "Do you now," she said.

"Am I okay?" she asked.

Dr. Mayhew looked to Hanna's mother for permission, who

reluctantly and silently gave it.

"All signs say you're healthy." Dr. Mayhew was tall for a woman, taller than Hanna's mother, and spoke down to Hanna, even though Hanna was on the table. "You're well into the third month of *pons anno*. It's a little early for your age, but not out of the ordinary. You should expect to start showing in the next few weeks."

Hanna didn't know what the Latin meant. More words to look up when she got home.

"Will it be a boy or a girl?" Hanna felt a bit brave talking to Dr. Mayhew in this fashion.

Dr. Mayhew again looked to Hanna's mother for permission, and received it.

"We can't test the gender for a few more weeks," Dr. Mayhew said. "It's up to your parents to decide if they want to know the sex of their child before it's born."

"What if I want to know?"

Dr. Mayhew rolled the round stool over to Hanna and sat before her. Now Dr. Mayhew spoke to Hanna face-to-face.

"Hanna, you are the *pons*, the bearer of your parents' child." She reached forward and touched Hanna in the midsection, where she'd probed just a few minutes earlier. "This here," she applied pressure to the tender bump growing under Hanna's skin, "this is your *parents'*, not yours. They get to decide."

"I'm just a box for it," Hanna said. "Like a carton of milk."

Dr. Mayhew suppressed another smile—did she think Hanna was being cute?

"You're not a carton of milk," Dr. Mayhew said.

"I'm like a hen sitting on another hen's egg."

"You are your mother's surrogate, yes," she said. "Be it God or Nature, that is how human reproduction works."

Hanna's mother announced, "Thank you, doctor." Then, "Hanna, say goodbye to Dr. Mayhew."

"I want to talk to you more," Hanna said to the doctor.

"Hanna—" her mother warned.

"I want to ask you a question," Hanna said to Dr. Mayhew again. "Alone."

"Our time is up," her mother said.

"I wanna ask a question!" Hanna snapped.

After a moment to gather herself, Hanna's mother spoke in an even tone. "Your father and I decided thirteen years ago we'd treat you like a normal daughter. And we're very proud of how you've turned out. All we ask is you show us some consideration. Can you do that?"

Hanna, quivering, said, "Yes."

"What do you say, then?"

"I'm sorry for yelling," Hanna said softly. "May I please talk with Dr. Mayhew alone?"

Hanna's mother took a breath, emotionless, then stepped out to the hall, closing the door behind her.

Hanna couldn't believe it. She'd never been left alone with Dr. Mayhew, never left alone with another adult at all, save a few times with Aunt Azami or Uncle Rick. Now she was there with Dr. Mayhew and granted permission to ask anything she wanted.

"My mother said I will pass away," Hanna said. "She calls it 'the finality.'"

Dr. Mayhew nodded. "At the end of *pons anno*, when the child is born, the *cerebrum funiculus* is cut, severing your tie with the infant—"

"You mean the umbilical cord?" Hanna asked, recalling the term from *Mother & Baby*.

"No," Dr. Mayhew said, "an umbilical cord connects a mother to her bridge daughter. Here, look."

Dr. Mayhew took a plastic scale model from the rear counter; a headless, armless, legless midsection of a naked pregnant female. It was cut lengthwise to reveal the uterus, placenta, ovaries, and fetus within. Dr. Mayhew used the tip of her ballpoint pen like a lecturer's pointer.

"When you were *in utero*, an umbilical cord connected you to your mother. Now, while you were in there, a pouch of cells in *your* uterus began developing. This pouch of cells is the genetically identical embryo within you today."

"A twin," Hanna said.

"The gemellius," Dr. Mayhew said. "Your genetic uniform, although its gender is not yet determined." She closed her eyes and waved a hand. "It's complicated." Then she placed her hand on Hanna's belly again. "Because you both are genetically uniform, there's no need for a placental barrier." Hanna didn't know what that meant; another phrase to look up at home. "That's why you don't have an umbilical cord."

Dr. Mayhew turned the plastic model around. Like a magician's box, the other side of the model displayed the internals of a bridge daughter: the uterus, similar to a normal woman's, but no ovaries, no Fallopian tubes, and no placenta. The fetus was connected to the bridge daughter by a thick eggplant-colored cable that originated from somewhere in the model's spine.

"The gemellius and you are in a symbiotic relationship," Dr. Mayhew said. "That means you depend on each other. You cannot live without it and it cannot live without you. When it reaches the fetal stage, it'll begin processing hormones in your bloodstream and, in turn, emit a different set of hormones back into your body."

Hormones—another word to look up in the encyclopedia at home.

"The *cerebrum funiculus* inside you is like an umbilical cord," Dr. Mayhew continued, "but it connects your brain and spinal cord to the fetus' cortex." She ran the pen up and down the eggplant-colored cable inside the model, curled like a telephone cord. "At birth, when the *funiculus* is severed, your brain functions will cease and you'll pass away." Dr. Mayhew said it matter-of-factly, as though it was no more dramatic than pulling a tooth.

"You mean I die."

"The finality. What started fourteen years earlier in your mother's womb concludes with the birth of the gemellius, your genetic duplicate."

Dr. Mayhew's authority was damning, but Hanna remained unsatisfied. "Why does the funcu—funick—"

"*Funiculus.*"

"Why does it have to be cut?"

"Once the infant exits your body, the connection must be severed. The infant won't survive outside your body with it attached."

Hanna mustered her next words. "Then maybe don't cut it."

"It's a symbiotic relationship only up to a point," Dr. Mayhew said. "It has to be cut at birth. There's no alternative."

"Doctors can change hearts and give people new legs," Hanna said. "Why can't they fix this?"

"What do you mean, 'fix this?'"

"Fix it," Hanna insisted. She waved a hand at the plastic model. "Stop this from happening."

Dr. Mayhew returned the pen to her breast pocket, replaced the model on the counter, and rose from the rolling stool. She had an air about her now, as though the conversation had become distasteful. "There's nothing to fix," Dr. Mayhew said. "This is going exactly as intended, Hanna. This is how humans have procreated for a hundred thousand years."

"But it's not fair," Hanna said softly, almost to herself.

Dr. Mayhew opened the door. Hanna's mother waited in the hall, purse over her shoulder, fuming.

"Vitamin B_6 will take care of that nausea," Dr. Mayhew said to Hanna's mother. "Make sure she stays hydrated. And don't forget to have that blood drawn before you go."

SIX

HANNA LOOKED UP Sadako Sasaki in the children's encyclopedia her parents allowed her to keep in her room. There she found the story Aunt Azami had relayed to her, but with dates and more detail. The entry confirmed Sadako was a bridge daughter. When Hanna looked up "Bridge Daughter" in the A–D volume of the encyclopedia, she discovered that page had been removed, sliced out with a razor blade so close to the binding she never would have known it was missing.

The children's encyclopedia had no entry for *pons anno*, but her dictionary defined *Anno Domini* as "the year of our Lord." Dr. Mayhew said she'd entered the third month of *pons anno*. *Maybe,* she theorized, *I have nine months remaining.*

Hanna was not in the habit of shoplifting, but now she had stolen two things from Cullers' Pharmacy. First it was the pregnancy test, now a pocket notebook; a pad of blank lined paper bound between indigo leatherette covers. Although her parents supplied her a weekly allowance (a progressive idea, something not traditionally given to bridge daughters), her mother kept Hanna's meager stipend in her purse and only allowed Hanna to purchase approved items. The pregnancy test obviously had to be obtained covertly. The notebook would have been innocent enough, but it too would soon hold a kind of secret Hanna did not want to share with her parents.

Alone in her bedroom, Hanna printed her name and address and phone number on the inside cover of the notebook so it could be returned in case she ever mislaid it. At the top of the first page, using the cleanest cursive script she could muster, she wrote:

Tsuru

The night of Dr. Mayhew's examination, Hanna stayed up late making paper cranes just as Aunt Azami had instructed her. She wanted to fall into bed, bury her face in the pillow, and cry, but she resolved she would not give in so easily. She thought of her friend Alondra, who'd been so strong when she was pregnant. Before the birth, she'd told Hanna she was moving to Massachusetts to spend the next few years with her grandparents. Hanna thought she was terribly strong to make such a move. Plus, she was due to give birth in just a month or so. Travelling across the country and living in a new city was a huge change. Hanna had always been a bit jealous of Alondra's courage. Could she be that strong?

Folding her twentieth crane at her desk, it dawned on Hanna what a fool she'd been. Alondra was a bridge daughter. She wasn't in Massachusetts. She was dead. Hanna's parents no longer socialized with Alondra's parents. No doubt Alondra's parents were raising a new baby, the child Alondra had given them right before she died.

Head down, Hanna folded faster and with more focus, burning off the worry-energy and determined to become as good as Aunt Azami at making cranes. The night of her birthday, she had decided she would number each crane so she would know when she reached the one thousandth. Through trial-and-error, she learned exactly where to write the number on the sheet of origami paper so it would be visible on the underside of the left wing when finished folding. She wrote it in the tiniest of numerals to keep her serialization scheme from tainting the beauty of the *tsuru*. By the time she reached number thirty, Hanna had her little system down pat.

Then, in the pocket notebook she'd stolen from Cullers' Pharmacy, she wrote consecutive numbers down the first page, each on its own line. Most of the numbered lines were blank. That meant she had kept the paper crane for herself. Beside some of the numbers, she wrote a name. For number *16*, she wrote *Dr. Mayhew*. For number *14*, she wrote *Mother* and beside number *15*, she wrote *Father*. Mr. Cullers, the owner of the pharmacy, received number *17*, unaware that the gift of a crane was a furtive partial payment for the notebook Hanna had pocketed from the stationery aisle.

Hanna doubted her wish would come true when she reached one thousand cranes. It would be the same wish she'd made as she blew out the candles on her birthday cake. She did not believe in magic candles and she did not believe in miraculous paper cranes, but she was willing to try anything if it meant one more breath of life.

When the second invitation for Cheryl's bridge party arrived in the mail, Hanna fought her mother hard for permission to attend. Hanna's mother steadfastly refused. Hanna switched tactics and pled with her father for intercession. Her father was as reluctant as her mother but agreed with Hanna's logic. If Cheryl was not going to be with the living for much longer, Hanna deserved a chance to say goodbye.

"I'll agree to it," her mother finally conceded, fuming, "but you can't tell Cheryl she's passing away. Not one word about her finality. That's not for you to say. Promise?"

"I promise," Hanna said softly.

"Liz registered at Macy's," her mother said, flicking the invitation with her finger. "We'll go tomorrow after lunch."

"I'll make a gift," Hanna said, thinking it would appease her mother, which it did not.

Two days later, Hanna's father drove Hanna to the Vannberg house for the bridge party. "That was nice of you to put together those flowers for Cheryl," he said from behind the steering wheel. "And the paper birds too. I'm sure she'll like them."

The bucket of flowers Uncle Rick had brought were just about done for. Most had wilted and shed their petals days before. Hanna had salvaged for Cheryl a decent bouquet of carnations and sagging California poppies. They surrounded the last sunflower Uncle Rick had included in the farrago of blooms. Hanna was not fond of sunflowers. They had almost no scent to enjoy. Their centers were rough and scaly, like an alligator's hide. Hanna figured she could gift the sunflower to Cheryl and be done with it, throwing in some color to liven it up. She knew none of them would last much longer before wilting and turning crinkly brown.

The *tsuru*, however, had been a fair amount of work. She'd stayed up the night before without watching any television to complete twenty of them. She recorded their numbers in her pocket notebook—64 to 84—and printed "Cheryl Vannberg" on each line.

Hanna said to her father, "I wish she'd asked me when we got the first invitation," meaning her mother. "Why don't I get to decide if I go to a party?"

"Well..." Hanna's father made it a practice to see things from other people's perspective. Or, Hanna later realized, to ask people to see things from other people's perspective. "Look at it from your mother's point of view. She and Liz don't see things eye-to-eye. I don't know if you remember, but we were at their house a few years ago for dinner. Liz and your mother kind of got into it at the table."

Hanna did recall that, but didn't understand what they were arguing over. It had to do with raising children.

"Can I ask you something?" Hanna said.

"Of course you can," he said.

"When were you going to tell me?"

Hanna's father blew out air from pursed lips. He'd not seen that one coming. "I promise, we were going to tell you soon. I think your mother wanted to wait until after the birthday party." Seeing Hanna's dissatisfaction with his answer, he added, "You know, some parents tell their bridge daughters when they're young. And those bridge daughters are expected to play a certain role in the family."

"Like Erica across the street?"

"That's right. But your mother wanted to raise you like a normal child. She has strong opinions about how bridge daughters should be raised. She did a lot of research before you were born."

Really? "What kind of research?"

"Just her own research," he said. "As you know, your mother and your Uncle Rick were raised in a...peculiar way. Your grandmother raised her bridge daughters different than most people would. Your mother has taken your grandmother's ideas and mixed them with more traditional thinking. A blend, kind of." He quickly added, "But that's different than what Cheryl's mother is up to. Completely different."

"But Cheryl's mom does all these great things for her. They go on trips together, and Disneyland, and they get their hair done, and—"

"Liz is lying to Cheryl every day," he said evenly. "Liz is telling Cheryl that when the baby is born, they'll both raise it. They've fooled that little girl." Hanna's father said this with some bitterness. "Liz is actually doing something very cruel to Cheryl."

"How? Cheryl has *everything*."

"Hanna, I know that if you look at it from Cheryl's point of view, you'll see just how little she really has." He gripped the steering wheel tighter. "Are you sure you want to go through with this? It's not too late to turn around."

"I want to see Cheryl one last time," Hanna said.

Then, after a few minutes, she asked, "What does *pons anno* mean?"

"'Bridge year,'" her father said. "The most important year of your life, honey."

Hanna was not excited about the party, or cake and ice cream, or the chance to ride a pony again. Although Cheryl's glamour wowed Hanna when she was eleven and twelve, she'd grown to see Cheryl's presence as souring and annoying. Cheryl made everything about herself, always, no matter the situation.

It only got worse when Cheryl's bump grew visible. She treated her pregnancy as an elevated status, a sign she was graduating to adulthood while the other girls remained little children, as though Hanna and the rest were still playing dress-up dolls and making mud pies. Once, cradling her sheer round belly, Cheryl told Hanna, "God chose me." Hanna later realized Cheryl was actually saying *God didn't choose you.*

Hanna's father guided the car around a corner. "Oh—you are kidding me."

Although the street was not blocked by a pony corral this time, the entire front of the Vannberg house was made up like a circus tent, red- and yellow-striped fabric down over the front with thick ropes projecting out from the corner eaves. A clown in full regalia, right down to the oversized maraschino-red shoes, blew up balloons and dispensed candy from a bag. A juggler in the driveway spun hoops about his arms, wrists, and ankles. Cheery organ music came from the house. Legions of kids swarmed in and out of the wide-open front door and ran circles about the lawn. It looked nothing like the bridge parties on television— tasteful adult-only dinner parties with roast beef and wine.

Hanna took a helium balloon from the clown and laughed when he honked his nose and waddled off. One of the boys on the other end of the front lawn waved to Hanna; she'd met him at Cheryl's birthday party last year. Hanna did not feel like seeing him again, and told her father they should go inside.

In the entry foyer, Cheryl's aunt sat at a folding table acting as the party greeter. Hanna traded her invitation for a colorful paper sack of goodies and tickets for a raffle being held later. She also received a stick-on badge with her name written in sparkly cursive script. Hanna's father placed his nametag on the pocket of his button-down shirt, hiding the old ink stains there.

"Cheryl is in the back of the house," the aunt said, and she pointed them down the hallway. "You should say hello."

The living room was a somber affair compared to the circus outside. The drapes were shut and two shaded side-lamps were on low, making the room oddly dim for one o'clock in the afternoon. Only adults were present. Most wore the kind of clothes one would wear to church or a funeral. They sat on the couches and in a circle of high-backed dining chairs, while the remainder stood. One way or another, each managed to balance a small paper plate of hors d'oeuvres on their laps or armrest while drinking wine from plastic cups.

At the far end of the room, Cheryl sat in a cushioned chair with extra cushions for back support. Her feet were up on a maternity footstool. Like her mother, she wore a flowing, flowery dress, one most likely purchased for this occasion and none other, and an excess of make-up. Her hair was up. Hanna could smell the hairspray from across the room.

"Come in," Cheryl said to Hanna and her father. "Mom, it's Mr. Driscoll and Hanna."

Cheryl's mother greeted them both, shaking Hanna's father's hand warmly. "Dian couldn't make it?"

"Under the weather," Hanna's father said.

It had only been a few weeks since Hanna saw Cheryl at the bakery, and yet she'd gained considerable weight. Most of it was around her neck and face and in her upper arms, exposed by the sleeveless dress. The garland in Cheryl's hair reminded Hanna of the green ferns Hanna's mother placed on the turkey each Thanksgiving.

Hanna offered Cheryl the bouquet and said, "Congratulations."

Cheryl accepted the flowers with a warm smile. She put her nose to the sunflower and drew in deeply. "They smell wonderful."

"These are for you too," she said, offering a paper bag of *tsuru*.

Cheryl raised a marigold paper crane from the bag for everyone to see. A few of the adults *ooo*'d at the craft. "Did you make these?" she asked Hanna.

Hanna nodded, tempering her proud smile. Then, "Are you feeling okay?"

Cheryl slumped a little, a weak deprecating smile her admission. "I'm feeling fine, but I'm taking some medicine for the baby." She looked down on herself. "It made me balloon."

"It's just a precaution," Cheryl's mother intervened. "The weight will come off after the delivery, honey."

"I'm so glad you came," Cheryl said to Hanna, sounding surprisingly sincere. "I wish I could see you after the baby comes, but I'm taking her to Oregon." She rubbed her distended belly through the loose flowery dress. "We're going to go live with my aunt and uncle until she's four."

"Fresh air," Cheryl's mother said.

Hanna surveyed the room. The adults sank back into the couches and chairs, giving each other knowing looks, little raised eyebrows and suggestive grimaces. Hanna felt a tinge within her, a kind of revulsion she'd lately started to experience more and more often.

After the raffle, adults and children gathered in the dim living room to watch Cheryl open the gifts that had been stacked about the brick fireplace. Just like on television, the gifts were largely for the coming infant, little booties for the feet, rompers for carpet-crawling, and so on. Most of the boys looked bored, and they snuck out to play tag on the front lawn. The girls watched Cheryl through intrigued, fascinated eyes, most a bit jealous of Cheryl enjoying the center of attention once again. Hanna wondered how many of them were bridge daughters, how many of their bodies were ticking down the days until they too began to taste a salty queasiness in the back of their mouths.

Then it hit Hanna. None of them were bridge daughters. Bridge daughters would be dressed like Erica Grimond, wearing functional gray dresses of flannel and linen, not festive party skirts. Bridge daughters only left the house to help with errands, never to attend festivities and eat frosted cake. Even *the* bridge daughter, the girl the party was honoring, wasn't supposed to be there, the center of attention. Cheryl was supposed to pick up dirty plates and answer the door and put out a hot supper when the time arrived. The adults' stiffness and arched eyebrows, the other girls' fascination with a glamorous bridge daughter preparing for birth—what was going on here was not the norm. Hanna recalled her mother calling Mrs. Vannberg "brazen." Without consulting her dictionary, she now had an idea what that word meant.

Once the gifts had been unwrapped and Cheryl's thank-yous and hugs distributed around the room, Cheryl's mother announced cake and ice cream. The kids rushed for the kitchen. Hanna's father was talking to Cheryl's father, Carter Vannberg. He had a perfectly round head, bald and car-wax shiny on top. Hanna had never seen him in anything but a vest and tie and white shirtsleeves rolled up to his elbows, just as he was dressed now.

With the help of a female relative, Cheryl rose from the chair, one hand on her back for support. She took tiny steps while regaining her balance. "I just need to stretch my legs." Hanna was stunned. Cheryl was huge, much larger than she appeared sitting.

"Can you help me decorate my room?" Cheryl said to Hanna. "With your paper cranes."

Hanna couldn't recall a single time where Cheryl asked for Hanna's private company. Puzzled, she said, "Of course." She offered a hand. "Do you need help?"

"I'll do okay," Cheryl said, walking in slight steps down the hall, right hand out for balance.

In Cheryl's bedroom, they took the cranes from the bag and distributed them around the room. Cheryl wanted a few on her bed stand, so she could see them when she awoke. She asked Hanna to place others on a high shelf alongside photos of Cheryl and her mother posing before California's trademarks: the Hollywood sign, the Golden Gate Bridge, Disneyland; all sights Hannah had never visited. Cheryl placed three cranes on the windowsill positioned so they appeared to be gazing longingly out at the backyard swimming pool and the children splashing about.

"I wish I knew how to make these," Cheryl said wistfully.

Unthinking and a bit nosy, Hanna picked up a bottle of prescription pills on the bed stand. Along with warnings and doctor information, the label read GEFYRAPROGESTAGEN.

"They make me feel sick," Cheryl said. "I never want to eat."

"Not even cake?"

"No," Cheryl groaned. "I never eat, but I keep getting fat."

"Maybe it's the baby."

"That's what my mother keeps telling me, but I don't think so. It's those pills." Cheryl dropped her voice. "Can I tell you a secret?"

Cheryl put a finger over her lips. She motioned for Hanna to close the door, which she did. Then Cheryl went to her clothes closet and drew back the sliding door.

"I can't bend down," she said quietly. "Reach in the back, in the corner. Pull up the carpet."

Hanna got on her hands and knees and felt around the back of the closet. The bedroom's peach wall-to-wall carpeting extended to the rear of the closet. Just as Cheryl indicated, the carpet was loose in the corner. Hanna pulled it back and, without Cheryl's prompting, felt around the hard exposed flooring. A board was loose.

"It should come right up," Cheryl said.

Hanna got a fingernail under the board and pried it up. She removed it and set it beside Cheryl's feet.

"You shouldn't have to reach down very far," Cheryl said.

Hanna reached her hand in the hole, then retreated, worried about rats. *Don't be dumb*, she told herself, and reached in again. She pulled out a compact wood box with a hinged top and a simple brass latch. Cheryl took it from Hanna and popped it open.

In the box rested a ream of leafy light-green cash, more money than Hanna had ever seen at one time. Cheryl scooped it out and fanned it. Singles and five-dollar bills, but also some tens and twenties. Hanna saw two or three fifty-dollar bills in the arrayed bills. A crisp, never-folded hundred-dollar bill crowned the top of the stack.

"Don't tell anyone, okay?" Cheryl asked.

"Where'd you get all that?"

"My parents," Cheryl said. "Every so often, I take a little money from my father's billfold or my mother's purse. Or keep some of the change when my mother has me buy something."

How much money do the Vannbergs keep around the house? Hanna thought.

In response to Hanna's facial expression, Cheryl said, "I'm not stealing!" in a high whisper. "They won't miss it."

"What's it for?"

"A few months ago, I started to think I should have some of my own money."

Hanna's eyes goggled. "You got all that in just a few months?"

"My parents use cash for everything," Cheryl said. "My father says that's how you get the good service." She stuffed the money back in the box and snapped the lid shut. "Do you know how babies are made?"

Hanna nodded. "I read a book about it. I could give it to you."

"Does it have pictures?"

Hanna nodded, although she didn't find the pictures in *Mother & Baby* as useful as what was written beneath them.

"I have to be with a boy, don't I?" Cheryl bit her lip. "I've kissed a couple of boys." She named them for Hanna as proof. "But that's not enough to make a baby, is it?"

Hanna, mindful of her promise, said, "What does your mother say?"

"God put it there," Cheryl said. "'Nature's way,' my father says. My mom calls her 'little Cheryl' sometimes." She shook her head, looking almost ready to cry. "I don't understand..."

Hanna replaced the wooden box in the hole and returned everything in the closet as she'd found it.

"If I phone you," Cheryl said, "can you come over and get the money for me?"

"For what?"

Cheryl's parents had placed a maternity chair in the corner of Cheryl's bedroom. A padded footstool allowed her to rest her ankles. She almost fell into the chair. She started crying, the first time Hanna had ever seen her do so.

"I might call you from the hospital." Cheryl pointed at the head of her princess bed. On the embroidered pillows sat a stuffed cartoony lion with a pink mane and a rainbow-colored ball at the end of its tail. "I might call you and say I want Mr. Fluffens. Can you come over here and get the money and bring both of them to me at the hospital?"

Hanna sat on the floor at Cheryl's feet. "What will you do with the money?"

Cheryl wiped her face dry, using fingertips to avoid smearing her makeup. "I've been a good daughter," she said. "Me and my mother, we talk about everything. But I feel like something bad is going to happen to me. I feel like my mother's hiding something."

Hanna took a chance. "Have you ever read about bridge daughters?"

"I've seen them on TV," Cheryl said. "But I'm not like them. I'm different."

"But this is a bridge party."

"Just for fun," Cheryl said. "My mom calls it that to make it sound more sophisticated. But it's not a *real* bridge party. Like my rodeo last year? That wasn't a *real* rodeo."

Hanna said, "Maybe I can get you a book," thinking she might have to steal *Mother & Bridge Daughter* for Cheryl. "You should read it."

Cheryl's cheeks were bright red from the crying. Strawberry-blond curls dangled down both sides of her face, their ends sticky-wet. They got into the foundation on her cheeks, now starting to cake up.

"I can't read books," Cheryl said. "My mom has always been there for me."

SEVEN

EVERY SURFACE IN HANNA'S bedroom overflowed with loose *tsuru*, all numbered. Cranes were in the hallway bathroom too, in the medicine cabinet and in the green fern hanging from the ceiling and around the toothbrush rack. Hanna wanted to showcase each and every one of them. Bath steam had deformed many of the cranes.

When her mother complained about them, Hanna convinced her to allow her to distribute *tsuru* as gifts around the neighborhood. It would allow Hanna to relieve the pressure of finding new places for the little paper birds. Without more room, she was going to have to start storing them in a box or suitcase under her bed. She hated the idea of keeping them where they couldn't be admired, even in passing.

Hanna's mother advocated and practiced a reformed method of raising bridge daughters, but nothing so unorthodox as to allow Hanna to run around the neighborhood unattended. Together, they dropped in on nearby homes with unsolicited offerings of origami cranes. It posed more of a problem than Hanna expected. Some of their neighbors seemed put out by the gift, as though taking in ten paper cranes was akin to storing the Driscolls' spare furniture in their garage. Hanna's mother explained Hanna was "going a little crazy" with origami and assured no gift was expected in return. From her mother's facial expressions, Hanna developed the suspicion she was communicating to the neighbors that they could destroy the cranes after they'd left. This bothered Hanna at first, but she placated herself by remembering that the goal was to fold a thousand cranes. What came of them was secondary.

Back at home, Hanna obsessively noted in her register which neighbor received which run of numbered *tsuru*. She flipped the pages of the notebook with a distinct sense of pride as she tracked the whereabouts of each crane. She had crossed the 200 mark, one-fifth of the way to her goal and her wish.

She was also down to the last few sheets of the origami paper Aunt Azami had gifted her. Once her supply was exhausted, she would have to start cutting writing paper into perfect squares. With this new source, her next cranes would be of flimsier bluish-white paper with thin college-rule stripes. Hanna hated the idea of quantity over quality, but when you're making a thousand of anything, expediency takes on a logic of its own.

Alone in her room, she finished four cranes from the last of the Aunt Azami's paper. From the two hundred and fifty sheets in the ream, she'd produced two hundred twenty-one cranes. The rest of the paper had been used by Aunt Azami on Hanna's birthday to teach her how to fold (which didn't count toward the one thousand, Hanna decided) and the various cranes Hanna had botched and couldn't salvage. She used the final sheet of Aunt Azami's paper as a template to cut squares from her pack of writing paper. The downtown stationery store might carry origami paper, but her mother refused to buy more without good reason.

"You've got too many of those things around the house already," she told Hanna. "Honestly, why do you need any more?"

Of Hanna's gift-giving throughout the neighborhood, she'd avoided the Grimonds across the street. Erica knocking on the window was not the only source of discomfort Hanna had experienced with the family. In the few months they'd been in the house, the Grimonds remained distant from the rest of the neighborhood. Their twin sons, kindergarten-aged, were as shut-in to the house as Erica. When Mrs. Grimond and Erica pulled down the driveway in their Plymouth, off to the supermarket or some other errand, Mrs. Grimond failed to make eye contact with Hanna, even when Hanna waved. Erica, on the other hand, stared back intently from the rear seat, saucer-eyed and expressionless. She failed to wave too.

Hanna's mother used the morning hours and the afternoon to home school Hanna. Her kitchen-table curriculum for Hanna included reading, writing, penmanship, arithmetic, treating others with respect, and America. For the lesson on respect, they would together read an excerpt from the newspaper or a book and discuss how the people in the story had been treated. Hanna's mother always emphasized that people shouldn't be judged by their outward appearances but by the content of their character. The phrase had an elegant ring to it—*the content of their character*—and Hanna took its meaning to heart as best she could.

One afternoon, while going over respect, Hanna realized she had failed Mrs. Grimond and Erica. She was not judging them on the content of their character. How could she? She'd never even spoken to them.

After school, Hanna collected ten *tsuru* in a paper bag and went to her mother. "Can I give some paper cranes to the Grimonds?"

Hanna's mother sat at the kitchen table, paying household bills. "That's fine. Let me finish and we'll go over in…fifteen minutes?"

"I can go myself," Hanna said. "It's only across the street."

"I'll go with you."

"Why can't I just walk across the street once, by myself, just me, by myself?"

It popped out just like that, a rambling spurt of objection, not exactly talking back, but brusque all the same.

Hanna's mother remained hunched over the household checkbook writing the latest entry in its register. "I told you I'll be finished in a few minutes. We'll go to the Grimonds' together."

Hanna crunched the top of the paper bag up, sealing the cranes in tight. "I'm going right now. By myself."

What could her mother possibly be worried about? Walking across the street by herself? They lived on the quietest of suburban roads.

"I want you to go to your room," Hanna's mother said without looking up from the bills. "Lie on your bed and close your eyes. I want you to think of your favorite flowers, or your favorite book. I'll be in in ten minutes, and then we'll talk."

Hanna's face felt hot. She could hear her pulse in her head. "Are you going to paint my room?"

"What's that?" Hanna's mother said, looking up from the checkbook for the first time.

"What color are you going to paint my room?" Hanna said.

"Where did you hear that?"

It was a phrase Hanna had heard on television many times, a technology she'd begun to realize was her most useful conduit of outside information. "That's what they say at bridge parties. 'What color are you going to paint the room?' My room, right? What color are you going to paint *my* room?"

Her mother's pink lips made a crimped suppressed smile. "Hanna, you don't know what you're talking about."

Again, just as in Dr. Mayhew's office, Hanna felt the hot streak of shame within her. Now her mother was patronizing her. Hanna rushed to the front door. She bolted down the lawn and across the street, not looking either way for traffic. Before she knew it, she was on the Grimonds' front porch. Panting and exhilarated by adrenaline, she dared not look back across the street. The sight of her mother would break her resolve now. Seal broken, she pressed ahead.

Up close, the Grimonds' double doors were not the dead-black they appeared from the street, but more like a rich coffee color. Their brass knockers, however, were as mighty and weighty as they seemed from afar. Hanna stood on her tiptoes and rapped the left one. She got off two sharp *cracks* before dropping back to her heels.

"Erica!" came a call from the inside, muffled by the imposing doors. "Get that!"

Hanna sensed her mother was across the street, arms crossed, watching the scene play out on the Grimonds' entryway. Hanna dared not turn around and verify this. Her mother's stern glare would magnetically reel her back to their house, where she would spend the evening in bed thinking hard about the decisions she'd made that afternoon.

Erica Grimond opened the door. She wore a heavy gray dress of straight lines and right angles. Her empty expression was framed by the pageboy cut of her dark brown hair. The rhythmic laughter of a television sitcom's studio audience came from somewhere in the house. Without a word, Erica held the door open and stared at Hanna.

"I brought you some origami I made," Hanna finally said, so soft she was unsure if Erica heard it. "There's ten of them." Still too soft.

Erica stared for a moment, then turned and went to the rear of the house. Hanna remained on the porch, feet itchy from the anticipation of assured punishment later that evening. Erica returned trailing Mrs. Grimond, a wiry-haired woman markedly older than Hanna's mother. She bore a moon-colored face marked with umber lipstick. She wore a dark blue muumuu and house slippers and carried an oversized coffee mug with a spoon handle sticking up from it. The mug was filled with a brothy noodle soup.

"What is it, yes?" she said to Hanna.

"I brought you some origami that I made," Hanna said, again too soft. She offered up the paper bag.

"You live across the street?" She peered over Hanna's head

and brought up one hand to make a slight wave. Hanna knew her mother was behind her, but how close? "You tell your mother she shouldn't be letting her bridge daughter just run around the neighborhood." Mrs. Grimond opened the bag and looked into it. "Are you selling these?"

"How did you know I was a bridge daughter?"

"Women know these things," Mrs. Grimond said. "Is this for a church drive?"

"I'm making a thousand of them," Hanna said. "I'm giving them away."

Mrs. Grimond wadded up the top of the bag. "We don't need any."

"No, they're a gift—"

"We're fine, thank you." She pushed the bag back into Hanna's hands. "Thank you, good night. I'll stay here and watch you cross the street. Your mother's waiting."

Hanna felt the shaming burn of patronization again. She looked to Erica, standing upright behind her mother, exactly as Hanna had been trained to present herself since a child. Erica looked back with a dull stare.

"Would your daughter want them?" Hanna said.

"My daughter?" Mrs. Grimond said. "You mean my *bridge* daughter?" She turned to Erica. "Well, what say you?"

Erica wilted a bit from her mother's forceful, presumptive tone. Erica meekly made a nod of her chin.

"Run on home now." Mrs. Grimond took the bag without asking and handed it to Erica in an offhand manner. "Tell your mother if she wants to come over for coffee some time, I'd love to have her."

Hanna said goodbye and retreated down the walkway. Ahead of her, Hanna's mother stood at the open front door of their house, arms crossed and a dark cloud hovering over her head. Hanna was going to get a talking-to tonight.

Behind Hanna, Mrs. Grimond yelled, "Erica!"

Hanna swiveled about. Erica ran down the walkway to Hanna,

her soft-soled shoes slapping on the paved cement. The paper bag swung wildly from her clenched fist. The flat expression on her face and her glaring white eyes—as wide as fifty-cent pieces—gave Hanna the sense of a madman bounding at her with the intent of violence. Hanna instinctively raised one arm to protect herself. Erica hugged Hanna and squeezed tight.

"Thank you," she whispered in Hanna's ear.

"Erica!" Mrs. Grimond said. "Get back here!"

"Please come over," Erica whispered. "We should talk about Hagar."

Hanna said, "Hagar?"

Erica released her and put a finger over her lips, indicating silence. Then she turned and bounded up the steps, the bag of *tsuru* again pendulous with each awkward jerk forward, the unpracticed loping of a girl who got precious little exercise. Erica ran into the house past her disapproving mother, who slammed the door, shaking her head.

EIGHT

THE EMBOSSED SIGN on the examination room door was of the variety cheaply produced at office supply stores. It was a plastic rectangular plate with *faux* wood grain and white rounded embossed letters. It read *Linda Mayhew, M.D.* on the top line, *Gefyriatrics* below.

In Dr. Mayhew's examination room, wearing a gown of the thinnest cloth tied loosely in the rear, Hanna lay back while the doctor prodded her belly with bony, cold fingers. Dr. Mayhew queried Hanna's mother about diet, nausea, pain, or discomfort, and so on, which Hanna's mother answered more or less to her satisfaction.

Dr. Mayhew once again extended the arms and stirrups from the bottom of the examination table. "Feet on the rests, please," she told Hanna.

Flush with embarrassment, Hanna did as Dr. Mayhew asked. She'd hoped, almost prayed, she would not have to go through this ordeal again. She consciously knew the opposite was true, that she would be exposing her genitals regularly over the next months, right up to the last day when Dr. Mayhew reached her gloved hands fully inside Hanna's body to extract the baby.

Dr. Mayhew rolled on the wheeled stool between Hanna's

spread legs and folded the hem of the gown up over Hanna's knees. She explained to Hanna that she was inserting a speculum, a word Hanna was unfamiliar with but guessed had something to do with vision. Cold steel inside her body, Dr. Mayhew peered into Hanna's womb with a penlight. She hummed and *mm-hmm'*d, then removed the device and pulled down the gown.

"Well," she said to Hanna's mother, "she's definitely passed *ponte primus*. As I said last time, she's advancing faster than expected."

"What's *ponte primus?*" Hanna asked softly.

"I need an ultrasound," Dr. Mayhew told Hanna's mother. "As a precaution. It could be nothing. I'll phone Oakland and let them know you're coming."

"What's *ponte primus?*" Hanna asked more forcefully.

"You can't do that here?" her mother asked Dr. Mayhew.

"We're just a clinic," Dr. Mayhew said. "We don't have the equipment."

"I can't ask one question?" Hanna demanded.

Hanna's mother stared at Hanna. "You'll at least show some respect," she said evenly, "to me and the doctor."

Hanna, heated, said, "Dr. Mayhew, may I ask a question?"

"Dian?" the doctor said.

"It's fine," Hanna's mother said, sounding a little exhausted.

"*Ponte primus* is the first full month of fetal development," Dr. Mayhew explained to Hanna. "The cells have passed the embryonic stage and are now a fetus."

"So how much longer do I have?"

"The finality usually occurs six months after *primus*."

Six months? "But I thought it took a year!"

"The final gestation cycle takes a full twelve months," Dr. Mayhew said. "But we didn't detect *pons anno* until it was underway."

Hanna pressed her fingers along her waistline. The pressure in her belly was palpable now, a sore knot much like indigestion. The lump was visible when she stood naked before the mirror.

Without knowing, she would have mistaken it as a little extra weight. The floppy sweaters and loose T-shirts she'd worn for years hid the bump well, but her jeans had grown tight about the waist, and she'd started leaving the top snap undone.

Dr. Mayhew said to Hanna's mother, "The receptionist has directions to the Oakland facility. Hanna should have a full bladder before she arrives. Have her drink two glasses of water before leaving the house." Dr. Mayhew offered Hanna a sugar-free lollipop. "You're doing great, Hanna. So far, everything is normal."

"Hanna," her mother said behind the wheel of the car, "that's twice you've embarrassed me in front of Dr. Mayhew."

Hanna flushed. She receded into the car seat. "I'm sorry."

"Your father and I have let you talk to adults without asking permission first. We've taught you to read and write, how to handle money, let you wear normal girls' clothes, and so on. It's not right for you to talk back to me in front of Dr. Mayhew."

Hanna, slumped in the seat, brooded. *You taught me to read*, she thought, *but only the books you picked. And you never let me ask Dr. Mayhew questions until I demanded it.*

"I could start being like Erica's mother," her mother said. "We could stop our lessons. You could start washing clothes and cleaning the house every day."

Why not stop our lessons? Hanna thought. *Why should I learn anything new now?*

"You want that?" Hanna's mother said. "No more parties, no more going to visit your friends?"

What friends? Hanna thought. *Alondra's dead. Cheryl's going to die soon.*

"I'll bet you," she told Hanna, "Erica's mother searches Erica's room every few days."

That fished Hanna out of the deep pond of her inner turmoil. "What?"

"Turns over her entire room," she said. "Checks under her bed and inside her closet. If she has one. Checks for little cubbyholes and hiding spots around the house. That's what mothers do when they have bridge daughters. Bridge daughters steal."

"I don't steal," Hanna said quietly, forgetting for the moment her acquisition of the pregnancy test and *tsuru* notebook.

"Bridge daughters steal money and hide clothes and food," her mother continued. "And they can't be left alone because they might try to hurt themselves. That's what Mrs. Grimond thinks of Erica. She thinks Erica's always planning to hurt herself. Would you like it if I treated you like that?"

Hanna couldn't imagine her parents searching her bedroom. Such an invasion was unthinkable. Did Erica really face that from her own mother? Or was her mother saying it to frighten her?

"You don't know," her mother said, voice fading off. "You just don't know."

Pen in hand, Hanna wrote with careful strokes *Dr. Mayhew* beside the number *358*. She'd only left one *tsuru* at the office for the doctor, mostly because she didn't care much for her and her cold probing fingers.

Hanna had tired of folding origami cranes. The process had become rote. The folds came easily now, although her cranes never came out quite as crisp and regal as Aunt Azami's. She still wished she could produce the origami as well as her aunt, but with this plateau in her skill level, she'd started to wonder if she should let go of her goal. After all, in six months, nothing would matter any more. A thousand paper cranes weren't going to grant her more life.

For two years now, Hanna had imagined going to high school and then on to college. She wanted a college roommate. She wanted midnight bull sessions with her roomie in the hallways while they wore snuggly college sweatshirts and sweatpants and drank hot cocoa. She wanted to study under professors who'd spent a lifetime classifying stamens and pollens and stigmas, lecturing and answering her questions and leading her through her thesis. Then on to a job, a biologist or a horticulturist or even a florist like Mr. McReddy, but better than him and his greenhouse tulips with cheap dry gyp.

Would she have a boyfriend? Maybe in college. Wasn't that what bull sessions were, talking about boys? College women should talk about other things too, though. They could talk about navigating thesis committees and career opportunities. She supposed she would have a boyfriend, though, eventually. Would he become her husband, like her father to her mother? Or would she meet her husband later, when she owned her floristry? Maybe he would come in looking to buy a bouquet. For who? *For me*, she thought, and she flushed hot.

She did not feel an ounce of desire for a child of her own, but she knew you were expected to have one. After all, a child made a couple into a family, and that sounded good to her. She would teach her daughter just as her mother had taught her, at home, sitting together at the kitchen table. She would look over her daughter's shoulder while she practiced forming her letters on lined paper.

A family would be her choice. A husband, a daughter, her choice. *Choice*; she loved the way the word sounded spoken, crisply assertive at its introduction, then softening as it faded off. The *choice* to marry, the *choice* to raise a family.

If those thousand cranes granted her a wish and let her live to adulthood, she wouldn't bear a child. She would raise a bridge daughter. Her bridge daughter would crawl, walk, spit up food, grow feverish and ill, throw a ball, read a book, smell a flower for the first time. Then she would turn thirteen and grow round in the belly, a little chubby, a little sick in the morning. And Hanna's bridge daughter would plan out her twin's life—college, boyfriend, career, family—and die a little before age fourteen after giving birth to Hanna's baby.

Still on her back, Hanna rolled her most recent paper crane between her fingers. *379* was printed on the bottom of its left wing. Six hundred more to go. What did Hanna have to lose folding a thousand cranes? Little. What did she stand to gain? The world and more.

Wouldn't she love her bridge daughter? Could she stand watching her bridge daughter die so she could selfishly have a real daughter?

Am I not a real daughter? she thought.

When Hanna's bridge daughter turned eight, Hanna would teach her how to fold *tsuru*. That gave her bridge daughter six years to fold a thousand of them. Then she could wish herself into adulthood, just like Hanna was going to. And then she could have her own bridge daughter, and she would teach her how to fold origami.

Hanna would be the first of a line of bridge daughters who lived to old age. Bridge women bearing bridge daughters bearing bridge daughters, and there would be no more finalities.

NINE

HANNA FELT BAD about her gift to Cheryl Vannberg, the bouquet of a fragrance-free sunflower and the weak, leftover blooms from Uncle Rick's bucket, little time-bombs who undoubtedly relinquished their petals the day after the bridge party. More than that, she felt bad not telling Cheryl the truth about bridge daughters and what lay ahead for her. Didn't she deserve to know? Hanna had kept her promise to her mother not to discuss sensitive things with Cheryl, and now she regretted it. She'd always been jealous of Cheryl's oversized life, her confidence and glamor-girl looks, and now could see her own pettiness. She wanted to make things right.

Once again riding in the passenger's seat beside her father, Hanna held the vase of flowers with both hands, careful to prevent the water within from sloshing out. She'd purchased the flowers from Mr. McReddy's florist shop with the gift certificate her parents had given her on her birthday, but she'd arranged the flowers herself. It largely pleased her, although she felt more carnations would have filled out its base further and created a cornucopia effect, that is, the luxurious sense of an overabundance of flowers.

The ride was a quiet one until Hanna chanced to break the

silence. "Why doesn't Mom like Mrs. Vannberg?" He had mentioned this before, on their last drive to Cheryl's bridge party. "Because she's spoiling Cheryl?"

Hanna's father, off-guard, needed a moment. "No. Well, yes, she is spoiling her. Keep that to yourself," he added with his mock *sotto voce*. "That's not the reason. What your mother objects to is..." He scratched around his neck, from his nape to under his chin. "Since the old days, bridge daughters were taught to tend to the home, to cook and sew, and always stay close to their mother. It comes straight out of the Bible."

Hanna never heard her parents talk about God or the Bible, and it surprised her to hear her father discuss it so easily. They were not religious people. Hanna's late maternal grandmother, Ma Cynthia, never prayed or went to church either. Sundays were for working in the garden, which Ma Cynthia relished. Sundays, she wore her big, floppy-brimmed hat and loose blue jeans with the pant legs rolled up to her shins. On hands and knees, she worked the soil, weeding and transferring green plants and flowers in and out of her garden.

Now, Hanna's father's mother, Grandma Driscoll, *she* prayed and read the Bible and went to church each Sunday. So her father would have been raised to read the Bible, whereas Hanna had heard enough sharp comments from Ma Cynthia to know she had little respect for the book.

"The story of Abraham," her father continued. "Abraham and Sarah had a bridge daughter named Hagar."

That caught Hanna's attention—it was the name Erica had whispered in her ear. "What did she do?" Hanna asked cautiously.

"Well," her father said, "Hagar ran away one night. When everyone was asleep, she took a bag of food and fled." He searched the air before him, his eyes momentarily off the road. "'Two jars of honey, three figs of Haran, and four loaves of bread.' I always remember that part from Sunday school," he told Hanna with a flash of a smile.

"Where'd she run away to?"

"Into the desert," he said.

"Why?"

"Well, I think she thought it was her baby, and not Abraham's and Sarah's."

"So what happened to her?"

Hanna's father shook his head. "I shouldn't have brought it up. I just wanted to explain why bridge daughters are raised the way they are. Some things change more slowly than others."

"Hagar died, didn't she?"

He reluctantly said, "The Bible says Hagar was punished for sinning."

"For running away?"

"Hagar gave birth to Abraham's son in the desert. God cursed Hagar with her finality." He added, "But God punished normal women too, because of Eve. He punished lots of people. It wasn't just bridge daughters," as though that equaled things up.

The drive continued on, quiet again. Hanna stared down into the vase, watching the stalks jostle and water slosh about with each turn of the car. The fragrance of the bouquet was rich and lovely. She put her nose into the flowers, the petals tickling her face, so she could fill herself with their admixture of scents. *Flowers sing*, she thought. *They sing aroma.*

Mr. Vannberg greeted them at the front door. He wore wool trousers and a brown banker's vest and a white pressed shirt with the sleeves rolled up. He had a glass of whiskey and ice in one hand. "Come in, come in," he said, waving them inside with the glass. "Did Liz call you?"

"I wanted to bring Cheryl some fresh flowers," Hanna told Mr. Vannberg. "To replace the old ones."

"That's considerate of you," Mr. Vannberg said. "Go on back. Liz and Cheryl are in the bedroom."

Seeing Cheryl again excited Hanna now. Learning about Hagar gave her a tingling sensation akin to the camaraderie of soldiers or poets—she was part of an ancient path, a sisterhood shared by Cheryl and Erica and countless more bridge daughters in history, all the way back to Hagar. Her father trailing, she stepped quickly down the hall, eager to surprise Cheryl with the arrangement.

Hanna entered Cheryl's room bearing a bright, enthusiastic smile over the trumpeting bluebells tall in the vase. Mrs. Vannberg sat in the maternity chair with her feet on the stool, rocking. An infant lay in her arms, its miniscule hands and toes curled and clenching at the air. Its head lolled with each rock of the chair. Its skin looked like fresh pink rubber.

"Hello!" Mrs. Vannberg said, obviously surprised at Hanna's presence. "How did you hear?"

"Where's Cheryl?" Hanna said, her bubbling enthusiasm reducing in an instant.

"Right here," Mrs. Vannberg said, nodding to the infant. "Isn't she the most beautiful little slice of heaven?"

Hanna, fallen, felt her father's assuring hand on her shoulder.

"Congratulations, Liz," he said. "We're all very happy for you and your family."

"That's Cheryl?" Hanna said.

"Of course. Thank you for those," she said, meaning the flowers. "Just put them over there."

Hanna took the vase to the nightstand. The pungent smell of sour milk filled the room, accompanied by the rhythmic squeak of Mrs. Vannberg rocking the chair. A few of Hanna's origami cranes were arranged in a circle on the nightstand as though holding a meeting. The other cranes lined the shelf over the bed. Mr. Fluffens sat tall on the pillows. His polka-dot jacket, straw hat, and saber-toothed smile seemed inappropriate at the moment.

"Carter's going to move the bed out of here later today," Mrs. Vannberg explained to Hanna's father.

"You already have a crib, then."

"Oh, of course. We meant to set it up last weekend, but the time got away from us. Before we knew it, the day arrived and we had to get Cheryl to the hospital."

"When did it happen?" Hanna asked, the sobering details crashing down on her.

"Last night," Mrs. Vannberg said. "We brought the baby home, maybe two hours ago."

"I thought it took a day to have a baby," Hanna said, recalling what she'd learned from *Mother & Baby*.

"Oh, no, honey," Mrs. Vannberg said. "For a bridge birth, an hour, never more. Now, look at you." Mrs. Vannberg waved Hanna closer. She placed her hand on Hanna's belly, fingers splayed to maximize the amount of Hanna's distension she could grip.

Hanna retreated a step at the touch. Dr. Mayhew could touch her like that, but no one else.

Mrs. Vannberg said to Hanna's father, "Is she in *ponte primus*?"

"About a week past *primus*," Hanna's father said.

"Such a beautiful bridge daughter," Mrs. Vannberg said. "So you don't know if you're painting the room or not, then?"

"Not yet," Hanna's father said.

"Make sure she drinks a glass of whole milk every day," Mrs. Vannberg said. "Puts some weight on her. Good for the bones too."

Hanna went to her father, her long grim expression signaling she wanted to go home. Her father made the perfunctory goodbye and led Hanna to the bedroom door.

"Tell Dian I said hello," Mrs. Vannberg said to their backs. "I'll be sending announcements soon. We'll be having a little party in a few weeks, dinner and some wine. Carter's going to make his Manhattans."

Hanna stopped at the jamb. She swiveled out of her father's guiding hands to face Mrs. Vannberg.

"Do you miss Cheryl?" she said in an almost demanding tone. "The old Cheryl?"

"Oh, honey," Mrs. Vannberg said in a mock pitying voice. "My bridge daughter was my best friend. I miss her. But now I get to watch another Cheryl grow up, all over again. It's like having two best friends. It's a blessing."

Her father's sure hands turned Hanna around and guided her down the hall. *They didn't have to paint the room,* she thought, now understanding this adult encoded language. Cheryl's pink wallpaper and cream trim and plush dolls could remain for the next Cheryl, the real Cheryl. Cheryl was dead and Mrs. Vannberg could use the remodeling money to make the celebration even more lavish.

Seated in the car, engine idling, it came out in a blurt: "Will you miss me?"

Again, Hanna's father scraped his fingers around his neck, from nape to under his chin. "Hanna," he said, "your mother and I—you're carrying our child." He gently lay his cupped hand on the back of her head. "We're trusting you with our baby. That's so very important." He added, "Can you see how we see things?"

Hagar's curse, Erica's confinement, and the blessing of the two Cheryls, twins born fourteen years apart. This was the tradition Hanna had been born into.

TEN

WHEN HANNA STEPPED DOWN from the bus to the sidewalk, the sky-high hotels and six-story apartment houses were blocking out the setting sun, making it seem much later than five o'clock. Without so much as a goodbye, the bus driver slammed the folding doors shut and the bus heaved forward into traffic, joining the rush hour throng of cars, motorcycles, taxis, and airport shuttles.

She'd tracked her money with care since leaving Oakland. The five-dollar bill had dissolved quickly, broken into three singles and loose change by the train ride under the bay, then one of those singles broken up into more loose change when she purchased a prepackaged sandwich from a news vendor in the underground Montgomery Station. She ate one triangle of the sandwich on a street-level marble bench, the chill of the stone seat numbing her butt. The remainder of the loose change paid bus fare up Geary Street. When she realized she'd gone too far, she jumped up and asked the driver to let her off, which earned stiff remarks from him about learning to use the pull cord and kids these days thinking they didn't have to wait for stops. In her haste to alight the bus, she left the other half of the sandwich on her seat.

All she knew was, this was San Francisco. Grimy, rude, cold, busy. Panhandlers on the corners asking for spare change, bus drivers griping, people of all stripes walking home from work to cramped apartments looking down on the congested streets below. She loved it. But she would love it more if she had a few extra dollars in her pocket.

No purse, no backpack, nothing but a light jacket over her sweater and the Geary Street wind twirling her hair in arcs, Hanna studied each entrance's wrought-iron gate as she walked past it. After travelling two blocks, she fretted she'd travelled the wrong direction—that she'd not overshot her destination, as she'd panicked in the bus—and reversed course to begin her search in the other direction. She was convinced she was on the right side of the street, but within a block of travel, she worried she would have to search both sides, and maybe the surrounding streets as well.

Worse, what if Uncle Rick and Aunt Azami had moved? It had been a couple of years since they'd visited them in the city. If they'd moved, how would she know?

Then she found it. The wrought iron gate had an off-centered sunburst for its interior design, each shooting beam like the strut of a spider's web. She tried the latch, but the gate held fast. The sun had set now; it really was dark, and the incessant wind down Geary Street had turned bitterly cold. It penetrated her clothes and nipped at her skin. Searching the faces of the passersby, she wondered if she should ask someone for help, or ask if they knew how to get inside the apartment building. But why would they know? They didn't live here. If they did, they would open the gate.

Looking about, she discovered a residence listing. It was posted in a box mounted on the entryway brick. Down the list she found "Hashimoto, Azami – 114." Below the box was a keypad like a telephone's. A weathered scrap of paper gave handwritten instructions in fading blue ink. Hanna pressed the pound key and typed *114*.

A speaker beside the keypad clicked twice. "Yeah?" came out a tinny male voice.

"Uncle Rick?" Hanna said.

"Yeah?" Then: "Hanna, Christ, is that you?"

It all crushed down on her now, what she had done. Hanna burst out crying. She looked around out of embarrassment, not wanting these sophisticated adults to see her in this state. They didn't. They kept walking to their next destination, and none of them were looking at her at all.

Uncle Rick cradled the handset on the wall-mounted phone. He looked down on Hanna with a wide-eyed, disapproving expression.

"You scared the hell out of your mother," he said. "The hospital security was just about to call Oakland P.D. That would've been really bad."

She'd pled with Uncle Rick not to call her parents, but Rick wouldn't hear it. He tried Hanna's home phone first, then called her father at his office, where the receptionist gave him a beeper number. This phone roundabout finally led to a call from her mother. Through the phone's handset, Hanna could hear her mother raging and crying, and every time Rick tried to get in a word edgewise, she cut him off.

"Your mom's going to call back in twenty minutes," Uncle Rick told Hanna. "You're going to have two options, I think. You can go home tonight or you can stay until tomorrow."

"I can stay?"

Uncle Rick checked the clock hanging on one wall of the narrow kitchen nook. "Your father dropped you and Dee off in Oakland, right?"

"That's right." In an attempt to be efficient, he'd driven them to Oakland around lunchtime. Her father had a business meeting of some sort in Berkeley, so by combining errands, they could take one car and avoid parking and traffic hassles. After the ultrasound at the hospital, Hanna and her mother were to do some shopping at Jack London Square. They'd meet her father around five, have an early seafood dinner on the bay, then they'd all drive back to Concord together.

"It sounds like your mother and father are jammed up at the hospital sorting through the mess you left there," Uncle Rick said. "So, that and traffic over the bridge, then an hour back to Concord. They might let you spend the night. *Might.*"

Uncle Rick motioned for Hanna to sit on the couch. He sat on the other end. "Why did you run from your mom, squirt?"

The question made Hanna scrunch up. "I don't know," she said. "Maybe to see Aunt Azami?"

"That's what I thought," he said. "Well, she's working tonight. If your parents drive out, you probably won't get a chance to talk to her."

The adrenaline of running away and the anticipation of seeing Aunt Azami again, and the crying fit she had on the street; it all brewed up a strange, contradictory mixture of feelings within her, an emotional sugar imbalance. Seeing Aunt Azami would have stabilized her, she was sure. Now to hear she wouldn't even have a chance to say hello was crushing.

"If you want," he said, "I'll talk to Dee and see if she'll let you sleep here tonight. You can talk to Azami tomorrow morning over breakfast. How's that?"

Hanna scrambled across the couch to throw a hug around Uncle Rick's wide frame. He hugged her in return, murmuring, *I'll do what I can, squirt.*

After the second phone call with Hanna's mother—calmer than the first and, in the end, more successful—Uncle Rick told Hanna she could stay. While Hanna jumped around the apartment in joy, he went to the kitchen to make dinner.

"What're you up for tonight?" he called out.

Hanna listed off her favorites, mostly dishes her mother would make for her. Uncle Rick had to turn down each on the grounds that they didn't have the ingredients, he didn't know how to make it, or simply that he wasn't a very good cook. Finally, Hanna offered spaghetti with meatballs. Uncle Rick lit up.

"I can do spaghetti," he said. "We've even got a jar of good sauce, I think."

Hanna waited at the stove while Uncle Rick assembled the ingredients and cookware. Getting the water boiling on the stovetop seemed a milestone in the process, and Uncle Rick popped open a can of beer to celebrate.

With his shirt sleeves rolled up, Hanna could inspect his tattoos up close. One was a pinup model with curly hair posing sexily in front of the ocean. Behind her, a toothy shark leapt from a spray of seawater. On the opposite arm, a black widow nested in the eye of a thick web. She wanted to ask why he would permanently mark up his body like that, but Hanna refrained, just as she refrained from asking him why he drank so much when he opened his second can of beer.

The apartment smelled musty, and the carpet was pilled and worn in many places. Hanna spotted cigarette burns in one corner. The plaster walls were bone-white save for one wall painted deep blue. Art hung on them all; abstract work and more realistic paintings, each heavy with earth tones and umber accents. Up close, Hanna realized they were Aunt Azami's handcraft, signed "Hashimoto '83" and so on, depending on the year she'd finished it.

The kitchen was the smallest Hanna had ever seen. The utensil holders and cutting boards and spice racks left not a free square inch of counter space. The refrigerator door couldn't fully open, as it banged into the stove opposite. A deep sink was at the end of the kitchen, but no automatic dishwasher and no garbage disposal. The oven would not hold the butterball turkey Hanna's mother cooked every Thanksgiving.

Hanna did not miss the conveniences. *This* was the apartment she wanted to live in while she worked on her horticulture degree. *This* was the neighborhood she wanted to inhabit, reading the Sunday newspaper at the cafe downstairs and shopping every evening at the green grocer across the street for her dinner fixings.

Uncle Rick piled fist-sized knots of sauced spaghetti on two plates, set them on the petite table next to the window, and placed a canister of powdery parmesan cheese between the settings. Hanna drank a glass of milk with her spaghetti, which she devoured in big mouthfuls. By the end of the meal, red sauce tinted her lips and the corners of her mouth. Uncle Rick ate heartily too, but not as ravenously as Hanna. He laughed when she tried to force too much pasta into her mouth at once.

Uncle Rick crushed his empty can of beer with a squeeze of his hand. "You want to go see Azami?" he asked, then grumbled a burp.

"Can we?"

"So here's the deal. We can go, but you have to do everything I say. *Everything.* If I say we have to leave, we leave. No asking twice. Understand?"

Of course, of course, Hanna assured him. She bounced up and took their dirty plates to the sink. She cheerily started the hot water and squeezed green liquid soap on the scrubbing side of a sponge.

"Forget that," Uncle Rick said. "We'll do them later."

"I don't mind!" she called over the *shoosh* of the tap.

"Well, just come back here and let's finish talking."

She dried her hands and returned to the table.

"This is really important," he said. "You *cannot* tell your parents we went to see Azami at her work. Got that?"

"Why?"

"Because your mom will go ballistic," he said. "I'll be in so much hot water, Dee will never forgive me. Do you promise?"

Uncle Rick extended a curved pinkie finger to her. She hooked it with her pinkie and tugged. "I promise," and she bounded back to the sink.

ELEVEN

UNCLE RICK LOANED Hanna one of his thick flannel shirts, giving her one more layer of welcome warmth, as well as a black knit wool cap that made Hanna feel like a sailor. They walked six blocks down misty Geary Street, headlamps and late-night restaurants lighting their way. She loved seeing Uncle Rick's neighborhood up-close and only felt more attached to it. The walk felt good after gorging on spaghetti, but she was shivering and covered in the fog's fine mist by the time they reached Aunt Azami's workplace.

The bar was dim, only illuminated by a jukebox in the corner and the muted orange uplights behind the bar. Thankfully, the room was quite warm. The distinct odor of cheap cigarette smoke hung in the air, which Hanna did not appreciate.

"Well, well, well," Aunt Azami said from behind the bar. She looked Hanna up and down to evaluate her in full. "So Rick wasn't pulling my leg."

Hanna said hello, but so softly it couldn't be heard over the country-western song twanging from the jukebox. Then she coughed into her fist.

"Catching a cold?" Aunt Azami said.

Hanna shook her head. "Smoke."

"Hey, guys." Aunt Azami went to the other end of the bar. Two men in jackets and baseball hats occupied stools there. Bottles of beer and empty shot glasses were arrayed before them. "Cool it a while," she said, nodding toward Hanna. They shrugged and stubbed their cigarettes into an ashtray between them.

"We'll hang out for an hour," Uncle Rick said, pulling off his jacket, "then we'll get out of here."

Uncle Rick directed Hanna to a stool at the other end of the bar, in the corner beside the jukebox. Rick sat beside her, his body mass blocking her off from the rest of the room. She felt a little trapped there, but didn't object.

Without him asking, Aunt Azami presented Uncle Rick with a glass of foamy golden beer. She set a shot glass before him, reached behind the bar, and came up with a bottle of whiskey. She poured it in a fancy way, moving the bottle up and down while a thin stream of the brown liquid zipped into the glass. She asked Hanna if she wanted a Coke and Hanna nodded yes. At the cocktail station, Aunt Azami filled a squat glass tumbler with a generous amount of cubed ice and added cola from an already-opened can. Aunt Azami presented the drink with two short cocktail straws and a maraschino cherry nestled in the jutting ice, carbonation bubbles sizzling on its taut red skin.

Hanna watched the entire process, amazed. This was not the Aunt Azami she knew. She glided behind the bar with elegant efficiency, utterly in charge of the liquor, the ice, the cash register—the entire establishment. And Hanna was surprised at Aunt Azami's work clothes, a black sleeveless cotton top that did not quite reach the waistband of her black muslin pants. The tight outfit outlined her thin, lithe figure. Every time she reached for the bottles behind the bar or into the floor cooler for another can of mixer, the wan supple skin around her midsection was a beacon to the men. The two men seated at the end of the bar emotionlessly followed Aunt Azami's movements, especially when skin was displayed. Uncle Rick seemed less interested in the men and more concerned with his beer and whiskey.

Hanna picked the maraschino cherry out from the cola and ate it, nibbling it off the stem with her front teeth. "Does Aunt Azami own this?" Hanna softly asked him.

Uncle Rick laughed, showing his teeth. He wiped froth from his beard with a cupped hand. "From the hours she puts in, she might as well, but no. She just works here."

Hanna sipped Coca-Cola through the narrow cocktail straws. It was more sugary than expected. Azami had added something sweet to it.

"Are we going to get into trouble?" she asked him.

"For what?"

Hanna pointed to a sign on the wall:

ABSOLUTELY NO ONE UNDER 21
ALLOWED

"We've got an in," he told her. "Don't worry about it."

Hanna sipped more of the sweetened Coca-Cola, thinking it felt very city-like to have an "in" at a bar. A few hours in San Francisco and she was connected.

Across the bar, Aunt Azami stood before the two men in baseball caps, arms akimbo. "If you want to give me a hand, buy one of my paintings."

"Yeah," Rick hollered across the bar, "help out a starving artist."

The adults all laughed. Hanna scrunched a little more in her stool and kept sipping her Coke. She had the strange feeling one of the men had suggested something to Aunt Azami, a proposition, and it made Hanna feel sticky inside thinking of it. That and Uncle Rick laughing along with them. Why wasn't he hurt, or angry?

"Ted's a scientist," Uncle Rick told Hanna. "He studies cows."

"Cows?" In San Francisco?

"I'm a biologist," he called across the bar. "Get it right."

Ted and his friend kept their eyes on the small color television jammed into the ceiling's far corner. A baseball game played out behind an electrostatic fog of TV interference.

"This is my niece," Uncle Rick called over. Ted hooked his bottle by its neck and moved down the bar to join them. "Hanna loves flowers," he told Ted. "You should see her. I bring scraps from the Flower Mart to her house, and in an hour, she's made an arrangement."

"Good, huh?"

"Puts the florists in this town to shame," Uncle Rick said. "These boneheads that come into the Mart every morning, all they want to push in their cases is roses and tulips, roses and tulips." He said to Hanna, "You want to be a florist some day, right?"

Hanna, bent over her cola, shrugged. "Maybe," she said, straws between her teeth.

"Horticulture," Ted said to her. "The best florists have horticulture degrees. Especially if you want to specialize in orchids."

"I don't like orchids," Hanna said.

"Why not?"

"They look weird," Hanna said.

Ted and Rick laughed together. Aunt Azami arrived with the whiskey bottle and refilled Rick's shot. She set a glass tumbler filled with roasted peanuts before the three of them and glided away.

"What kind of cows do you study?" Hanna asked Ted.

"Dairy science." He scooped up a handful of peanuts and tossed two in his mouth. "Milk safety. I work for McKesson."

Hanna recognized that name—her mother bought their milk by the gallon at the supermarket.

"Did you go to college?" Hanna asked.

"New York," he said. "My father wanted me to be an evolutionary biologist, but that's a fast track to a teaching job. No thanks."

"You don't want to teach?" Hanna asked, incredulous.

Teaching at a university sounded amazing.

"He didn't want to teach theory," Uncle Rick said to her. "He wanted a *career*," he added mockingly.

"Oh no," Ted said to Rick. "Evolution isn't a theory."

"What do you mean?" he said. "It's a theory."

"No. Evolution is *not* a theory."

"I mean, I believe in evolution," Uncle Rick said, "but it's still only a theory."

"Fine," Ted said, chewing on more peanuts, "tell me what evolution is. Tell *me* what *you* think evolution is."

Aunt Azami glided back. Hanna, who had watched Aunt Azami intently so far, sensed that one part of her job was to act as a kind of cop around the bar.

Uncle Rick, flummoxed, waved around his whiskey glass. "Evolution is...you know—"

"I know what it is," Hanna said.

"What is it?" Ted, standing this whole time, pointed down at her. "Explain to me evolution."

Hanna receded in her stool, back against the bar wall. She wished she'd kept quiet.

"Go ahead, Hanna," Uncle Rick said. His smile offered her some confidence.

"Evolution," she said after a moment, "is the process where species change over time. They change each generation due to random genetic changes." She mentally rummaged around in her memory, worried she'd forgotten something. "Any gene that allows an animal to live longer means it can pass more of those genes on to its children."

Ted peered down on her, jaw loose. Bits of chewed peanuts pimpled his lips. He turned to Azami. "I want to buy that girl a drink."

Aunt Azami smiled across to Hanna and gave her a wink. She placed an upside-down shot glass beside Hanna's Coke and glided away.

"How did you know that?" Ted said to her.

"I dunno." Hanna shrugged. "I read it."

"That's a smart girl," he said to Uncle Rick.

"Takes after me," he said back. "And I still say it's a theory."

"Okay, okay, it *is* a theory," Ted said, raising his hands in defeat. "But I learned a long time ago to quit admitting that. Religious nuts in this country have taken the word 'theory' and made evolution into a fiction. So I just say evolution is not a theory. There's too much evidence. Even people who say they believe in evolution don't understand it." He pointed again at Hanna. Ted liked pointing. "You got it right. Most people say evolution makes animals 'better.'"

"What's wrong with that?" Rick said.

"It's random," Hanna said.

"Listen to the girl," Ted said. "There's no guiding hand adding 'good' mutations and removing 'bad' mutations. Evolution is constant uncontrolled experimentation. Every time an animal is born, dice are rolled. If that animal procreates, its genes get another roll of the dice in the next generation. No good or bad in it. It just *is*."

Hanna felt warm and bright inside. She'd never heard an adult so effusive about something she'd said. Uncle Rick beamed at her. He reached over and mussed her hair.

Ted was on a roll now. "Look at humans," he said, moving his hands to help illustrate. "No other mammal produces bridge daughters. Evolution rolled the dice, and we got *pons viviparous hemotrophism*. You know what that means?"

Hanna nodded, eager to hear more. In contrast, Uncle Rick's warmth faded. He cleared his throat and leaned toward his drinks, moving between Ted and Hanna. Ted, standing, leaned around him so he could talk to Hanna.

"Well, *pons vivo* worked, and it was a huge success," Ted continued. "A six-month gestation period meant women could produce more bridge daughters. Sure, it takes those bridge daughters fourteen years to produce, but you have them around to help out until the real child is born. Evolution gave humans loaner children until the real ones were ready."

Uncle Rick, grim, leaned in farther, but Ted moved with him. "I think the Giants just got a man in scoring position," he murmured to Ted.

"Today, people have one, two children," Ted said to Hanna. "But back in the day, people used to produce ten or twelve. Have you ever seen photos from the nineteenth century? Those old sepia pictures of farm families?" Ted held his arms out wide, like he was bragging about the fish that got away. "Bridge daughters lined up in feed sack dresses, each of them holding the children the older bridge daughters had given birth to."

"You mean the bridge daughters had to take care of their brothers and sisters?" Hanna said.

"Of course!" Now Ted contorted like a gymnast to lean around Rick's bulk. "Bridge daughters practically ran home nurseries by themselves. All those pregnant little girls stuck inside the house all day were ready-made for taking care of children. As well as the household and the farm. Some even ran nurseries at the churches while the adults prayed and sang. I know a guy who wrote a paper on—"

"Bridge daughters had jobs?" This responsibility, as constrained as it may be, was foreign to Hanna's experience.

"Ask any farmer. Kids are free labor. Bridge daughters doubly so, because you don't send them to school. Evolution gambled and stumbled on the perfect way for humans to dominate this planet. I mean, can you imagine what the world would be like if women were like dogs, going into heat twice a year—"

"Ted," Uncle Rick said forcefully, "why don't you go watch the baseball game."

Ted retreated two steps, confused. "Whatever you say." He returned to his stool at the other end of the bar. Hanna watched him, knowing Rick had offended him. She could see the biologist grumble under his breath, then knock a cigarette out from a pack and light up. Hanna knew why Uncle Rick did what he did, but she was dying to go over and learn more.

Uncle Rick continued drinking past their allotted one hour. The bar grew busy around nine thirty, with almost half the stools occupied and more patrons standing behind them. Outside on the street, the fog thickened. Water dripped from the eaves above the entry.

Hanna noted the bar's patrons were mostly men, arriving alone or in groups. The occasional woman appeared, but never alone. She would be with a man or two, or with a female friend. Hanna instinctively understood why, or at least thought she did. This place was warm and cheery, but drab as well, with the slight tang of must in the air. Everything seemed to be coated in the thin grease of age-old grime mixed with cigarette ash. Hanna's mother would hate this place and tell her father they needed to leave.

Hanna also noticed how men grew brash here. Not out of control, but each drink reduced their inhibitions by a tick. At home, her parents never swore. The men here used foul language like punctuation marks. It cut through the cigarette smoke when uttered. Uncle Rick seemed not to notice, but Aunt Azami would make a worrying glance at Hanna when the basest of the English language was invoked by the men.

So Hanna paid great attention to a young woman who appeared in the doorway a little after ten. She wore a camel coat and a headscarf of mottled red, yellow, and orange silk. With slight, petite movements, she unraveled the scarf and removed her coat and placed both on the hooks beside the entryway. When she approached the bar, she was all-but-ignored by the other men in the room, who either watched the baseball game or Aunt Azami. When the woman drew close, Hanna saw she was elfin and not terribly taller than herself. The bags beneath the woman's eyes made her appear exhausted. Her thin pale lips drew into a pinkish smile when Aunt Azami recognized her.

"I want to introduce you to someone special," Aunt Azami said to the woman. "Maureen, this is Hanna, my niece. She's staying the night."

Uncle Rick leaned back so Maureen could offer Hanna a

delicate, bony hand. "Nice to meet you," she said. The bony hand was quite cold. "Azami has told me all about you."

Hanna admired how this woman carried herself, the elegant way she removed her outer garments, the quiet purposefulness of taking her wallet from her purse and extracting a fresh unfolded ten-dollar bill to pay Azami for her first drink. It was a Coca-Cola in a squat tumbler with a maraschino on top, just like Hanna's. Certainly there must be alcohol in hers, Hanna believed.

Uncle Rick got up and offered his stool to Maureen. "You two should talk," he said. "I'm going catch the last couple of innings." And he joined the men at the other end of the bar, whiskey and beer in hand.

"How do you like San Francisco?" Maureen asked her as she settled on the barstool.

"I love it here," Hanna breathed. "I wish I could live here."

"It's a singular city," Maureen said. "You can be whomever you want to be in San Francisco."

"Really?" Hanna thought for a moment. "Can I be super-rich?"

"Well," Maureen said, smiling, "some people certainly try to look that way here."

"I don't really want that," Hanna said quickly. "I was just saying."

"Azami told me you love flowers."

Hanna cocked her head, surprised to hear this.

"She shows off your arrangements," Maureen said. "She brightens up the bar with them, you know." Maureen pointed to a wall inset over the cash register. "She places them right there. Everyone who comes in, she tells them all about you and your love of flowers."

Hanna, touched, looked to Aunt Azami to thank her, but she was busy at the cocktail station. No one else showed off her bouquets. She made them for her father, but he never took them to the office.

"My aunt makes beautiful origami," Hanna said to Maureen. "She taught me how to make paper cranes."

"Ah, yes," Maureen said. "I love them too."

"I'm making a thousand of them this year," Hanna said. "I'd make you one, but I don't have any paper."

"Next time," Maureen said.

"Wait—" Hanna checked her back pocket. Sure enough, in her tiny notebook accounting for every *tsuru* she'd made, she found a square of paper. It was her template for cutting more origami sheets. She pushed her cola aside and wiped the bar dry with the sleeve of her sweater. She numbered the crane just as she'd numbered hundreds of cranes before. Then she set about folding it. Maureen watched on with mild interest. When Hanna gingerly pulled the crane's neck and tail, Maureen's eyes livened and sparkled. The crane's wings extended as though in preparation for flight.

"You get number four hundred twenty-six," Hanna told her.

"Like a serial number," Maureen said, accepting the crane. "Thank you very much."

While Maureen admired the crane, Hanna studied her closer. The hollow under Maureen's throat was deep and round and bluish-gray, like a moon crater. Maureen's upright posture and the careful, direct way she spoke seemed practiced to Hanna and unnatural. Hanna never considered Maureen frail, but she had the characteristics of a dry twig, a judgment Hanna felt ashamed to entertain.

Hanna told herself to stop staring. "Are you meeting someone here?" she asked.

"Your aunt," Maureen said. "I came to see her."

"You're friends?"

"I've known Azami for six years now," Maureen said. "She's a very sweet person."

Aunt Azami joined them. "Are you two having a good time?"

Hanna nodded several times. Maureen murmured, "Of course."

"You two should talk," she said to Maureen before gliding away. "*Really* talk."

Maureen took a slight sip from her tumbler of cola. She only used the straws to stir. The maraschino cherry remained in her glass, unthinkable to Hanna, who devoured them as soon as Azami presented her a fresh drink.

"Your aunt tells me you're a bridge daughter," Maureen said.

Hanna shrank in the stool. She nodded once.

"I am too," Maureen said.

Hanna furrowed her brow and looked closer. Maureen was elfin and slight, yes, but she had the distinct face of an adult, a woman in her twenties, albeit a wan and gray one. She simply could not be thirteen years old.

"I had a procedure," Maureen said. She spoke guardedly, although the baseball game and the occasional cheers from the other end of the bar muffled their conversation. "Two months before my finality, I had my *pons anno* halted. It's called an intrauterine bi-graft. Have you heard of it?"

"I've heard about abortion," Hanna said slowly.

Maureen drew her lips in, acknowledging the weight of the word. "I don't see my bi-graft as an abortion," she said, voice remaining low. "But a lot of people do."

"I don't understand. Everyone tells me—"

"Everyone will tell you lots of things," Maureen said. It was the first time she interrupted Hanna, and it felt sharp. "They're not telling you all the facts."

Maureen turned on the stool toward Hanna. Facing each other in the corner of the bar, this afforded some privacy. She took Hanna's hand and placed it on her own belly. Through her loose blouse, Hanna's splayed fingers touched Maureen's prominent ribs. In her palm, Hanna felt a rigid tension the size and shape of a shallow ice cream bowl. Hanna placed her other hand on her own tight bowl to compare.

"The fetus is still inside me," Maureen said. "Its development has been arrested. I'll never give birth."

"How old are you?"

Maureen gingerly released Hanna's hand. "I'm twenty-four,"

she said, chin raised. "I have a full-time job. I work at a supermarket. I pay all my bills and rent, and on time."

College libraries and dorm room bull sessions, thesis committees and horticulture degrees. Hanna would set all those dreams aside just to lead Maureen's life of bagging groceries and visiting her bartender friend every few nights.

Hanna fell forward and hugged Maureen. Maureen, surprised, returned the hug. Finally, Hanna released her. She stretched her sweater sleeves over her hands, making improvised mittens to wipe the moisture from her face.

"I'm not telling you what to do," Maureen said to her. "You deserve to know your options."

"I want to do it."

"You need to really think it over," Maureen said.

"Where do I get it done?"

"I don't know," Maureen said. "I had it done ten years ago. I've never seen that doctor since. You'll have to find one on your own. And Hanna—" She took Hanna's hand again, holding it between her two icy palms. "You'll never see your family again. You have to leave home. You can never look back."

"You're not from San Francisco?" Hanna said.

"I can't tell you where I'm from," Maureen said. "I can't tell anyone. But it's far away from here. And you would have to run far away too."

"Why?"

"Bi-grafts are illegal," Maureen said.

"I don't care."

"Hanna," Maureen said, "you would be taking your parents' child away from them. You would be attacking some very basic instincts within them."

"But they would have me. *I'm* their child."

Maureen squeezed Hanna's hand tighter. "Your mother wants the child you're carrying. That's the motherly instinct, one of the strongest instincts in the world. I've never heard of a mother seeing it any other way."

TWELVE

AUNT AZAMI GLIDED over around ten thirty with another sweetened Coke for Hanna. "I got someone to take over for me," she said. "We'll get out of here in about half an hour. Are you hungry?"

"A little," Hanna said, still drained from her talk with Maureen.

"There's a good pizza place around the corner."

"Pizza!" Hanna sat straight up.

Azami's relief arrived ten minutes later, an older woman with bright blond hair in a ponytail. Aunt Azami told Uncle Rick to help out, which he did, bleary-eyed and full of whiskey and beer. He hauled buckets of ice from the back room to the metal tub under the bar counter, then carried out six-packs of beer to restock the reach-in fridge. Aunt Azami counted money from the till and explained the situation to her relief, in particular who owed how much money, who was paid up, and who didn't need any more alcohol.

Then Aunt Azami began counting the tip money stored in a brown glazed honey pot beside the cash register. Her hands came out with leaves of loose green cash, one fistful after another. She straightened and squared the thick stack of bills and pocketed it.

The three of them departed the bar after eleven, Uncle Rick stumbling along and Hanna holding Aunt Azami's hand. Azami was now clad from neck to knees in a black wool overcoat, straight and stern with doorknob buttons down the front.

Hanna had never visited a by-the-slice pizza counter, and she eyed the wondrously large pies displayed under heat lamps. Unlike her family's visit to the parlors in Concord, where Hanna never had any input on the toppings, Aunt Azami invited Hanna to pick out the exact pizza she wanted. Hanna asked for a slice of vegetarian pizza on whole wheat crust, while Uncle Rick got a pepperoni slice and Aunt Azami ordered one with pesto.

The gigantic slice was too much for Hanna. She moaned she was full. Without a word, Uncle Rick reached across the stand-up counter and took the remainder. He was drinking a beer with his pizza, eyelids drooping and his bulk swaying. Aunt Azami couldn't finish her pizza either, and Uncle Rick confiscated her remains as well.

"Where does Maureen live?" Hanna asked Aunt Azami.

"In the Richmond," she said. "It's a short bus ride from here."

"Can I see her tomorrow?"

"I don't think so," Aunt Azami said. "Your parents will be here in the morning."

Hanna had already forgotten that. She was ready to move in with Aunt Azami and Uncle Rick and start a new life on Geary Street.

"Remember," Uncle Rick said, mouth full of pesto and cheese and chewed-up crust, "don't breathe a word of this to your mom."

Uncle Rick unlocked the door, stumbled lead-footed across the apartment, and fell onto the bed face-first. Within a minute, the buzz saw of his snoring consumed the apartment.

Aunt Azami, unprepared for Hanna's visit, hurried around the apartment tidying up. Other than the kitchen nook and bathroom, the apartment was a single-room deal, with a couch, coffee table, and a television set on one side and a queen-sized bed wedged into the opposite corner. Makeshift drapes hung around the bed created a sense of privacy.

Aunt Azami started the shower. She helped Hanna out of her outer layers of clothes. When steam was rolling out the door of the tiny bathroom, Hanna went inside, finished disrobing, and stepped into the shower. The trip down Geary Street had injected another chill into her. Now the hot water soothed and relaxed. She scrubbed herself, thinking of Maureen's revelations. It seemed improbable she would find a way to have a—what was it called?—an intrauterine bi-graft…especially if it was illegal.

Swabbing the cake of soap across her distended belly, she asked herself if she could muster the will to hurt the child inside her. When she dreamed of college and career and marriage, no one was hurt. Would she hurt her parents' child? Before, in her dreams, she wanted the child to simply disappear, taking with it her problem. The sore tightness in her, a mosquito bite abnormally swollen—Maureen had shown her the child was something she would have to live with, bi-graft or otherwise.

She peeked out the bathroom. Uncle Rick's snoring continued. "Is it safe?" she said to Aunt Azami.

"He's out," Aunt Azami said. "He won't see you."

With a towel wrapped around her from armpits to knees, she trod barefoot across the carpet to Aunt Azami. The hissing steam radiator made the room nice and warm, even with a window cracked open for fresh air. Aunt Azami put a square orange pillow on the floor, huge with a giant button in the middle. Hanna sat on it cross-legged, careful to cover herself with the towel. Aunt Azami sat behind her. She began to carefully pull a brush through Hanna's brown hair.

"Maureen is super nice," Hanna said.

"She's my favorite person in the world," Aunt Azami said. "She's very strong." Then, "Do you want to see the Flower Mart tomorrow?"

Hanna turned around, causing a sharp tug on her hair. "Can

I?"

"I'm going to call your parents early in the morning. I'll ask if they want to meet us there."

Hanna, elated, turned back so Aunt Azami could resume brushing.

Aunt Azami said, "Why did you come here?"

If Aunt Azami had asked the question earlier, Hanna probably would've blurted out the story in a wet, breathless flurry of details, sobbing about everything being unfair and scared stiff of the punishment she faced. Now, after all the heady events at the bar, Hanna explained the story in a more level manner.

That afternoon at the Oakland hospital, after the ultrasound, the doctor told Hanna to step out to the hallway while he gave his conclusions to her mother, just as Dr. Mayhew would. Hanna had no idea if it was good or bad news, but she certainly wanted to know. Her mother, however, had warned her on the drive to Oakland not to step out of line. She did not want more rudeness or another interruption in front of the doctor. They would discuss the doctor's findings a day or two after the visit.

For the first time in her life, Hanna could tell her mother was lying to her. She was counting on Hanna forgetting to ask later. Even if Hanna did remember, she sensed her mother wasn't going to be completely truthful. Was it good news or bad?

After visiting Mrs. Vannberg and meeting the new Cheryl, Hanna now felt all news was bad news when it came to her pregnancy. Each stage of *pons anno* was just one more milestone closing in on her own mortality. No more hospital visits, she told herself. No more adults probing her insides and sending her out of the room to discuss her health with her mother. Hanna was more than a milk carton, she was more than a hen warming another hen's eggs. Hagar ran. Hanna could run too. And she did.

Unattended in the hallway, with no plan but to flee, Hanna hurried to the stairs. She might have to wait precious seconds for an elevator car, so she descended the wide staircase. The hospital was in an old building, one with old-fashioned porcelain drinking fountains built into the walls and transoms over the doors. The oak staircase took her down four flights to the lobby. Walking past the receptionists' station, she resisted the urge to look anyone in the eye, fearing it would reveal her guilt. She was out on the Oakland downtown street in under two minutes. If they'd not discovered her missing by then, they would quite soon. She bounded down the block and descended another set of stairs to an underground train station. Less than thirty minutes later, she was in San Francisco.

"I didn't know what to do," Hanna confessed to Azami. "I think I just wanted to talk to someone."

"Your uncle?" Aunt Azami said, smiling.

"I wanted to talk to you," Hanna said. "I don't want to go home."

Aunt Azami, for the first time since Hanna had known her, looked saddened. "I'm sorry."

"Do I have to go?"

"Your parents are worried sick, Hanna."

"I want to get a bi-graft," Hanna said firmly. "Like Maureen."

"I can't help you with that," Aunt Azami said.

Something inside her collapsed. "You can't?" The walk home from the bar, she'd started to count on Aunt Azami's help, thinking she was an ally. She thought Aunt Azami introduced Maureen to her specifically to learn about bi-grafts.

"Hanna," Aunt Azami said, "I can't get between you and your parents. I mean, taking you to the bar tonight, that was one thing. They'll probably never forgive me—"

"Where can I get it?" Hanna said, meaning a bi-graft. "Where do I go?"

Aunt Azami said, "I don't even know where to look. And, really, I shouldn't be talking to you about it. Like I said, your mother..."

Uncle Rick's snoring deepened and grew louder. He slept on his belly, face smooshed against the wool blanket. Hanna put her hand over her mouth to hide her laugh. Aunt Azami stifled a laugh too.

"Your uncle has stolen more hours of sleep from me than you can imagine," she said. "Here, let's get you dressed for bed."

Aunt Azami dug through a dresser and came up with one of Uncle Rick's old Jefferson Airplane T-shirts. On Hanna, it hung straight to her knees like a go-go dress. Then Hanna and Azami took to the couch. They sat cross-legged, facing one other and sharing a blanket.

"Why does Uncle Rick drink so much?"

"He says it's the only thing he's good at," Aunt Azami said reluctantly. "I don't believe that, though."

With the barrier dropping between them, Hanna ventured closer.

"Why don't you have children?" she asked. *Would you raise me?* Hanna wanted to ask.

Aunt Azami spoke even more reluctantly about children than about Rick's drinking. "Your uncle and I don't feel like we want any."

"Why not?"

Aunt Azami grimaced. Hanna rushed to take it back.

"I'm sorry," she said. "I guess that's personal."

"I'll tell you something you probably don't know," Aunt Azami said. "Do you know how much older your uncle is than your mother?"

Uncle Rick *felt* younger than her mother, from the way he talked and the way he seemed to find fun—or alcohol—in everything he did. Aunt Azami too, although she was much more stoic than Uncle Rick.

"He's six years older than your mom," Aunt Azami said. "Think about that for a minute. That means your mother's bridge mother was almost eight when he was born. All Rick's young life, there was this older girl taking care of him. They went on walks, she made him lunch. She even changed his diapers."

"He remembers diapers?"

"No, but I'm saying she was a second mother to him. They

would sing songs and dance in circles in your grandmother's farmhouse. She cooked all his meals and taught him the alphabet. Your grandmother was busy with her gardening and her photography. She expected a lot from her bridge daughters."

Ma Cynthia loved being outdoors, especially tending her garden, but Hanna knew other things about her. She refused to enroll her mother or Uncle Rick in public school, homeschooling them part-time and having them work the farm the remaining daylight hours. The "farm," as Hanna's father put it, holding his fingers up in the shape of quotation marks, as Ma Cynthia's "farm" had no livestock or fields. Ma Cynthia's house was a cabin on the edge of the woods of Marin County with a garden that produced table vegetables and trees that yielded canning fruit. The remainder of their diet came from a farmer's co-op in Sonoma County. Hanna never met her grandfather, but a slip at the dinner table years earlier suggested that her mother and Uncle Rick had different fathers, men Ma Cynthia never married.

Ma Cynthia had kept a picture on the fireplace mantel. Hanna loved it dearly. It was her mother and Uncle Rick as children, both in overalls and no shirts and no shoes, hair long and frazzled wild, with a black Labrador named Debs panting at their feet. Ma Cynthia took the photo with an old-fashioned Brownie camera. She developed it in the ramshackle chicken house, which served as her photo lab and painting studio. She hand-tinted it to give the children rosy cheeks and bright blue eyes. Over the intervening years, the tint had bleached away, making the photo looked overexposed and weathered, ancient.

"Understand something," Aunt Azami said. "Your uncle loves your mother. There's nothing that gets between them. They're as close as any two people can be. Okay?"

Her mother and Uncle Rick seemed to argue a lot, and her mother seemed dismissive of Uncle Rick's career path, using a tone of voice that suggested he had none. But the way her mother called him Ritchie when no one else could, and the way she kissed him on the cheek whenever he arrived at their house…Hanna could see what Aunt Azami meant about their relationship being close. It was so evident, it was easy to overlook.

"As much as Rick loves your mother," Aunt Azami continued, "he never got over his bridge sister, the girl who raised him. She was named Dian too, you know. She died giving birth and her baby grew up to look just like her. It tears him apart to talk about his bridge sister. It tears him apart that no one will talk about her."

"Even Ma Cynthia?"

"Especially Ma Cynthia," Aunt Azami said. "She never spoke of her bridge daughters. She was a strong and stubborn woman, but she was traditional in her own ways. Do you know that she delivered your uncle and your mother? She didn't take her bridge daughters to a hospital. She led the labor right there at the farm."

"Like a doctor?"

"More like a midwife. In that farmhouse out in the woods, she midwifed both her children. No painkillers, no medicine, nothing but hot water and warm towels. She had a special curved knife for cutting the *funiculus*. She used it for Rick's birth and the second time for your mother's. She used that knife twice. Two cuts. Then she mounted it on the wall in her kitchen."

Hanna remembered that knife. It seemed appropriate out in the woods, like having a rifle on the wall. She always was a little scared of Ma Cynthia. She spoke her mind whenever they visited the farm. She criticized everyone, her mother, her father, Uncle Rick and Aunt Azami, even Hanna. No one did anything right, according to Ma Cynthia. But now, with this one revelation, Hanna beheld her grandmother with a fresh measure of awe. Gardening, vegetables, hand-tinted photos, midwifing—how did she learn all these things?

Aunt Azami peered across the room, verifying Uncle Rick was still asleep. "Before your grandmother delivered your mother," Aunt Azami said softly, "she drilled your uncle on everything he was to do when the time came. He was only six, but living on that farm, he grew up pretty fast, as you might imagine. When the time arrived, he prepared the water and soap and towels while Ma Cynthia began coaching her bridge through the delivery."

Aunt Azami's eyes were veiny and pink. "Your Uncle Rick held his bridge sister's hand through the entire labor. He was just a child. She died right there in front of him. Her hand was clenched so tight, his little fingers went numb. Then her hand relaxed and...fell away. And there was Ma Cynthia swaddling your mother and rocking her in her arms. He told me, it was like she didn't notice her dead daughter lying before her."

She continued after a moment. "Your Uncle Rick, he did everything he'd been told to do. He pulled the blanket over his bridge sister's face and got up and went to the next room. He called the county and told them to bring the morgue van. Then he began heating bottles of milk and drawing water for the baby's bath."

Aunt Azami looked over at Rick again, longingly. "Ma Cynthia caught him when he was eight or nine crying over his bridge sister. She told him he could cry that once and no more."

She reached over and stroked the side of Hanna's head. "I'm not telling you all this to scare you. I really don't know why he drinks so much. But I think, somewhere deep down, that's where it started."

After a long silence, Aunt Azami said it was time to turn in. She and Hanna stripped the back cushions off the couch and placed pillows at one end. Aunt Azami tucked in Hanna between layers of blankets. Within a minute, Hanna was toasty-warm, from toes to neck. Aunt Azami changed into a long shirt herself. She hit Uncle Rick on his ribs until he rolled to one side of the bed. Then she slipped under the covers.

"Don't worry about the radiator," she said across the room to Hanna. "It talks in the middle of the night. It's normal." And she turned off the light.

A great clanging of hollow metal awakened Hanna. Off in the corner, the cast iron steam radiator banged twice again, then rattled. She remembered Aunt Azami's assurances; she told herself it was an old building and old buildings do this kind of thing, but she could not return to sleep.

In her unwinding imagination, someone or something lived in the basement. It slammed the flat of a heavy wrench against a lead pipe, one of hundreds of pipes snaking through the basement, a pipe for each dwelling in the building. Its banging was delivered up the walls and into the apartment, like sending a message through an old-fashioned pneumatic tube. An ominous telegraph from below addressed to Hanna and detailing things to come.

THIRTEEN

WHEN HANNA AWOKE, it all came to her at once: lightheadedness, the golf-ball lump in the back of her throat, the taste of old pennies in her mouth. She bounded barefoot across the thin carpet and made it to the bathroom in time.

"You okay?" Aunt Azami called from the kitchen.

"I'm fine," Hanna called back, vomit dripping from her lips. She spit out the last of it, flushed, and washed up. It was a one-vomit morning. She felt better now.

The bed curtains were tied to the walls and the bed was made. Food was on the table; a glass of pineapple juice and a plate of eggs and toast. Aunt Azami washed dishes in the kitchen, wrapped in a lavender cotton robe cinched tight around her waist.

"Good morning," she said, hands in the sink's sudsy water. "Can you eat? I made some breakfast for you."

"Where's Uncle Rick?"

"He left for work at five."

Hanna couldn't imagine rising that early, and not understanding hangovers, she barely conceived of the willpower it took for him to do so five days a week.

She fell into the chair before the plate of eggs and dug in. Her empty stomach beckoned. "I can't wait to see the Flower Mart," she said. "I've wanted to go there for so long."

"Hanna," Aunt Azami said cautiously, "your parents will be here any minute."

Hanna felt something drop out of her insides.

"I spoke with them this morning," Aunt Azami continued. "They didn't want to wait any longer. Your mother is all torn up."

Hanna set down her fork. She had no more appetite. She drank the pineapple juice for its sugar, to get her engine started, but it tasted acidic and had the consistency of whole milk, and nothing seemed pleasurable that morning.

Hanna's mother rushed inside and hugged Hanna. She felt around Hanna's back, repeating, "Are you okay? Are you okay?"

"Thanks for watching her." Hanna's father stood in the hallway beyond the front door. "We're sorry to put you out like this."

"It's no problem," Aunt Azami said. "We're happy to have her."

Hanna stood in the entryway, arms hanging at her side, while her mother crouched on her knees and continued hugging her deeply. Hanna felt like she was being pressed into her mother, as though she wanted to return Hanna to her womb. She knew the outpouring of affection and her mother's question—"Are you okay?"—were not directed at Hanna but the child inside her. A miser hugs the lockbox tight to his chest, but he does not love the lockbox, only the precious gold inside.

In the car, her father navigating downtown traffic, Hanna made one more play. "Can I say goodbye to Uncle Rick?"

Hanna's mother turned around in the passenger's seat to look Hanna in the eyes. "Were they smoking in front of you?"

Hanna, off-guard, truthfully shook her head no.

"Were they smoking in their apartment?"

"I didn't smell cigarettes," Hanna's father said.

"Hanna?"

Hanna shook her head again, beginning to realize where this

was leading.

"There's tobacco smoke in her sweater," her mother said to her father.

Her father chuckled and looked at Hanna in the rearview mirror. "You better tell your mother where you went last night."

"Did your uncle take you to a bar last night?"

Hanna sank into the backseat cushions, shoulders collapsing inward, head down.

"I want to go to that Flower Mart right now," her mother said to her father. He was smiling a puckish smile, one even Hanna could see from the backseat.

The San Francisco Flower Mart took up an entire city block, most of it fenced off. Through the chain link, Hanna watched panel trucks and pallet lifts in action, moving boxes and crates of blooms from loading docks into the main building, a flat, featureless warehouse with sliding metal gates wide open for foot traffic. A smaller, more personable building ran along the street with florist business names above each door. From years of listening to Uncle Rick's gripes about work, Hanna knew the florists and downtown flower stands used these offices to transact business with the wholesalers inside the warehouse.

As the trio crossed the floor of the warehouse, Hanna gawked at the flowers around her. Pallets organized by variety and color filled each wholesaler's portion of the sales floor. Some specialized, such as an orchid dealer with hundreds of the weird plants on stands and tables. Another wholesaler decorated its sales area with red Chinese paper lanterns and a twisting dragon kite strung to the rafters. Cincotti's Flowers was in the rear of the warehouse, its floor area lined with long rows of annuals and perennials in buckets. Hanna ran her hand over the top of a field of penstemon plants, leafy and tall, their elongated stems lined with umber blossoms like velvet trumpets.

"Ritchie!" her mother called out. Across the warehouse floor, Uncle Rick pushed a stack of boxes with a hand truck. A quick grin split his beard. He left the boxes to trot over to Hanna and her parents.

"Hey, Dee." He kissed her on the cheek. "Barry, good to see you."

"Thank you for taking care of Hanna last night," her mother said with an unmistakable terseness.

"No problem at all. Right, squirt?"

"Did you take Hanna to Azami's bar last night?"

Uncle Rick's grin slowly collapsed, like a circus tent deflating. Hanna felt squishy and embarrassed—embarrassed for herself, embarrassed for Uncle Rick, embarrassed to be seen with her lecturing mother.

"I thought we could go see Azami," Uncle Rick said. "She wasn't getting off until two, so, yeah, we went and visited for a little bit."

"You took her to a *bar.*"

"It's not what you think," Uncle Rick said. "It's a neighborhood place. People bring their kids in sometimes," although Hanna did not see any other children there.

"What if the police found her?" her mother said.

"They'd look the other way. Dee, the cops know the bar, they know Azami. They're not going to—"

"Her sweater smells like an ashtray," her mother said, tugging at the elbow of Hanna's sleeve. "I don't want her around smokers, you understand? Or people *drinking,* of all things."

It went on like this for another minute, Uncle Rick taking the drubbing, nodding, admitting he did wrong, and finally asking for forgiveness.

"But it was all my idea," he said. "Don't blame Azami. Or Hanna. Please."

Hanna's mother chewed on that for a second, considering all that had been said, then asked Rick for a hug. They embraced for a long moment, swinging a bit. Hanna's father looked down on Hanna with a blank expression. He winked and she knew it was okay.

"Okay," Hanna's mother breathed out, wiping the corners of her eyes. "We will talk about this when we get home," she said to Hanna.

"Can I see the rest of the Flower Mart?" she asked.

She could not. It was time to go.

Hanna's father followed the signage directing them to the Bay Bridge. Once they were crossing the bay, Hanna's mother turned to face Hanna again.

"When we get home, we're going to have a talk," she said. "There's going to be some changes."

Hanna nodded meekly, feeling the weight of judgment lowering in the car.

"Your father and I had a long discussion last night," her mother said. "This 'experiment' of ours, this experiment of raising you differently than other bridge daughters, we're now reconsidering that."

Hanna, shrinking down as far as she could in the car seat, shrugged.

"We're going to cut back your school hours," she said, meaning the time Hanna spent at the kitchen table being homeschooled. That sounded like a pretty good deal, until her mother continued. "Instead, we're going to have you follow more traditional roles. You'll be taking more responsibility about the house."

Hanna, throat dry, thought back on what the biologist had told her in the bar. "But we don't have any other children."

"What do you mean?"

"I thought bridge daughters took care of the other children."

"Long time ago," her father said.

"Don't worry," her mother said. "There will be plenty for you to do. And there will be some new rules."

"Like what?"

"Speaking only when spoken to," her mother said. "Asking for permission. You'll always be at my side when we're out of the house."

Reading and writing, the freedom to speak her mind, books of her own, and a real allowance, pittance it may be—this hybrid of bridge-rearing, her mother's blend of tradition and new thinking, this was the experiment her parents abandoned while Hanna sat on a barstool munching maraschino cherries.

Hanna turned in the backseat to admire San Francisco's skyline one last time. The pyramid, the tower, the prison on the island, the Ferry Building's great neon sign proclaiming SAN FRANCISCO—the car shot into the tunnel and all of it was gone.

FOURTEEN

HANNA AWOKE with her mother standing over her. She had a grim, almost imperious air.

"You'll be making breakfast today," she told Hanna. "We'll have pancakes."

Hanna, sullen, rose and followed her mother to the kitchen, still in her pajamas. She retrieved the box of dry mix from the pantry. At her mother's prompting, she read the directions on the side of the box, located the necessaries in the refrigerator and cabinets, and whipped up the batter. A side of bacon was in the bottom drawer of the refrigerator, and with her mother looking on, she got four strips sizzling in a pan.

Satisfied with her progress, her mother sat at the table with her coffee and unfolded the newspaper before her. Hanna wordlessly prepared the breakfast and poured apple juice for them both. Food on two plates, she brought the meal to the table.

"You need to set the table," her mother said without looking up.

Hanna returned the hot plates to the countertop and set the table. Her mother held up the newspaper so Hanna could put the utensils and placemat before her. Hanna then presented the meal.

She wondered if she had to wait for her mother to start eating, but her mother indicated it was fine for her to begin.

"Is this my punishment?" Hanna said down to her pancakes.

"This is how other bridge daughters are raised," her mother said.

"I said I'm sorry."

"Actually, that's not true," her mother said. "Traditional bridge daughters would eat in the kitchen, standing up."

That confused Hanna. "Why?"

"Your place is not at the table," Hanna's mother said coolly.

They ate quietly for a few minutes, facing each other. Hanna's mother did not look at Hanna, finishing the newspaper while eating.

"There's a reason we let you stay with your aunt and uncle last night," her mother finally said. "I was *furious* at you for running off. Your father suggested we let you stay in San Francisco so we could discuss the situation between ourselves. Maybe, I told him, maybe we should have stayed with the old ways, like how Ma Cynthia raised her bridge daughters."

"I don't like it," Hanna said softly.

"I don't care for it either," her mother said, "but the way you've been acting lately and running off like that—running away, exactly like I've been warned you would since before you were born. I always told myself, *My bridge daughter won't do that. I'll raise her right.* And then you go and do it, threatening the life of my child..." She shook her head. "When you finish, we'll start making cookies."

Hanna brightened. "Cookies?"

"We're going to the Grimonds' for coffee," her mother said. "You'll be expected to act properly there too."

On the Grimond's front porch, the door opened to reveal a drab Erica Grimond. She stared at them with saucerous eyes. Hanna wore a featureless dress much like Erica's, gray and unadorned, tight about her neck and hanging straight to her shins. Her mother had purchased it and more like it the day before, at the end of their drive back from San Francisco.

"Please come in," Erica said blankly, standing aside. Hanna's mother entered, followed by Hanna, who kept close behind her and careful to maintain her posture.

Mrs. Grimond swept into the room wearing a taupe blouse and bright red toreadors. Hanna thought the pants made her look hippy, but said nothing.

"I'm so glad you could make it," she said to Hanna's mother. "What are these?"

Hanna stepped forward and offered the plate. "I made cookies."

Mrs. Grimond raised her eyebrows and grimaced at Hanna's mother as though a tad embarrassed for her. Hanna's mother pinched the back of Hanna's arm. Hanna receded like a touched snail returning to its shell.

"I hope you like chocolate chip," Hanna's mother said.

"Of course," Mrs. Grimond said. Then, to Erica, "We'll have cookies with our coffee." She looked to Hanna's mother. "And sandwiches after?"

"You shouldn't have."

Erica took the plate from Hanna and went soundlessly to the kitchen, her soft flat shoes like moccasins on the carpeted floor. Hanna's mother pushed her by the arm. Hanna followed Erica's path, looking backward at the women as they took their ease on the living room couches.

The kitchen's heavy swinging door completely cut them off from the rest of the house. Coffee already brewed, Erica deftly poured two hot blacks into *tasse à café* cups. A service tray with saucers and cubed sugar in a bowl stood ready on the counter. Erica saucered the coffees and filled a creamer with half-and-half from the refrigerator.

"Are you going to help?" she finally said to Hanna.

Hanna jumped. "Of course!"

Erica pointed at the cabinets on the other side of the kitchen. "I need a salad plate and two smaller plates." She pointed to the countertop. "Fold two napkins. And there's a thin vase in that cabinet. We'll add a flower from the bunch." A spray of yellow daisies cheered up the kitchen from their perch over the sink.

Hanna instinctively prioritized. She retrieved the flower vase first. Long-necked with a bulbous base, like an elongated gourd, Hanna added cold water, then selected the best daisy she could find in the bouquet. She looked through drawers for a pair of scissors to trim the daisy's stem. When it was prepared, she turned and realized, red-faced, Erica had finished the other tasks, folding the napkins and plating the chocolate chip cookies. Erica stood in the center of the kitchen, lips crimped, smoldering while Hanna dawdled with the flower.

"Put it on the tray with the coffee," Erica said. "You carry the cookies."

When Erica had the coffee tray in two hands and Hanna had the smaller tray of cookies and napkins in hers, Erica nodded for her to follow. Erica pushed through the swinging door and held it open for Hanna, who was having trouble balancing the tray of plates. They proceeded to the living room, Erica leading, and set the refreshments on the table running before the couch. Hanna grew red-faced when she realized her mother and Mrs. Grimond were discussing runaway bridge daughters.

"She had taught her bridge daughter to read and write," Mrs. Grimond said, scandalized. "When the girl ran off, she was shocked, even though everyone had told her she was playing with fire. You wouldn't do that, now would you, dear?"

Hanna looked between Mrs. Grimond and her mother, attempting to decode the situation. She shook her head once, for appearances.

"Very good," Mrs. Grimond said to Erica. "We'll be ready for sandwiches in about thirty minutes." The women resumed their conversation. Hanna stood waiting for some recognition from her mother. None arrived. Erica took Hanna by the arm and led her out of the living room.

"You're welcome," Hanna muttered.

Erica smushed a finger over her lips, indicating silence. She led Hanna back to the kitchen and through a pocket door in the rear corner. It hid a narrow windowless hall that smelled of dog food and bleach. Sure enough, the shelving on the walls stored various household goods, cans and jars and plastic bottles, along with economy-sized bags of dry kibble and laundry detergent.

Hanna followed Erica into a dark room off the hallway. It had no door. Erica flicked on the light to reveal a twin bed covered with gray wool blankets and a hardbacked chair jammed in the corner. The carpet was not the luxurious shag of the living room but stiff bristle, the kind marketed for its easy-to-clean features. A few toys were lined up on the floor against the wall, simple dolls and a coloring book and a big box of crayons with a safety sharpener built in the side. There was no radio, no shelf of books. A doorway lacking a door led to a bare bathroom. It was nothing more than a showerhead sticking out from the wall, a floor drain, a toilet, and a hardware store vanity.

Erica faced Hanna with a grim expression, as though challenging her to say something about her living quarters. Hanna, aghast, stared back.

"What do you want to do?" Erica finally said.

"I don't know," Hanna said. "Can we watch television?"

Erica made a scoffing snort. "Are you joking?" She flopped onto the bed. "That's right. You get to do what you want."

"That's not true," Hanna said quietly. "I don't get to go to school."

"You're probably one of those bridge daughters that got to go to bruckegarten when you were little."

"Everyone goes to bruckegarten." Only when the words left her mouth did Hanna realize, no, everyone did not go to bruckegarten—only bridge daughters with mothers who raised them differently. "But I didn't get to go to kindergarten," Hanna added, thinking that somehow recovered her from the slip.

Erica lay back, hands behind her head, and stared up at the ceiling. "We have twenty minutes," she said, "then we have to start preparing the lunch."

"Sandwiches?"

"I've taken care of all of it," Erica said. "We just have to build them. You don't even have to help, if you don't want to. I can do it." Erica twisted on her side to face Hanna. "But you should help serve them. It won't look good if you don't do that."

"Is this what you do all day?" Hanna said. "Make food and sit in here?"

Erica emitted another of her deprecating snorts. "No, I should be doing the wash right now. My mother *generously* said I could play with you. I think it makes her look better. So you can tell your mother I entertained you."

"I wash my own sheets," Hanna said.

"What else?"

"That's it," Hanna said, realizing the insignificance.

"That's. It," Erica fumed. "Do you mend?"

"Mend what?"

Erica twisted back around to stare at the ceiling.

Hanna didn't want to be big friends with Erica, but she did want to pass the time as amicably as possible. She felt doubly stung now, and that drove her to think of some commonality between them. She came up empty.

"My mother says you got in big trouble." Erica twisted around to sit up on the edge of the bed. "What did you do?"

"I ran away," Hanna said. "To San Francisco." So Mrs. Grimond did know—she was being catty when they served the coffee.

Erica nodded. "And?"

"My parents came and got me."

"You didn't have a plan."

Hanna almost felt stung again, but this time, Erica sounded helpful, not deprecating.

"Do you know Marie Devlin?" Erica said. "She goes to our church. She ran away." Erica's voice quickened. "She had a plan. She saved up some money and hid food under her bed. It was a pretty good plan. She got to San Diego."

Hanna's eyes widened. San Diego was hundreds of miles away. "How did she do that?"

"My mother says it was because she could read and organize things in her head. They caught her, though, and brought her back. She had her finality about a month ago." Erica shrugged. "What about Michelle Kahn? You know her? She goes to our church too. She ran away last year. No one's found her yet. Her mother is really upset about it. Michelle should have had her finality by now."

"Well," Hanna reasoned, "that means Michelle's dead."

"Or she had a bi-graft," Erica said.

Hanna jolted. "You know about bi-grafts?"

"Of course," Erica said flippantly.

"Do you know where to get one?" Hanna asked.

"Why?" Erica said.

Hanna suddenly realized this might be a trap—that Erica was under instructions to relay everything said back to her mother, who would then pass it on to Hanna's mother. Was this part of her punishment, this new way of life? Perhaps it was common for traditional bridge daughters to rat out other bridge daughters. Hanna, always trusting, experienced a taste of paranoia for the first time.

"I heard about bi-grafts once," she answered Erica. "But I don't know what they are."

"It means no finality," Erica said. "It means you get to grow up like everyone else."

Hanna scooted closer to Erica. "I want to talk about Hagar," referring to the time Erica had hugged her and whispered the name in her ear.

Off in the distance, a dainty bell tinkled. Erica sighed and hopped up from the bed.

"They're early," Erica said. "Let's make those sandwiches."

After replenishing the women's coffee cups and clearing the plates, Erica led Hanna through the lunch-making process. From the refrigerator, Erica produced packages of supermarket cold cuts and cheese slices wrapped in butcher paper. She instructed Hanna to toast the bread – tiny loaves, one white and the other wheat, a size of bread Hanna had never seen before. Meanwhile, Erica took an egg salad from the refrigerator and placed cutting boards on the countertop. With the fillings before them, the duo deftly prepared a stack of finger sandwiches cut into triangle halves. At Erica's behest, Hanna snapped open a bag of ridged potato chips and poured them into a large bowl.

"No, no, no," Erica said, "you have to pick out the best ones. No crumbs in there."

"You're kidding."

"For guests," Erica told her. "We don't eat like this when people aren't around."

Hanna poured the chips back into the bag and dumped the remaining crumbs into the sink. "How do you normally eat?" She began hand-selecting the largest chips from the bag for the bowl.

"You know, normal food," Erica said, still assembling sandwiches. "We'll probably have pasta tonight. I'll use the leftover vegetables from last night to make a primavera." She nodded at the chopped lettuce, onions, and tomatoes before them. "A dinner salad from this."

Hanna didn't know what *primavera* meant, but she was more taken aback at the idea of planning meals, from leftovers or otherwise. Erica really was in charge of the kitchen.

"Do you tell your mother what to buy at the supermarket?"

"No," Erica said. "When we go, I just take what we need and put it in the cart."

"Does she help?"

Eric shrugged. "She pays."

Erica poured iced tea in tall glasses with lemon trees painted on their sides. She searched the pantry for straws, but they were out. Together, they assembled the tray and presented the luncheon together, Erica carrying the tray and Hanna bringing the drinks.

"Lovely," Mrs. Grimond said. "I hope you like egg salad," she said to Hanna's mother, who nodded her approval. "We'll be finished in thirty minutes," Mrs. Grimond announced, taking a sandwich from the stack. "You can clear up then."

The girls retreated to Erica's room once more. They sat cross-legged on the bristle carpeting, facing each other.

"What was San Francisco like?" Erica asked.

"It was *great*," Hanna breathed. "I saw my uncle and aunt."

"Your uncle and aunt?" Erica extended her arms in exasperation. "No wonder you were caught!"

"I didn't really run away," Hanna said. "I just wanted to be alone for a little bit. They're always hovering over me. My parents, I mean."

Erica nodded. She fully understood that feeling.

"It's private back here," Hanna said. "That's nice."

"But I always have to listen for that bell, or the front door," Erica said. "Or one of my little brothers hollering he's hungry."

Hanna knew the twins Jason and Jed would be at kindergarten right now. Kindergarten, the bruckegarten for normal children. "Do you play with them?" Hanna asked.

"It's more like I have to watch them," Erica said, digging a finger into the bristle carpet. "It's okay. They're not that bad. I guess."

"It's like you run this house. You're the boss." She hurried to add, "My grandmother, Ma Cynthia, she told me that in this country, the people who get the work done are never recognized. They're invisible."

Erica dug her finger deeper into the carpet. Hanna knew it was the kind of cheap carpet that left rug burns if you slid across it barekneed.

"Can I tell you a secret?" Erica said.

"Yeah." Hanna scooted closer.

"You can tell no one," she said. "*No one.* Promise?"

"Promise."

Erica wiped the back of her wrist across her nose. "I know where to get a bi-graft," she whispered. "I'm going to get one." She swallowed hard. "And when I run away, I'm not going to visit my uncle and get caught. Because I have a plan. Just like Hagar."

FIFTEEN

"WHAT KIND OF PLAN?" Hanna asked, mesmerized.

"You promise you're not going to tell your mother, right?"

Hanna nodded, still taking in Erica's revelation. Could this be a trap of some kind? And how could Erica know where to get a bi-graft?

"Where can you get one?" Hanna asked.

"You have to have money." Erica paused for effect. "One thousand dollars."

Hanna almost jumped up. "A thousand dollars? Where would I get a thousand dollars?" she said, forgetting she was trying to be coy. Then: "Where did you get a thousand dollars?"

"I don't have all of it right now," Erica said, motioning for Hanna to lower her voice. "But I'm not due for over a year now." She ventured, "When is your finality?"

"They told me six months. Probably five by now."

Erica nodded at Hanna's midsection. "Can I see?"

Hanna hesitated, shy about letting Erica see her in her underwear. Maureen was strong. It was time to be strong too. She lifted her new bridge dress up past her waist. Her oval bump had grown pronounced, her belly button a bit off-center.

"You can touch it," Hanna said.

Erica tenderly placed her fingers on Hanna's belly. "You have to get a bi-graft soon," Erica said. "If you wait until the last month of your *pons anno*, it's too late."

"Why?"

"The baby has grown too much by then."

Hanna felt the skin on her face grow hot and well up. She was going to cry. How could she collect a thousand dollars in time? Maybe she could sell each of her origami cranes for a dollar—but no one would buy the little things for that amount, and even if they did, her parents would collect the money and keep it from her.

Hanna let the dress fall back into place. "How do you know all this?"

"Church," Erica said. "There's a lot of us bridge daughters. We talk when the mothers aren't around."

"Like in Sunday school?" Although Hanna had never attended church, she knew about Sunday school. Other girls talked about it, including Cheryl Vannberg.

"We don't get our own Sunday school classes," Erica said. "We have to sit behind our mothers while they're in class."

"Your mother goes to Sunday school?" Wasn't it only for children?

"Sure," Erica said. "My father too. At our church, everybody goes to Sunday school. It's like real school. Everyone goes to a different room, depending on their age." She added, "Except us. The bridge daughters. They don't want us out of their sights."

"Did you know Cheryl Vannberg?"

Erica pished and waved the name away with a dismissive hand. "Oh, she got to go to Sunday school by herself. She even went to church camp by herself."

"How?"

"They're Unitarians."

One more term for Hanna to look up in her encyclopedia when she returned home. "How much money do you have?" she asked Erica.

"Some." Erica's tone of voice shifted between defensive, authoritative, and secretive so often, Hanna had trouble making inferences. "Enough."

"A thousand?"

"I'll have a thousand when the time comes." She added, "I have about four hundred dollars right now."

Four hundred? "Where did you get all that?"

"Our church has a Wednesday evening supper," Erica said. "It's a Susanna dinner. Our church has the bridge daughters put it on."

"Susanna?"

"Don't you ever read the Bible?" Erica said a bit haughtily. "Mary's bridge daughter? Susanna gave birth to Jesus."

Hanna was thoroughly out of her depth. The more she heard about bridge daughters from the past, the more she wanted to read about them.

"What does Susanna have to do with any of this?" she asked Erica.

"We put on a dinner every Wednesday," Erica said. "People have to buy a ticket to get their meal. One of us sells the tickets at the front door. Then the people wait in line and give the ticket to one of us serving food at the kitchen counter. I save some of the tickets I get in the kitchen and add them to the cash box the next week. Then I can pocket as much money as I want."

It sounded sacrilegious to Hanna, stealing from a church, but she could see how Erica would raise four hundred dollars if they held these dinners every week. And she certainly understood why Erica would do it, be it stealing or sacrilege or otherwise.

Erica crawled on hands and knees to the meager line of toys on the floor against the wall. She extracted a crayon from the box and returned to Hanna with it and the coloring book. In the back cover, she'd drawn short strokes in assorted colors, an organized but abstract jumble of tiny, carefully crayoned lines boxed into sections. Erica explained her system.

"These are the times I've brought home money, and this is the amount I made each time. I should have a thousand dollars a year from now. Right?"

Decoding Erica's expression, Hanna realized Erica's abundant confidence had reached a ledge. She only *thought* she would have enough money, but she was not certain, not as certain as she was of the other details she'd relayed to Hanna so far. Hanna checked the numbers, did some quick mental arithmetic, and shook her head.

"I can't believe you can bring home this much money each week," Hanna said.

"They're dumb," Erica said. "The church people; they're just happy to raise enough money to pay for the food we're cooking. I'm careful, though. I never take too much."

Forty dollars in one week seemed a lot to Hanna, but maybe the church brought in so much money at once it could easily be missed. Or the church assumed the bridge daughters had miscounted, easily true if they weren't schooled. Hanna turned to an uncolored page in the coloring book and performed some quick crayon arithmetic in the margins. Erica watched closely, lost in the process, confused when Erica carried values from the bottom of one column to the top of the next.

"You won't have a thousand dollars a year from today," Hanna announced.

"No?" Erica said, stunned.

"You'll have over two thousand," Hanna said, pointing to a crayon figure on the page. "But only if you don't get caught."

Erica sat back, wide-eyed. "That means when I get the bi-graft, I should have money left over."

"You'll need it. You'll have to run away." Just like Maureen.

Erica jumped up and jumped around. She danced like a marionette on tangled strings, a little girl who wants to dance out of sheer joy but doesn't know how.

Hanna smiled at the awkward celebration. Looking about the sparse room, she said, "Where did they go? The cranes I gave you?"

"My mother threw them away," Erica said, grinning for the first time in Hanna's presence.

Hanna felt bitten hearing it. As long as she made a thousand of them, she reasoned, she would get her wish, no matter how silly that sounded, the idea of paper birds granting wishes.

Back at home, Hanna's mother told her to sit at the kitchen table so they could talk.

"Well," she said, "what do you think?"

Hanna squirmed. "Erica has to do a lot of stuff around the house."

"And?"

"I don't want to do all that stuff."

"I bet you don't," Hanna's mother said. "Did you see her room?"

"She doesn't have any books," Hanna said. Coloring books didn't count.

"She probably can't read," Hanna's mother said. "Or she can only read little children's books and food labels."

"But she can count," Hanna said.

"Counting's important when you're tending to the house and the larder. Does she have a *wenschkind*?"

Hanna, confused, shook her head.

"That's a baby doll they give bridge daughters," her mother explained. "They'll probably give her one on her thirteenth birthday. Very traditional. It's for bridge daughters who want to know what it's like to hold the baby inside them. Do you want one?"

Hanna shook her head.

Her mother spoke carefully now. "I'm now going to do something very distasteful. The Grimonds do it to Erica every week. I don't like doing this, Hanna, but I will do it."

Her mother rose from the table and instructed Hanna to follow. They filed down the hall to Hanna's bedroom. Her mother instructed Hanna to stand in the doorway and remain still and quiet. Then, Hanna aghast, her mother began opening every drawer in her dresser and rifling through her clothes. She pressed each article of clothing between her fingers, searching for hidden pockets and anything sewn into the seams. She ran her hands up under the lid of the drawer for secreted items. She replaced the clothes as she finished searching them, folding them back up if necessary. Hanna kept a tidy room; at least her mother was not disrupting that.

"What are you looking for?" Hanna said.

"Quiet, please," her mother said.

Once completed with the dresser, her mother went to work on Hanna's bed. Pillowcases were removed and felt through, just like the clothes, and the pillows themselves were squished to discover anything that might be sewn into them. The covers and sheets were stripped and checked. Her mother swept an arm between the mattress and box spring. Hanna had confessed to that hiding spot months earlier and no longer considered it a safe place for illicit goods.

She had nothing to hide, though. The pregnancy test had been thrown out, and her copy of *Mother & Baby* was now openly stored in her bookcase, as she'd confessed to buying it with her mother's money. She received no punishment for it, but future infractions would not be so easily forgiven. She had nothing to hide, Hanna reasoned, but it alarmed her watching her mother search her room so wantonly and without discretion or apology.

"Help me make the bed," she told Hanna, and Hanna obliged. Once finished, she told Hanna to return to the doorway.

The bookcase was next, then her closet. Her mother retrieved a stepladder and flashlight from the kitchen so she could search the top shelf of the closet, where old toys and clothes were stored. Hanna's alarm faded with each new location rooted through. She told herself that this was the new reality. She was living far better than Erica, who was housed with dry dog food and boxes of All Temper-Cheer.

Mind wandering, she didn't realize until too late that her

mother was flipping through the pages of her ledger, the register of every origami crane she'd folded to date.

"Where did you get this?" Hanna's mother held it out to Hanna. "I don't recall buying this for you." Hanna, wide-eyed, took too long to answer, her mouth dry from surprised guilt.

"I got that a long time ago," she stumbled. "From Uncle Rick."

"He never gave you this," Hanna's mother said. "I would have remembered. Tell me the truth."

Hanna hung her head. Her face felt hot. *Can't be soft anymore,* she thought. *What would Maureen do? Have to be strong now.*

"I took it from Mr. Cullers," she said. "I'm sorry."

Hanna's mother nodded to herself, looking about the room. "How many of these cranes have you made?"

Hanna pointed to the notebook. "I think I'm up to six hundred and twenty."

"And where'd you get this?" Hanna's mother held up an unopened packet of origami paper.

"Aunt Azami gave that to me! In San Francisco. For real!" It was the truth.

Hanna's mother went about the room, tapping the spine of the notebook against her fingers. The only items she'd not searched were the origami cranes themselves, hundreds of them, a paper sea of sharp lines and colorful patterns. They filled the windowsill, the top of the dresser, and the back half of Hanna's writing desk. Her mother took a random one from the sill and considered it.

"I'm tempted to throw all of these out," she said to Hanna.

"No!" Hanna crossed the room and wrung her hands together. "Please stop doing this!"

"I'm worried you could hide money in them," her mother said. "Maybe you already are."

"I'm not!" Hanna took one from the desk and unwrapped it as fast as she would a candy bar. "There's nothing inside."

Her mother took the unfolded crane from her. "Why do you number them?"

"I want to make a thousand," Hanna said.

"A *thousand*?" Hanna's mother took in the sheer number of cranes again. Hanna had never revealed her project, fearing her mother would learn about the thousand cranes' attendant wish. "No, you're not keeping a thousand of these things here. Why a thousand, of all things? This has gone on too far."

Hanna pressed her hands tighter. "Don't! Please!"

She took Hanna by the upper arm. "Go back to the door," she said. "Stand there until I'm finished."

The earth was slipping out from under Hanna, a complete loss of control. When would this tectonic rumbling end? Her mother, so patient with her when homeschooling, firm but willing to listen, was now resolute in changing every assumption Hanna held, right down to the simple idea she could fold a thousand *tsuru* without needing to ask permission.

"You can throw them away," she told her mother, remaining at her side. "But let me keep making them."

"You don't mind me putting them in the trash?"

"I just want to fold a thousand of them," Hanna said, "then I'll stop."

After a moment of consideration, Hanna's mother said, "I'm not going to take your books, although I should. I'll let you make your flower arrangements from time to time. But I don't like the clutter."

Hanna's mother lay the unfolded crane and the pocket notebook on Hanna's desk.

"I won't throw your cranes away," she said to Hanna. "You worked too hard. But I'm going to put some of these in a grocery bag and store them in the garage. When you finish a thousand, we'll talk about what we'll do with them all."

Hanna, drained from panicking, now felt warm gratitude filling in its place. She told her mother thank you, and she meant it.

"I'm going to search your room once a week," she told Hanna. "Now go wash your hands. You need to start dinner."

SIXTEEN

WIPING A DUST RAG across the dining room table, Hanna felt something inside her fighting to get out. At week thirty-six of her *pons anno*, her belly was like a volleyball pressed up against her pink skin. The pressure came again—a soundless thump, the baby in her punching to get free. Hanna made a noise of surprise and staggered to a high-backed chair for support.

Her father rose from his easy chair and approached with both hands out. "Hanna?" he said. "Are you okay?"

"It's moving," she said.

"Dian," her father called out, "we need you in here."

Her father watched on, all but helpless, until Hanna's mother arrived and inspected her. "It's kicking is all," she told them both. "There's nothing to worry about."

"It's going to keep doing this?" Hanna said.

"It might," her mother said. "You sure did, all the way to the end."

Hanna took deep breaths and massaged her belly until she felt she could stand straight again. It seemed she could do nothing without the thing inside her fighting back.

After drawing blood at the clinic's lab, Hanna and her parents ate lunch in the first floor deli, a Reuben for her father and the soup-and-half-sandwich special for her mother. Hanna took sullen bites from her plain hamburger, no cheese, no dressing, no vegetables. Food had lost its taste. Even the pleasure of ice cream had abandoned her. She was gaining weight too, and not just about her midsection. Her wrists and ankles and knees had swollen up. Her old comfortable jeans would not zip up, even if she sucked in her gut.

Not that she wore her old clothes any longer. Hanna's mother took her clothes shopping the day they returned from San Francisco, and as she gained weight, they shopped again for larger sizes. They no longer visited the Misses section of the department stores. Instead, they went to the back corner of the stores' basements, a few unattended racks of frumpy dresses and soft-soled shoes. The mannequins about the section were girls Hanna's height frozen in various stages of *pons anno*. A sign of all-capital lettering hung over the dressing rooms: BRIDGE. Hanna had seen this section in the upscale department stores too. Those establishments tastefully labeled the section *Passerelle* in cursive script, even though she didn't understand what that word meant. In those stores, the racks were stocked with frillier dresses and bonnets and flat leather shoes with decorative buckles across their tops.

Hanna's father took one of the French fries from her plate and popped it in his mouth with a playful smile. Before, Hanna would have protested playfully in return, but that morning, she didn't care. Eat them all. Starchy carbohydrates, bland ketchup, mealy hamburger meat, rubbery bun. More blood drawn from her right arm, the puncture hole gauzed and sore. More test results told in confidence to her mother, more instructions on what vitamins to take and what activities to avoid. More of the astringent odor of Dr. Mayhew's perpetually sanitized examination room, more of the crunching sound the waxy paper on the table made when Hanna climbed on it. And more of Dr. Mayhew's prodding and manhandling and peeking inside her.

"Do you like the flowers?" Hanna's father asked her. He motioned to the two carnations standing in a plastic vase beside the shakers and coffee sugar.

"They're fake," Hanna said.

"Really?" He reached over and rubbed a petal between his fingers. "I'll be."

The examination completed, Hanna requested her father turn his back while she slipped out of the hospital gown and into her bridge daughter dress. Today she wore a lavender frock, its corded neckline close about her throat and its hemline well past her knees. The soft flat slip-ons were not designed for running across lawns or through puddles, or running at all. That would be the point, Hanna reasoned. Her mother helped her with the dress, smoothing out creases and ensuring it was square on her body.

"Everything is textbook," Dr. Mayhew announced. "Hanna has definitely reached *ponte amplio*. The final twelve weeks of gestation," she added for Hanna's benefit. She opened Hanna's folder and scanned down a page. "Dian told me on the phone you'd changed your minds?" Dr. Mayhew said to Hanna's parents. "You would like to know the gender of the gemellius after all?" Dr. Mayhew added for Hanna, "That means your double. The baby."

On their way to the clinic that morning, Hanna wondered why her father had come along. Now she realized his attendance was to hear the baby's gender first-hand. He had never come to Dr. Mayhew's before.

"We had a change of heart," Hanna's mother said to Dr. Mayhew, looking to Hanna's father for a nod of agreement.

"Is this because of San Francisco?" Hanna said, but her parents ignored the question.

Dr. Mayhew double-checked the results before her. Smiling, she announced, "You won't need to paint the room."

While her parents embraced, a spout of bile rose up within

Hanna. Saved of the trouble of a coat a paint, her bedroom was prepped and ready for another little girl, one who happened to look exactly like her. She would inherit Hanna's books and blankets and clothes, even her *tsuru*. And her parents were so pleased.

"Are you going to call her Hanna?" Hanna said sarcastically.

"Hanna," her mother said, "do not start."

"Little Hanna to replace the old worn-out useless Hanna."

"Listen to your mother," her father said.

"What were you going to name him if he was a boy?" she said. "Harry? Harold?" She searched for more boys' names starting with H, but bitterness robbed her of her imagination.

"We would have named him after your father's father," her mother said calmly. "Armand."

Hanna never knew Grandpa Driscoll's given name. "Dumb name," she muttered.

"Young lady—"

Hanna's father touched his wife's shoulder. "I think Dr. Mayhew has something she wants to tell us."

Dr. Mayhew had watched the back-and-forth from afar. "Ah, yes. I'm recommending Hanna begin taking gefyridol." She continued talking while filling out a prescription. "It's merely a precaution."

Hanna, stewing, said, "More pills?" Dr. Mayhew had put her on a multivitamin regimen at week twenty-four, adding two dietary supplements eight weeks after that.

"I thought everything was textbook," her father said.

Dr. Mayhew said, "The bridge daughter who carried Dian had Hoff's Syndrome. It carries from bridge daughter to bridge daughter. It rarely leads to complications, but they're preventable. Actually, I'm surprised the bridge who carried you wasn't prescribed gefyridol."

"My mother believed in home remedies and homeopathic cures," Hanna's mother said dryly.

Dr. Mayhew tore the prescription from the pad and handed it

to Hanna's mother. "Gefyridol is injected subcutaneously. There's a cream, but it's not covered by your insurance and fairly expensive."

"Shots?" her father said before Hanna could exclaim the same.

"Twice a week," Dr. Mayhew said. "Have you given her injections before? No? All right, I'll give her one now, just to show you." Sensing the room tense up, Dr. Mayhew smiled broadly for all of them. "Really, it's easy."

Dr. Mayhew took a slender cardboard box from a glass-fronted cabinet and broke its seal. From it, she removed a flimsy plastic tray securing three vials. She demonstrated to Hanna's father how to sanitize the vial's rubber stopper with an alcohol swab. Then she unwrapped a disposable syringe and plunged its needle through the stopper and into the magenta-colored liquid. She tipped everything upside-down and withdrew one cc, showing Hanna's father the proper way to measure. Hanna's hands were gripped tight around the seat's frame.

"I hate needles," Hanna's father said to Dr. Mayhew, flushed.

"You get used to it," Dr. Mayhew said. "Hanna, please come over here."

"No," she said.

"It won't hurt," Dr. Mayhew said.

The needle looked long enough to go through her leg and squirt the liquid out the other side. "I'm not doing it."

"How much does the cream cost?" her father said.

"You said it's not necessary," Hanna said to Dr. Mayhew. "Why do I have to take it if it's not necessary?"

"It's to ensure the safety of the child," Dr. Mayhew said.

"I don't care," Hanna said eyeing the needle. A drop of purplish liquid hung from its tip.

"It'll be over in five seconds—"

"I don't care about little Hanna! What about me?"

"Hanna!" her mother snapped. Her gaunt face was Puritanical. "Come over here this instant."

Hanna hung her head and squirmed down in the chair,

fingernails digging into the bottom of the seat cushion.

"Now," her mother said.

What would Maureen do? Hanna shook her head once, defiant.

Hanna's mother strode two long steps across the examination room and smacked Hanna across the left side of her head. Hanna reeled, crying out, feet coming off the floor. Her hands had gone up to protect herself, and without support, the force almost knocked her from the chair. She cradled her head and stared up into her mother's granite, determined face.

There could be no crying now. It was more than being strong. She carried her mother's child. She'd consciously known that for months now, but here in the examination room, head ringing, the fullness of that statement revealed itself to her. She had to quit thinking of herself as her mother's child. She'd stopped being her mother's child when *pons anno* began.

No, Hanna thought, the bite of the slap seeping across her face, *I never was her child. I'm the soil around the seed.*

Her mother took the needle from her stunned father. "I'll do it," she said.

What would Maureen do? Be strong. Hanna rose and shuffled to the examination table.

"Just remain standing," Dr. Mayhew told her, as uneasy as Hanna's father. "I should've had you keep the gown on, but this will do."

Dr. Mayhew instructed Hanna to pull up her bridge dress. No longer caring what her father saw, she gathered its hem and bunched it below her nipples. She had thought—no, hoped—her breasts would develop as the mother's breasts did in *Mother & Baby*, but hers remained stubbornly flat throughout *pons anno*. Another aspect of evolution's genetic gamble, another dimension to God's plan for the human race: Mothers breastfeed bridge daughters but the gemellius receives all the nourishment it needs from the bridge daughter *in utero*. Little Hanna would be born ready for pureed apples and carrot-pea mush.

Standing as she would in public—chin level, eyes out

straight—Hanna waited with her dress up and panties revealed. Behind her, Dr. Mayhew instructing, Hanna's mother discarded the syringe's drawing needle into a sharps container, capped it with a thinner injection needle from its own sterilized package, and tapped the syringe to remove any air bubbles.

Then Dr. Mayhew advised her mother on the best places to insert the needle. Two sets of hands tugged and squeezed and stretched taut the skin on her lower back and upper buttocks. A firm hand pinched a roll of fat from the weight developing on her hips. A moist toilette sterilized a patch of the roll. The prick of the needle arrived, followed by a cold flush spreading across her lower back. She did not feel the needle removed. The ripping of paper sounded behind her, a Band-Aid package being torn open, and a hand smoothed the bandage over the sore, frigid spot.

"You'll need to do that twice a week," Dr. Mayhew said.

"For how long?" her mother asked.

"Until the finality," Dr. Mayhew said. "It's not a cure; it's prevention."

Hanna let her frock fall back in place and faced the adults. Although she couldn't see it—didn't even consciously realize it—she peered back at them with the grim expression of a soldier ordered back to the field for one more tour.

Dr. Mayhew offered Hanna a sugar-free lollipop and a supportive smile.

"No thank you," Hanna said. She strode behind her mother and straightened up, chin level and hands at her back. While her parents collected their things, she stroked the Band-Aid with the meat of her thumb, acknowledging the taut soreness now hidden from the world.

SEVENTEEN

ONE EVENING while washing the dishes, Hanna asked her father about Susanna.

"Susanna?" Sitting at the kitchen table, he held a spoonful of vanilla ice cream before his mouth. "I don't know that I've met her."

"She's in the Bible." Standing at the sink, Hanna had her back to him. "I think."

"Oh, *Susanna*." He savored the ice cream and nodded. "Mother Mary's bridge daughter. She bore Jesus."

"Can I read about her?"

"Not much to read," he said, gathering another spoonful from the bowl.

Hanna bounced imperceptibly against the edge of sink, her taut round belly springing against the counter trim. Maybe she should let go of the topic. She couldn't come up with a good reason for hearing the full story. Girls in the Bible, like paper birds, were not going to grant her more life.

After a quiet moment of scrubbing and rinsing, her father spoke up. "There's two bridge daughters in the Bible," he said. "Hagar and Susanna."

Hanna's scrubbing slowed. Back still to him, she said, "Only two?"

"Only two," her father said. "That's more than Shakespeare. He only wrote one bridge daughter." He searched the air before him. "I can't recall her name. The youngest daughter in *King Lear*. Anyway," he returned to his ice cream, "Susanna's only mentioned once. Matthew. Or Luke. I forget which."

"She has a pretty name," Hanna said.

He rose from the table. "The Bible only calls her 'the bridge.'" He set the bowl, still holding ice cream, by the sink. "I think the Church gave her a name later in order to venerate her." He added, "They made her a saint."

"For what?"

"For bearing Jesus," he said, as though obvious.

For not running away, Hanna thought, the more obvious possibility.

Hanna continued washing. She couldn't help but feel her father's presence as he stood behind her. He was awkwardly close. It made her slow her scrubbing and rinsing. She twisted her neck ever-so-slightly to locate him in her periphery. He was there, close and silent and watching her work.

She finished a plate, set it in the rack, and began on his ice cream bowl. She dumped the remaining frigid white goop into the rinsing sink and ran hot water to send it down the pipes. She waited for anything from him: a single word, a clearing of the throat, even the creaking of the soles of his shoes as he shifted his weight. The bowl remained ice cold in the hot sudsy water. Even though she scrubbed and rinsed it well, it was cold all the way to the drying rack.

She spun around. She glared up at him, daring him to say something, anything. Her dishwashing gloves dripped suds on the linoleum.

Her father had bunched himself together, like a washrag wrung out. His arms hugged his sides. He gazed down at her, eyeballs veiny and red.

"We're going to lose you," he said. "But then we get you back again." Then he said, "I know it's unfair. You just have to accept things as they are."

Hanna continued to glare up at him. She considered how to respond. It was useless. She returned to the sink.

Thankfully, he left the kitchen. She finished the dishes in short order, belly gently bouncing against the edge of the sink like a baby slapping a toy drum.

The summer heat had receded the last week of July but returned in force at the beginning of August. Hanna proposed iced tea, a tossed salad, and sliced fruit for the lunch, but her mother knew Mrs. Grimond would think she was skimping. She led Hanna through the preparation of a macaroni casserole. The oven heated the kitchen and the dining room so thoroughly Hanna had to throw open the windows and sliding glass door to allow air through. She felt faint preparing lunch, but told herself to push onward lest be subject to Mrs. Grimond's tongue-clucking when the food wasn't ready upon her arrival. The second time she felt faint, her mother sensed it and told Hanna to lie down in her bedroom, the coolest room in the house.

The doorbell jolted Hanna awake. In her stupor, she started to jump from the bed, then fell back to the pillows. Her swollen belly no longer allowed for such athletics. She pushed herself up on her elbows, swung her legs off the side of the bed, and slid out to her feet. Up, she checked her hair in the mirror and hurried to the entryway. Her mother was waiting.

"You look fine," she told Hanna. "I took out the casserole, and everything's on the countertop. We'll do this like Vivian did lunch at her house."

Vivian Grimond waited at the front door with her mask of a smile and darting eyes sensitive to any out-of-place detail. Erica stood behind her, posed as a bridge daughter should, back erect and hands hidden. Without speaking, Hanna opened the door fully and acknowledged them. The women exchanged pleasantries in the entryway. Mrs. Grimond complimented Hanna's mother on the decorating. She expressed she wished they'd done these lunches sooner. Hanna looked to Erica for some recognition, some secret signal of eyes or eyebrows or even a nod, but Erica remained expressionless behind her mother.

"How do you like your iced tea?" Hanna's mother asked Mrs. Grimond.

"Sugar and lemon," she said.

Hanna's mother nodded for their leave and the bridge daughters made a beeline to the kitchen. Their soft-soled shoes scuffled on the entryway tile and padded quietly on the kitchen linoleum. Hanna wished they could talk, but unlike the Grimond house, the kitchen had no heavy swinging door to seal them off while they worked. A second opening in the kitchen led straight to the combination dining/living room where the women relaxed. Hanna would be risking a great deal if she talked to Erica now.

Although they'd only worked together for one lunch, Hanna had learned quite a bit over the past weeks. Now they operated in lockstep. Erica used the stepstool to retrieve two tall iced tea glasses from the kitchen cabinet, requiring only a pointed finger from Hanna to hint which cabinet held them. Hanna took a plastic bucket of ice from the freezer and set it in the kitchen sink. They prepared four iced teas, two in specialty iced tea glasses with cartoon lemon wedges painted on their sides, and two in plastic tumblers for themselves. Although the oven heat had dissipated, it remained warm in the kitchen. Hanna's mother had started the house's forced air to help.

Lemon and sugar in Mrs. Grimond's glass, lemon in Hanna's mother's. Then Hanna took a flat glass pan of Jell-O from the refrigerator and began spooning portions.

"Slice it, slice it," Erica scolded under her breath. She went through the drawers until she found a metal spatula. She cut squares of red Jell-O from the sheet and slid them onto dessert plates, eschewing the bowls Hanna had brought out to use. Slices of bananas and grape halves floated in the Jell-O as though held in stasis for some future civilization to reanimate. Hanna detested anything in her Jell-O, but her mother had insisted.

Hanna strode out to the living room with the women's refreshments on a TV tray with the legs removed. Per decorum, Erica stood in the entry hall with her hands behind her, watching Hanna serve the Jell-O and making her own presence known.

"We'll call you when we're ready for lunch," Hanna's mother said to her. "You can have your Jell-O in your room."

"You let her eat in her room?" Mrs. Grimond said.

"It's fine," her mother said, motioning to Hanna that the quicker she left, the better.

Hanna closed her bedroom door and lifted herself onto her bed. Jumping onto the mattress was a small far-off pleasure now lost.

Erica peered around, taking in the toys, the books, the *tsuru*. Her jaw hung loose, making a faint frown. "This is your room?" she said. "You're so lucky."

Hanna didn't know what to say to that. She ate up the Jell-O in three bites; whipped cream and fruit, all of it. When she'd visited Dr. Mayhew, food had lost all its flavor. Now, this week, sweets and savories held intense flavors for her, the sugar so strong she could feel it sizzling on her tongue like Pop Rocks. Erica sat in Hanna's writing desk chair, feet swinging idly. She ate her treat with less relish.

"Why can't we just serve the Jell-O in scoops?" Hanna said, savoring the gelatin's artificial cherry flavoring. "That's how we do it all the time."

"It's a test," Erica said. "Like when my mother came in. Did you notice her looking at the floors? If something's not right, it's a point in her favor. That's what my mom does."

Hanna thought that sounded silly, a lot of trouble for no good reason. "Why?"

"She has her reasons," Erica murmured and pushed a blob of Jell-O into her mouth.

"Well, I don't care what she thinks or says," Hanna said.

"You will," Erica said.

"What's that mean?"

"Nothing." Erica shook her head. "If you're living like...*this*," she waved her spoon as though casting a spell on the bedroom, "then you've got nothing to worry about."

Hanna scraped up the last of the dessert in her bowl and licked the spoon clean. She wanted to press Erica for an explanation. From the last lunch, Hanna suspected Erica liked to pretend she knew more than she really did, to pretend that she was worldly and dark.

"Are you still doing those Susanna dinners at church?" Hanna asked.

"Did you tell you mother?" Erica demanded, all interest in her Jell-O disappearing. "You promised. You pinkie promised."

"I didn't say anything," Hanna said. "But I had an idea."

"What kind of idea?"

Hanna bounced a little on her mattress. "Promise you'll listen."

"I'm listening."

"Promise it."

"I promise!" Erica said, exasperated.

Hanna said, "I want to take a loan out from you."

"A loan? What do you mean?"

"You give me your money," Hanna said, "and I'll give it all back later, plus some extra as interest."

"Interest?" Erica said. "Interest in what?"

"I mean I'll give you more money back."

"No way," Erica said. "I'm not giving you my money."

"At your rate, you'll have enough for a bi-graft before you need it," Hanna said. "Even if I took all your money, you'll have more than you need. But I promise, I'll give it all back to you, plus more. Don't you see?" Hanna slid off the bed to her feet. "That means you'll even have more money when you run away. You'll need it."

"How can you give me all my money back?"

"I can work," Hanna said, lowering her voice. This was the big plan. "There's a huge flower market in Los Angeles. It's bigger than the one in San Francisco. I'll work every day there and give you the money I make."

"You're going to run off to Los Angeles," Erica said, "and then come back *here* with my money in time for me to get a bi-graft."

"I promise," Hanna said. "I don't even think it'll take a year."

"No," Erica said, shaking her head. "I don't believe you."

"Even if I run off and never come back," Hanna said, "you'll have enough for a bi-graft anyway. Please?"

"You should've gotten your own money," she said. "That's not my fault."

"My mother didn't tell me I was bridge daughter until I turned thirteen," Hanna said. "You've known for a long time, right?"

"Oh, how bad for you," Erica said, voice rising. "Poor little Hanna, stuck in this room all by herself, toys and books and her mom making her dinners each night."

Hanna, flustered, grasped for anything to toss back. "You have your own room!"

"Only after Jennifer's finality," Erica snapped, meaning Jason and Jed's bridge mother.

"Do you have to take shots?" Hanna showed Erica the place on her rump where the syringe was inserted every three nights. "This is for the baby, not me," she explained.

Erica stared coldly back. "Don't you get it? It's *all* for the baby," she said evenly. "And, no, I don't get shots. I get this."

She stood and turned her back to Hanna. Grabbing the bottom of her dress with both hands, she lifted it to her shoulders. She had beautiful pale skin discolored by a flurry of thin red welts like tally marks, from her shoulder blades down to her waist. Some were fresh, red like boils, while others had healed to faint scar tissue, the skin wrinkled like used-up Saran wrap.

"What do your parents do to you when you speak when not spoken to?" she said over her shoulder. "When you put too much detergent in the machine?"

Hanna crossed the room with her hand out to touch the welts.

Erica pushed her dress back into place before Hanna reached her.

"You're not getting my money," Erica said.

They stared at each other a long while. Hanna's mother called to them from the living room. The women were ready for their luncheon.

After serving the women the casserole and side dishes, Hanna and Erica retired to the kitchen to eat their lunch. This week, Hanna was famished at meal times, seemingly eating for three instead of two. She ate double portions of casserole and a healthy portion of fruit. Erica ate most of her casserole square and picked at her salad. As the kitchen had no stools or chairs, they ate standing, a traditional touch to their bridge daughter meal. Through the open doorway, Hanna listened to the women discuss the Grimonds' church. It seemed the Grimonds had no social outlet beyond it.

In Hanna's bedroom, door closed, Erica said, "You need to get your own money. If I help you, I have to help every bridge who asks."

Hanna, morose, went to her windowsill. She picked through the origami cranes absentmindedly. She located one she'd folded with Aunt Azami's new paper. It was a baby-blue checker pattern with dainty pink blossoms in the blue squares. She turned it over as though inspecting its sex. It was numbered *843*.

"Here." Hanna offered the crane to Erica.

Erica crossed her arms. "You can't bribe me with one of your paper birds."

Hanna went to her writing desk and peeled off the top sheet of the origami paper there. She opened her register and wrote Erica's name beside the number *966*.

"Why did you make so many of them?" Erica said. "Can't you fold anything else?"

Hanna's practiced fingers made quick deft creases. She no longer needed to refold lines. She didn't even need to be sitting or using a table as a folding surface. She could fold standing, just as they ate their lunch in the kitchen, just as bridge daughters back to antiquity took their meals and folded clothes. As the *tsuru* began to take shape, Erica's critical expression softened to mild wonder. Last creases in place, Hanna took the beak and tail by her fingertips and pulled. The wings gently spread as though preparing for flight.

Erica, unaware of herself, said, "Oh!"

Hanna held it out to Erica, who accepted the *tsuru*. She let it sit in the palm of her hand. With her other hand, she touched its side, rocking it back and forth, prodding it to animate and take flight.

"I should tell you," Erica said. "My mother is trying to convince your mother about something." She took in a deep breath and sighed it out. "It's called Susanna Glen. It's a camp in the Santa Cruz mountains. Our church helps run it."

"Camp? Like sleeping outside?" That sounded like fun.

"No," Erica said. "Susanna Glen is a place they keep bridge daughters. Out in the woods, gated, fenced, watched over by adults. They send bridge daughters up there until their finality. If your parents say yes, you'll probably go right away." Sensing Hanna's naiveté, she blurted, "It's so you can't run away. It's a big cage in the redwoods. They send you up there and they keep you there until you die."

EIGHTEEN

THE DRIVE DOWN Sainte-Beuve Way reminded Hanna how she used to cherish time alone with her father, a rare treat due to his work schedule and her mother's near-constant presence. This afternoon, Hanna did not cherish her father's company so much. Not in the least, she realized. His squeamishness about administering the shots and the uncomfortable moment in the kitchen did not endear him to Hanna.

Unlike the rigidness that had developed in her mother over the past few months, her father had grown withdrawn: at dinnertime, in front of the television, even when she brought him a glass of ice water as a break from mowing the lawn. Her parents had prepared for over thirteen years to detach themselves from their bridge daughter, and Hanna could sense her connection to them crumbling as her finality approached. They were not so different from Mrs. Vannberg after all, or even Mrs. Grimond. They would celebrate their new child when Hanna died. They would mourn the loss incurred, but only lightly, as a necessary price to be paid. They would surrender to an instinct injected into the human DNA chain millions of years ago—they would surrender to God's eternal plan for mankind—they would surrender Hanna in one heartbeat and embrace Hanna in the next.

The flowers in Hanna's lap made the car interior cloyingly aromatic to Hanna's father, who rolled his window down a touch for fresh air. Hanna pinched the bulging stamen of a daffodil laden with pollen and put the yellow dust to her nose. *Sweet Heaven.*

Liz Vannberg met them at the door. She accepted the bouquet with delight. "Let me put these in some water," she said to them both. "Won't you come in?"

"Hanna also brought some origami cranes she made for little Cheryl," Hanna's father said.

Hanna took one from the sack and held it up. Mrs. Vannberg nodded with less enthusiasm than the flowers, perplexed at Hanna's obsession with the little folded birds.

Hanna tugged at her father's sleeve. He gave her permission to speak.

"May I put these in Cheryl's room?" she asked Mrs. Vannberg. "Alongside the ones I brought last time?"

"Oh, honey," Mrs. Vannberg said, crestfallen, "I threw those all out when the baby came home. I hope you understand."

"That's okay," Hanna said, "but maybe I could put these in their place?"

"Well, go ahead, then," she said to Hanna. To her father, she said, "Coffee?"

Her father accepted the offer. Hanna moved quickly down the hallway to Cheryl's bedroom. The Vannbergs had not painted the room, just as the adage went. Cheryl's bed was gone, though, replaced by a crib with lacy pillows and blankets and a mechanized mobile of cartoony zoo animals. The sour-milk odor of baby powder was strong. She instantly worried little Cheryl might be in the crib sleeping—she dare not waken her and risk her crying out—but was relieved to see it was empty save for the bedding.

Hanna tossed the paper bag of *tsuru* on the changing table and went to the closet. She slid back the door and was confronted by its contents: designer misses clothes, teenage outfits, handbags of all shape and color, and shoes, shoes, shoes. All of it was tightly packed in the closet and wrapped in clear keepsake plastic, saving them for little Cheryl to grow to big Cheryl all over again. Such thrift seemed unlike Mrs. Vannberg, but Hanna supposed there was no reason to throw it out when the new Cheryl would slip perfectly into all of it, like interchanging outfits between two Barbie dolls.

With one hand supporting her engorged belly and another on the closet jamb, Hanna lowered herself to her knees. On all fours, she felt around the back of the closet floor. The weight in her gut swung about and distended her belly even further, making her feel like she'd eaten an enormous indigestible meal.

"Do you want to take a look?" Mrs. Vannberg called from the other end of the house. She always talked a little too loudly for Hanna's tastes. It sounded as though she was calling to Hanna's father from the kitchen, probably preparing his coffee while he reclined in the front room.

Hanna's fingers found the loose flap of carpeting in the back corner of the closet. She peeled it back and prodded the edges of the exposed floorboards. The rear one remained loose. A small notch gave her a finger-hold to pry it up. She set it aside and dipped her hand once again into the back of the closet, listening intently for anyone's approach. Her swaying stomach ached. Her heart was beating so hard, she could feel it in her jaw.

"Carter had someone come out and put it all together," Mrs. Vannberg called out again, meaning Mr. Vannberg. "You should poke your head in and see. It's just darling."

They were discussing the baby room. Leave it to Mrs. Vannberg to talk up the changes—all they'd done was remove Cheryl's princess bed and bring in a crib and a changing station. The old dresser and vanity remained in place. They didn't even bother to strip the shelves of Cheryl's old travel photos and memorabilia.

Hanna crawled deeper into the closet. The leathery smell of patent leather shoes and used-once handbags was overpowering.

"Maybe I'll just take a look," she heard her father say, being polite, as always.

Her fingers found it—her hand gripped the box. She scooted out of the closet for light. It was the same wooden box Cheryl had shown her months prior at the bridge party. Footsteps approaching, Hanna fumbled with the box's clasp. The lid sprung open.

In the box rested the pile of loose green bills with that crisp one hundred-dollar bill on top. She spread the stack in her hands. The twenties and tens revealed themselves like ranks and suits in a winning poker hand.

Bridge daughter dresses only offered utilitarian pockets on their fronts, flappy loose pockets like those found on aprons or smocks. No zippers, no buttons—no way to conceal money or goods from watchful eyes. On her knees, Hanna pulled her dress up and slipped the packet of cash into the front of her underwear. With her bulging belly, she hoped the dress would hang in such a way that the money would go unseen.

Footsteps padded down the carpeted hallway. Heavy footsteps—her father.

She snapped the box closed and crawled back into the closet. She dropped the box in the hole, set the floorboard, and patted the carpet back into place. Lacking proper light, she could only hope it would go unnoticed.

On all fours, she backed herself out of the closet, slid the closed door closed, and the bedroom knob twisted.

"Hanna?" Her father rushed to her with his hands out. "What's going on?" Mrs. Vannberg, mouth agape, entered behind him.

"She kicked," Hanna improvised, still on all fours. *Would it work?* "A good one too. I thought I was going to throw up." She made a weak apologetic smile. "I wasn't expecting it, I guess."

Her father helped her up. She placed both hands on the egg-shaped outline her belly made through her dress. She rubbed little circles over it, desperate to smooth out the material and ensure the money remained unseen.

"I'm fine," she told them both with a smile. "Really."

While Hanna prepared dinner, her father explained the afternoon's events to Hanna's mother. At the story's conclusion, Hanna's mother marched into the kitchen with her father in tow. She turned Hanna away from the stove before Hanna could set down the meat prong. She pressed the back of her hand to Hanna's forehead and cheek, then put her palm on Hanna's belly. The cash had long been stashed away.

"Do you feel sick?" her mother said. "You're not running a fever."

"I'm fine," Hanna assured her. "A little throw-up feeling came over me."

"A kicking baby shouldn't make you fall to the floor," Hanna's mother murmured.

Hanna's father held a *wenschkind* out toward them. "Liz gave this to Hanna before we left. I thought it was generous of her."

"Why?" Hanna's mother said. "Cheryl's her last bridge daughter. She doesn't need one anymore."

Her father turned the infant doll over in his hands. "She could've given this to anyone," he said. "It's not cheap."

The *wenschkind* was a realistic anatomical baby doll with skin of fine tan fabric and baby clothes that could be changed. Its hair was soft and fine, but spotty on the crown and not thick, just like a real infant. This was not the yarn-string hair of a Raggedy Ann doll. And the *wenschkind*'s clothes were modern, not the old-fashioned frilly dresses of the nostalgia dolls Mrs. Grimond displayed under glass in their living room. The *wenschkind*'s label indicated it was hand-manufactured in West Germany by the Schmidt Family Company, descendants of the brothers who'd crafted the first *wenschkinds* in Bavaria two hundred and fifty years earlier.

This indicator of quality and expense softened Hanna's mother's cynicism. "You're right," she said. "That was generous of her."

"*Why did she give me a doll?*" Hanna had stopped playing with dolls years before. They'd been replaced by dinosaurs, then books on the planets, then bees, before discovering flowers and flower arranging.

"A *wenschkind* is a wish child," her father said. "They're for bridge daughters your age."

"I don't like dolls," Hanna said. She couldn't imagine Erica playing with them either. It even seemed beneath girly-girl Cheryl, who may have loved plush animals, but baby dolls? Those were for *children.*

"You don't feel anything for her?" Hanna's father said.

"Who? That?" Hanna said, meaning the doll.

"Little Hanna," her mother said. "Inside you." She returned her firm hand to Hanna's belly. "You don't care at all?"

Hanna, reproached, stepped back toward the stove. The pork chops in the pan sizzled their desire to be turned.

"You'll start to feel things for her soon." Her father held the *wenschkind* out to her. "Don't you want to know what it's like to hold little Hanna in your arms?"

The doll's face was uncomfortably human, with glassine marble eyes and a dainty hard nub for a nose. Its mouth was slightly agape, ready to receive a nipple for nursing. Both arms were flopped wide, desperate for a hug from someone, anyone at all.

"I didn't ask Mrs. Vannberg for it," Hanna said.

"It's yours anyway," her father said. He quivered it with his hands to entice Hanna, like shaking a stick before a dog.

"You could try holding it," her mother said. "Ma Cynthia used to make her own *wenschkind*. She sewed them from old denim pants and worn-out shirts. And old pantyhose for the skin. I don't know where she got them; she never wore any." Her mother tapped a dull red fingernail on the doll's face. "She painted the eyes with tempera on seashells that she'd gathered at—"

"Whose wish is it?" Hanna said. "Who's wishing for the

child?"

Hanna stared up at them defiantly, meat prong in hand. She rubbed her free hand over her belly. She admired its ovoid tautness, tight like an overinflated tire.

Her father retracted the doll. Hanna faced the stove and turned the browned chops in the pan. Her parents' dinner was almost finished and she wasn't going to allow her parents to ruin it.

At the conclusion of every meal, Hanna's father produced a toothpick from his shirt pocket and cleaned his teeth at the table. He never seemed without a toothpick, even if they were eating a hot dog at a walk-up stand. Over the years, she'd seen him pocket two or three of the complimentary toothpicks from restaurant greeter stations on their way out the door. When Hanna washed the family laundry—another of her new bridge daughter duties— she learned to remove forgotten toothpicks from his shirts before tossing the load in the machine.

As he began to work the pick between his teeth, Hanna started clearing the table. "Don't do that yet," her mother said. "Sit down."

For all her mother's determination to fall back to traditional bridge daughter duties and roles, Hanna continued to eat at the table with her parents rather than in the kitchen, standing, as Erica did every night.

"Your father and I have been talking," Hanna's mother said. "How would you like to go to the mountains?"

"There's a place with cabins," her father said. "Very outdoorsy. Lots of flowers."

"Do you mean Susanna Glen?" Hanna said.

Hanna's mother, surprised, nodded once. "That's right."

"Erica told me," Hanna said. "She said it was a church thing." Hanna assumed that would immunize her from Erica's prediction, as her mother recoiled from anything associated with organized religion, and her father didn't seem particularly inured to it.

"It's nondenominational," her father said. "Sort of a co-op between a lot of churches and nonprofits in the Bay Area."

Hanna's mother went to the china hutch in the entry hall and returned with a glossy brochure. It featured color photography of birds in trees, towering redwoods, a stream running full, and a cluster of wood cabins in a clearing. The cabins surrounded a great fire pit ringed with granite blocks. A photo on the front of the brochure was of a semicircular birch sign over high metal gates. SUSANNA GLEN was burned into the wood in a fancy script. Below it was burned:

"And the bridge provided." – Matthew 1:25

On the back of the brochure were photos of sanitary bright-white examination rooms and expensive-looking medical equipment of uncertain purpose. Hanna peered at those photos the closest. Susanna Glen, the accompanying text gushed, featured a state-of-the-art clinic with a staff of doctors boasting thirty-five years combined experience in gefyriatrics and a team of round-the-clock nurses.

"We're going to live up there?" Hanna asked.

Her father peered across the table at Hanna's mother, indicating she needed to answer. "We won't be staying with you," she said to Hanna. "We'll be there for the finality, though."

"They have good doctors," her father said. "And the food is supposed to be something else. They told us there's a soft serve machine in the dining room, and you're allowed to have seconds."

Hanna turned the glossy brochure over again, looking for anything she might have missed. The meager amount of text printed alongside the oversized photos offered nothing substantive. No mention of *bridge daughters*, only the euphemisms she'd learned to spot: *pons* and *passerelle*. No mention of guards at their crow's-nests with spotlights and German shepherds prowling for pregnant thirteen year-old girls who fled into the night.

"So I don't get to come home," Hanna said.

Her mother said, "No, you won't."

Hanna pushed the brochure aside. "What did I do wrong?" Hanna said. "Just tell me."

"You did nothing wrong, honey," her father said.

"It's the decision we've made," her mother said.

Hanna breathed for a few moments, pouting, her hands folded on the table. She felt a hot swelling under her cheeks and behind her eyes, tears on their way, but, confusingly, she felt not a drop of sadness in her. "This is because I went to Uncle Rick's and Aunt Azami's," she said, her wet mouth making bubbles in the corners. "You're punishing me because I ran away."

"Now, Hanna—" Her father reached an assuring hand toward her.

"No, we won't sugar-coat this," her mother said to him. "Hanna, it's not punishment. We're doing this because we don't trust you."

Hanna gasped at the accusation.

"Dian—" her father said.

"Don't," Hanna's mother said to him. Then to Hanna, "You'll never understand what your father and I are going through. We've waited over *thirteen years* for our child. You are carrying *my* baby. How can we risk you running off again and putting our child in danger?" When Hanna started to protest, she said over her, "We raised you the way we did to avoid everything you've put us through these past months. You forced us into this."

Hanna dropped her head onto her folded hands and began crying. The wetness flowed, covering the back of her hands and pooling in the corners of her eyes. It all came out so hard she had trouble breathing, and she started wet-coughing. Her mother massaged her back. Hanna shrugged her off.

"What can't you have another one?" Hanna said into her hands, voice wet. "Just have another one."

After a long pause, her father said, "Your mother had complications when she had you. She can't have another bridge daughter."

Hanna raised her red swollen face from the table. "Really?"

"Really," he said softly.

"As soon as you were born, they took you away from me," her mother said. "They thought I was sick. They didn't want you exposed."

"They removed your mother's uterus," her father said. "For her safety."

The short sleeves of Hanna's bridge daughter dress prevented her from making mittens from them. She wiped her eyes clear with her fingertips, as the backs of her hands were soaked.

"When I held you in my arms," her mother said, "I wanted you to be my daughter so badly. You were so precious. I didn't want to wait fourteen years. I wanted to start raising you as my daughter at that moment. I understand why Liz did what she did to Cheryl. To raise her as her daughter and not the bridge. It is so tempting, Hanna."

She swallowed and continued. "I gave up a career, you know. My master's degree, just collecting dust now. Or the piano." She swept one hand toward the stand-up piano in the living room. Its top and bench were covered with green potted plants Hanna watered every other day. "I used to practice every morning and after dinner. Now I've lost my touch."

"Why didn't you tell me I was a bridge daughter?" Hanna said quietly. "Erica's known for a long time now."

Hanna's mother reluctantly nodded. "That was our mistake. I see that now. We were going to tell you when you reached *ponte primus*."

"It's my fault, actually," her father added. "I liked the little Hanna that got excited about dinosaurs and flowers. I thought when we explained the facts of life to you, I'd lose that Hanna."

"You're the one chance we have," Hanna's mother said. "We've done everything we can to protect you and keep you healthy. Thirteen years. That's why we need to send you to Susanna Glen. We can't risk all of that now."

Finally, after she'd dried her face, Hanna said, "I don't want to go to the mountains. This is my home too."

Her parents stared at each other for a long while. Her father broke the impasse.

"I say we sleep on it tonight," he said to Hanna's mother, "and discuss it over breakfast."

Her mother closed her eyes. She ran her hand over the middle of Hanna's back, as though divining the future within her.

Finally, she opened her eyes. "We'll discuss it first thing in the morning."

The mauve alarm clock on Hanna's bed stand started bleating at six thirty. It reeled her up from the watery depths of dreamy slumber to the world of oxygen and sunlight and blood and bile. The emotional force of the prior night's argument and her mother's revelations had sapped her little body, and she'd slept well.

Head slung from bleariness, she trudged to the hall bathroom. The cold floor gave her tender feet. She peed and washed her face and pushed a brush through her brown hair. Her hair had thickened over the past few weeks. Its mousiness had faded and a golden sheen had emerged, the color of pancakes perfectly done. Her fingernails, usually brittle and chipped, were each now firm and pearlescent. Her hips had rounded. Even her breasts had begun to fill in with pockets of fatty tissue behind her nipples. Hanna was undergoing pubescence and pregnancy simultaneously. Her body was swerving one direction to attract sexual partners and swerving another direction to nurture and deliver the double within her. There was no logic to Hanna's biology, but there it stood in the mirror staring back at her.

She'd committed theft before, but nothing on the scale of what she'd stolen from the Vannbergs. Was it their money, though? Or Cheryl's? What did her father sometimes say? "Possession is nine-tenths of the law"? The eight hundred twenty-three dollars belonged to her now. She would make an excuse to visit Erica across the street, beg for a measly two hundred dollars from her, and then she could flee for a bi-graft. It didn't matter what her parents decided at the table. Hanna was not going to Susanna Glen.

She padded barefoot to the kitchen. *Pancakes,* she decided to cook, *with sweet syrup promises and butter to butter them up.* Her mother splurged on the sausage links that week at the supermarket. Hanna would fry them up and serve them with the cakes and orange slices.

Although she'd never thought of herself as a cook, Hanna had discovered a personal satisfaction in her developing kitchen skills. *Handy for saving money,* she thought. *Too expensive to eat out every night when you live in the city,* thinking of Maureen. A slight smile, a pep in her walk, face tight and dry from the scrubbing, Hanna entered the kitchen ready for the world.

Her mother sat at the table wearing her plush red robe. Her hair was not mussed, but not kempt either. A steaming cup of coffee and a jar of powdered creamer were on the table before her.

Also on the table before her mother, between the coffee and creamer, lay a squared-off stack of cash. Fives and tens and twenties, loose and weathered and flimsy, with a single crisp hundred-dollar bill on top.

NINETEEN

HANNA PEERED UP at the ambitious brass knockers on the Grimonds' double doors and wondered if she would ever see them again. She would not miss them, not at all.

Hanna and her mother had not phoned, so they were unexpected. Erica appeared unsurprised all the same. She asked under her breath if they could wait and padded to the rear of the house in her soft bridge daughter shoes. She returned behind Vivian Grimond.

"Hanna is off to Susanna Glen tomorrow morning," Hanna's mother explained. "She wanted to give some things to Erica. If that's okay with you."

"You took my advice!" Mrs. Grimond said. "Jennifer had such a good experience there, I knew it would be a perfect fit for Hanna too." She said to Hanna, "Jennifer was my first bridge daughter. We'll be sending Erica to Susanna Glen when she's ready."

Hanna stepped forward and set the cardboard box on the entryway tile. Mrs. Grimond leaned over to rummage through it. She murmured the contents to herself. "Sweater, cardigan, shirts—oh, this one is cute—t-shirt, jeans—you can use those when you help in the backyard," she said to Erica. "Sneakers—oh, these might be a little small for you, Erica. We'll see. Toothpaste?" She looked up at Hanna's mother, taken aback at the idea that Hanna no longer needed to clean her teeth.

"Hanna doesn't like that flavor," her mother assured Mrs. Grimond. "She didn't want to throw it away, though."

"I see. Well, this is all very generous of you. We'll put it to good use. Thank you."

Mrs. Grimond told Erica to take the box to her bedroom. Diminutive Erica struggled a bit with its girth.

Then Mrs. Grimond leaned down to Hanna. "Now you have a good time at Susanna Glen. Cherish every moment. When your finality arrives, you'll see how blessed you and all bridge daughters really are." She told Erica to say good-bye, and Erica did so, chin on the top of the box.

After lunch, Hanna and her mother packed two suitcases full of clothes and shoes and so on. Hanna wondered what would happen to the things she left behind. Of course, she thought, they would save it all for little Hanna as she grew up.

When her father arrived home from work, he removed his coat and tie and opened a can of beer. He told Hanna to join him at the kitchen table.

"I want you to tell me where you got that money." His voice was calm but firm.

"I asked her three times already," her mother said.

With the questions and yelling at the kitchen table that morning, her father didn't have time to shave. His chin and neck were dark with stubble.

"What were you going to do, Hanna?" He waited a long while for her answer, drinking patiently. Finally, he heaved a hoppy, carbonated sigh and pushed himself to his feet.

"We'll have to lock her in her room tonight," he said to Hanna's mother. "We can't risk it."

"You can't do that," Hanna said. "What if there's a fire?"

Hanna's father shook his head. He left the kitchen with his

back hunched and a hand on his nape, the other carrying his beer. A minute later, he was in the backyard, smoking a cigarette in the dwindling dusk light and drinking from the can. Hanna had never seen him smoke before.

That night they had a silent dinner of delivered Chinese food. Her father chewed aimlessly, drinking his second can of beer with the meal. He carried in from the backyard the chemical, odorous tang of American tobacco.

"Your father won't ask this outright, but I will," her mother said, breaking the wordless evening. "Were you going to use that money for a bi-graft?"

"I'd rather not talk about this at the table," her father said.

"Did Erica tell you about it?" her mother demanded from Hanna.

"No," Hanna insisted.

"Do you know what a bi-graft does to the baby inside you?" her mother said. "Do you know what it makes you? Sickly and addicted to gefyridol."

Hanna stared straight ahead, mustering everything she could to avoid her mother's glare.

"Did your aunt tell you about bi-grafts?" her mother demanded.

Hanna involuntarily revealed something, a tic or darting eyes.

"I should have known," her mother said. "That bitch—" In four strides, she went from the table to the phone on the table beside the couch.

In a moment, she had Uncle Rick on the line. She vented at him, then demanded Aunt Azami be placed on the line. Hanna's aunt then got an earful as well. Hanna so wanted Rick and Azami to be her parents, living together in their tiny apartment on Geary Street, Hanna using the couch as a bed. Every night, they'd go out to the bars and meet up with Maureen and eat pizza, and every morning Hanna would greet them with breakfast in bed and fresh flowers in cut glass on the tray. The city would be theirs.

Hanna's father stood in the backyard, having one more cigarette before bed. Only the red firefly of his cigarette's cherry was visible through the sliding glass.

"I don't have any walking shoes," Hanna said to her mother. Both suitcases split open like cracked crabs, Hanna rooted through the folded frocks and shirts and socks and toiletries.

Her mother stood in the bedroom doorway with her hands on her hips, watching Hanna's frantic search. "You have shoes."

"These are house shoes," Hanna said. "We're going to walk through the woods every day."

"Don't you have an old pair of sneakers?"

"I gave them to Erica," Hanna said.

Her mother checked her petite wristwatch. "Let me call Vivian," she murmured.

Mrs. Grimond opened the door herself this time. Stepping out to the cone of porch light, Erica offered Hanna her old sneakers, the ones that had curled at the toes from runs through the dryer after rainy days.

"Not those," Hanna said, "the other ones."

"Other ones?" Mrs. Grimond said.

"I didn't see any others," Erica said.

"There was another pair," Hanna insisted.

"You should show me," Erica said.

With a bit of urgency in their step, Erica led Hanna though through the kitchen's swinging doors and down the rear hallway of laundry goods and dry dog food.

In her room, Erica spun around. "What do you really want?"

"Give me the address. For the bi-graft."

Erica, dubious, went to the adjoining bathroom. She opened the bottom door of the vanity cabinetry and crawled on her back under the sink, like an auto mechanic checking a clutch line. Hanna had hidden her money under the bathroom hall vanity as well, but she was apparently nowhere near as clever as Erica.

"Here." She offered Hanna a small business card. It read *Dr. Mark Hemming, Pastor*. Printed below it were the address and particulars of the Grimonds' church and Pastor Hemming's office phone number.

"On the back," Erica prompted.

Scrawled on the back of the card in the curly-perfect handwriting of a junior high school girl was this:

Hotel Mavis
555 Ellis St.
SF
"Arch"

"San Francisco?" Hanna gasped. "I thought it was here in town. Isn't there one closer?"

"This is the only one I know about," Erica said.

Hanna went to the cardboard box of her old things. Erica had not had time to unpack it, save for a few items on the floor she had removed to get to Hanna's shoes. Hanna was not lying; there was a second pair of shoes at the bottom of the box. She went through the rolled-up jeans, feeling at the denim tubes until she located one in particular. She unrolled the pair to their full length and reached inside the right leg. She pulled out another rolled-up tube of fabric, a backpack she used for trips to the library.

Hustling, Hanna stuffed a sweater, socks, and pairs of underwear from the box into the backpack. The toothpaste she supposedly didn't like the flavor of, she tossed that in the bag as well. She kicked off her soft bridge daughter shoes and tugged on a pair of socks and the sneakers. She pulled a colorful sweater down over her head. It effectively covered her bulging expectation and made the giveaway shape and plainness of her bridge daughter smock look more like a bland school skirt.

"You better hurry," Erica said. "They'll be down here any second now."

Hanna slung the backpack on. She went to Erica, uncomfortably close, almost nose-to-nose.

"Give me the money," she said.

"What?" Erica coughed a laugh. "No way."

"Give it to me," she said, "or I tell your mother about it."

Erica's mouth opened in protest. "You promised," she breathed.

"I'll tell her you have the money. I'll tell her you're stealing from your church."

"You pinkie promised!"

What would Maureen do? Hanna broke away and charged into the bathroom. The bottom door of the vanity was still open. Erica hadn't returned the card to its hiding spot yet. Hanna lowered to her knees, eye-to-eye with the plumbing and bathroom cleaners stored beneath the sink, and poked her head in.

Down the hall, from the kitchen door, Mrs. Grimond called, "Is everything okay down there?"

Two hands on her back and shoulders dragged her out. Erica stared down on her with a blaze of fury.

"You're such a brat," she muttered. "Always get your way."

"You can get more," Hanna said.

Erica dropped and crawled on elbows under the vanity. Hanna stumbled out to the bedroom and called to the kitchen, "Still looking!"

Erica slammed the vanity's bottom door shut. She held out a wad of cash to Hanna.

"You pinkie promised," she whispered.

Hanna threw her arms around Erica. "Thank you."

Then she hurried, out of the bedroom and down the hall, away from the kitchen. Mrs. Grimond called out again from the kitchen. Hanna reached a door to the backyard. The weight on her back swung left and right with each push forward, as did the ponderous weight in her belly, but she knew she had to keep pushing, and so she did, pushing out and into the cool quiet night.

She'd not planned to run under these circumstances, and she'd not planned to run to San Francisco. That night, planning gave way to urgent action. Hanna's hurried footsteps set the

Grimonds' dog barking when she passed the garage and compelled her to move faster. Out on the street, she gripped her backpack straps and hurried as fast as she could, waddling down the amber-lit sidewalk to the closest intersection.

She'd done some homework over the past week. She'd assumed the doctor performing the procedure—or whatever profession he might call his own—she assumed he'd be reachable by bus, if she needed one. Now the Concord train station was distant enough she had to use the bus. The spare change she'd hidden in one of the backpack's many zippered pockets would get her there.

At the first intersection, she turned the corner. Better to get off her house street and onto another one, out of the sight of her mother. And soon she'd have to worry about her father patrolling the neighborhood in the family car. Erica was probably now telling Mrs. Grimond and her mother that Hanna had run off. She'd fake innocence and point to the raided cardboard box as proof of her lack of complicity. Would Erica tell them of her destination? No, that risked Hanna being caught and blabbing where'd she gotten the money and information. Erica would save her own skin, but she had good reason to hope Hanna would not be caught and squeal.

Which Hanna would never do. Threatening Erica for the money had disgusted her. That would be one regret she'd carry a long time. With Cheryl's money, the morality seemed fuzzier and more theoretical.

Hanna's short legs were better at carrying her increased load than even she expected. She worried not so much about the bouncing as she did revealing her pregnancy. Her old plan, now blasted apart, relied on passing herself as an older teenager. She kept that in mind as she hurried onward through the nighttime air.

She cut through a park, one used by dog walkers to give their pets a chance to perform their business, and reached its other side out of breath and sweaty. She'd hustled four suburban blocks in fifteen minutes. More importantly, she had made her way to a different neighborhood. Her parents would be searching the streets at that moment, calling out to her from the car. They might even be calling the police now. Hanna had to keep moving.

Like most cities in the Bay Area, Concord did not offer particularly reliable public transportation. Bus routes were sparse and service spotty. At the bus stop on the edge of the park, Hanna stepped out on the quiet road and peered down its length. No buses in sight.

Over the weekend, when she was cleaning the bathrooms, Hanna had pocketed three items from the small wicker basket on her parents' vanity: a tube of lipstick, a cap of violet eyeliner, and a folding hand mirror. The basket was overflowing with old make-up, colors her mother no longer used, and the items were not missed. Under the streetlight, she rapidly applied the cosmetics, the first time she'd ever worn make-up. She wished she'd taken a pair of clip-on earrings too, but her mother would have noticed.

She kept walking, every two blocks stopping to look down the street for an approaching bus. The extended walking made her back sore, especially the pinprick knots left from her recent injections. At the fourth stop, she saw the bus headlights, big and bright, with the backlit destination sign across the top of the carriage. She dug out change from the backpack pocket. She had exact fare ready when she stepped up onto the bus.

"Kind of late, isn't it?" the driver said to her.

"I'm on the colors committee," she said, mimicking a phrase she'd heard high school students say in one of the television dramas she followed. "We were working late."

The driver looked her up and down. Hanna had tugged the loose, baggy sweater out away from her belly, hoping she presented as a frumpy high school student. As is the wont of girls her age, she'd applied too much makeup, but not so much to appear like a little girl who'd gotten into her mother's cosmetic kit one rainy afternoon.

The driver closed the front door. The bus lurched forward.

Public transportation was not only poor in most Bay Area cities, it was rarely used. Hanna sat in the cold bench seat shivering, happy she had the bus to herself.

TWENTY

HANNA STEPPED DOWN from a bus onto Geary Street for the second time in ten weeks. The driver indicated she should walk south two blocks to Ellis Street. She thanked him from the sidewalk. The doors closed and the bus eased forward into traffic.

It was now approaching 11:30 at night. A strong temptation took hold to go straight to Uncle Rick and Aunt Azami's apartment. They could give her a place to sleep until morning, when she could set out and find the Hotel Mavis. She knew she risked much going to them. Her mother would have phoned Uncle Rick as soon as it was obvious she was no longer in the neighborhood. Even if Uncle Rick and Aunt Azami sympathized with Hanna's decision, Hanna couldn't imagine Uncle Rick going against the wishes of his own sister.

On the train ride in the tube beneath the bay waters, she'd counted Erica's money using her body to shield her activity from the other passengers. It amounted to a little over four hundred dollars. The total was far below what the doctor was expecting for the procedure. She would have to beg for his consideration.

Unless she could trust Aunt Azami. *What would Maureen do?* Hanna tightened her grip on her backpack's straps and set off down Geary Street, walking with purpose.

The bar was not as busy as the first time she'd visited. A young man sat at the far end drinking a beer and watching the television, a late-night John Wayne western. A man and woman sat at the middle of the curved bar, closest to the entrance, drinking from stemware. All three were smoking, causing Hanna to cough when she stepped inside. Aunt Azami was behind the bar washing glasses.

"Oh, Hanna." She flicked excess water from her hands and picked up a rag. "You shouldn't be here."

Hanna approached the bar. She stood on the brass foot rail to elevate herself to Azami's height.

"If your uncle was here," Aunt Azami warned.

"Don't call my mother," she said quietly.

"Your mother is incensed with me already," Azami said, shaking her head.

Hanna's eyes adjusted to the amber votives running down the bar. Out of the corner of one eye, she caught a dim outline in the dark corner. It leaned forward and edged its gaunt, pale face into the light. "Hello, Hanna," Maureen said.

"I need money," Hanna said softly to both of them.

Aunt Azami reached across the bar and patted Hanna's wrist. She dipped her hand into the ceramic honey pot beside the cash register and brought Hanna a splay of dollar bills.

"It's been a slow night," she said. "I wish there was more."

Maureen unsnapped her purse. From it she produced a crisp bill neatly folded in half and offered it to Hanna.

"Thank you," Hanna said. "I promise I'll pay you both back."

"No way do you do that," Aunt Azami said. "I can never see you again. You have to run."

"Where are you staying tonight?" Maureen said.

Hanna shrugged. She still half-hoped Aunt Azami would invite her to her apartment.

"I have a couch," Maureen said.

"You don't have to," Azami said to her.

"One night won't do any harm," she replied.

Hanna pushed the new money into the pocket of her backpack, joining Erica's savings. She couldn't imagine the total was enough, but she had to try.

Aunt Azami came around the bar with red eyes. Azami and Hanna hugged for a long while, rocking slightly, Hanna's face buried in Azami's chest. Then Hanna made an improvised mitten with her sweater sleeve, wiped her face dry, and said goodbye to her.

Maureen and Hanna rode the bus for so much time, Hanna wondered if they were still in San Francisco. They traveled so far, the city stopped naming streets and simply numbered them, much like Hanna numbered her *tsuru*. Tenth Avenue, Sixteenth Avenue, Twenty-third Avenue. How high would the numbers go?

In the hard revealing light of the bus' interior, Hanna had her first opportunity to really take in Maureen. She was more sickly than Hanna estimated in the bar. She wore nice clothes, classically fashionable, her mother might say, her long skirt and blouse flaring to hide her emaciated frame. Hanna had seen women who looked like this before, but they were much older than Maureen, women who'd lived hardscrabble lives waitressing in diners or scrubbing corporate toilets in her father's office building. None as young as Maureen.

At Thirty-third Avenue, they stepped off the bus. Maureen lived two blocks off Geary Street, in a walk-up with no front yard to speak of, the stairway to the front door ascending right at the sidewalk. At the top of the stairs, Maureen keyed them into a surprisingly attractive apartment with hardwood floors, beanbags, and a rattan couch before a television and hi-fi. Maureen told Hanna she could place her backpack anywhere.

Maureen prepared ham sandwiches. Like Hanna, Maureen used a footstool in the kitchen to reach the upper shelves of the cabinets and the top of the refrigerator, where the bread loaf was stored. They ate the meal with glasses of milk in the kitchen nook. As on the bus, few words passed between them. Hanna gathered the plates and bowls when they finished and washed and set them in the drying rack.

The kitchen, and the rest of the apartment, was meticulous. The hardwood floors shined. Hanna felt hesitant to even sit on the rattan couch, where the throw pillows seemed placed with an eye for aesthetics and not comfort.

"My roommate may come in later tonight," Maureen said. "I'll leave a note on the door that you're here, so you don't surprise her."

"Thank you for this," Hanna said. "I saw people sleeping on the sidewalk tonight. I thought I might have to do that too."

Maureen led her to the rattan couch and motioned to sit. "What are your plans?"

Hanna hated to admit that she'd made little in the way of preparations. She was sure Maureen had gathered as much when she came into the bar asking for money. In Hanna's fervid imagination, ten years earlier, when Maureen was thirteen, she had systematically saved the requisite monies, had the bi-graft performed on schedule, and an hour later boarded a flight to San Francisco where a job and apartment waited as per her mailed instructions. Hanna couldn't even tell Maureen she was improvising, as improvisation at least suggests one knows the shape of the situation and not just feeling around in the dark. She bent her head and admitted to Maureen she had no plan at all.

"You know where you'll have the procedure performed?" Maureen asked.

Hanna nodded. "On Ellis Street."

"And then what will you do?"

Hanna shrugged. "I can't stay here, can I?"

"No," Maureen said firmly, "you cannot."

"There's a Greyhound station out by the docks," Hanna said. "I read in the paper they're running a special. I'm going to buy a ticket for Los Angeles."

Maureen nodded. "And where will you go then?"

"Isn't that far enough?"

"Maybe," Maureen said. "Maybe not."

"There's a flower market in Los Angeles," Hanna said. "A big one. I'm going to try and get a job there."

Maureen gathered her thoughts. "You can't do this alone," she said. "I'm not even sure L.A. is far enough, but let's say for now it is. You'll need to find help. There are women like me. Working together is the only way to survive."

"Who?" Hanna said. "I don't know anyone there."

Maureen went to the bookshelf and returned with a short pad of paper and a pen. "You need to look for this," she said, drawing on the pad. "It's Hagar's symbol. If you see it on the side of a building or a doorway, it means more of us are nearby. They can help you."

Maureen showed Hanna the outline of a portly water urn with a sharply curved neck. Elongated handles spread from each side like perked ears.

"It's a water jug," Maureen explained. "Hagar carried water her entire life. When you see it, look nearby. Find women who look like you and me. Ask them about Hagar. But be careful. Sometimes they're traps. Always be ready to run."

Hanna ran her forefinger along the outline of the urn. She'd been carrying water her entire life too.

"How much money do you have?"

Hanna opened her backpack and removed the cash: Erica's, Aunt Azami's, and Maureen's slim folded bill. She counted out loud. Then, thinking how her father counted money when he withdrew from the bank, she turned the stack upside-down and counted it backwards. She arrived at the same figure both times.

"Six hundred forty-five dollars," she said.

"How much do you need?"

"One thousand," Hanna said.

"I was afraid you'd say that." Maureen pursed her lips. "I'm sorry I can't give you more."

Hanna hurried to stop Maureen. "I know, I know," she said. "You've done enough."

"I know it looks like I live in an expensive apartment," Maureen motioned about the room, "but, really, this isn't my place. I rent a small room for cheap. My roommate is doing me a favor."

"Is she like you?"

"No," Maureen said. "But she's sympathetic to women like us."

"Can I ask something?" Hanna asked. "If this is illegal, aren't you afraid of being caught?" In Hanna's mind, Maureen should have been hiding out, like in the movies, sleeping in an abandoned warehouse or on a deserted dock.

"In San Francisco," Maureen said, "people look the other way. There's more of us here than you might think."

"Not on television," Hanna said.

"Of course not. Television isn't going to tell our story any time soon. Look," she said, "wherever you land, make sure it's a big city. You have a better chance of blending in there. Otherwise, make for the mountains or the high desert, someplace where people believe in live-and-let-live. Stay away from the suburbs. You don't have a chance there."

"Don't worry," Hanna said. "I'm not going back there again."

As Maureen warned, Hanna was awoken by the sound of a key scratching around the apartment's front door lock. The hinges creaked as it opened and shut. A woman whispered, a man whispered back, there was some giggling, and the pair moved to the rear of the apartment.

Hanna, lying on the floor, waited for them to disappear into the back bedroom. Soon she heard bed springs squeaking and gasps and exercised breathing. She rolled away and put her hands over her ears, wishing sleep to return.

Unable to drift off, Hanna's imagination began to run visions she'd begun to see in her mind over the past few weeks. She had begun to imagine her parents living their lives after she'd run away. She saw them eating at far ends of the dining room table, not saying a word to one another. She saw her father sealing off her bedroom from the rest of the house, locking the door and stashing the key in the garage with the gardening tools and the bicycles the three used to ride together. Her mother slept in the master bedroom while her father improvised a bed each night: on the couch, in the guest room, sometimes conked out on his easy chair at two in the morning while the television's dartboard test pattern irradiated the living room. So quiet, the house without her, and so still.

A beam of dawn light struck Hanna in the face, warming her cheek and forcing open her eyelids. She'd slept lightly. Anxiety acted as a kind of adrenaline, and she came alert in an instant.

She rose, folded the blankets, and piled them on the rattan couch. She used the bathroom and took a drink of water from the kitchen tap, mindful to clean the glass and return it to the drying rack. She tiptoed about the apartment. The two bedroom doors were closed. No one was up and about. It seemed for the best.

On the kitchen table, she left a brief thank you note to Maureen. In the bottom corner of the note, she drew to the best of her abilities Hagar's water jug. On top of the note, she set a bright yellow origami crane numbered *994*.

TWENTY-ONE

REACHING 555 ELLIS STREET required another extended bus ride, this one among the throng of Geary's morning commute traffic. Seemingly bumpier than the night before, the bus stopped at corners all the way back to San Francisco's downtown. Anxiety was in her neck. It gave her hands light tremors. She told herself she had no choice, this was what must be done. Otherwise, she would be dead in six weeks.

The Hotel Mavis was a six-story building done up in San Francisco's gaudy cake-frosting style, dark purple with banana-yellow windowsills and eaves, the colors having faded long before. High overhead, painted on the side of the building in flaking blanched letters, the hotel proclaimed "Rooms by the Night / Week / Month" and "Fully Furnished."

A rococo alabaster archway framed the hotel entrance. It was deep purple, the same paint as the hotel's exterior. Twin purple tornadoes composed its sides and curved to meet at a top point, in the style of a Turkish arch. Hanna scarcely noticed the carvings until she'd passed between them, then stepped back to study them closer. The motion lines of the swirling, violent tornados were ribbed deep into the gypsum. Caught in the wind's violence, tossed about casually by its gale forces, were molting breasty angels, sneering devils with engorged phalluses, and woodland satyrs, centaurs, and nymphs. All wore garlands on their heads, but otherwise were buck naked.

A hotel clerk sat behind a long tiled counter reading a copy of *Reader's Digest*. A beehive of mail slots covered the wall behind him, each cubbyhole numbered. It wasn't until that moment she realized she had no room number to ask for. The only clue on Erica's business card was "Arch." Was that a name to ask for? Or did it mean to look for the carved archway entrance?

"Can I do something for you?" The clerk was entirely bald with a white stubble chin and thick bags beneath each eye. His glasses sat on the top of his shining head.

"Arch," Hanna said.

"Thought so," the clerk said. He dialed two numbers on the house phone. After a moment, he said, "Got one down here for you." He hung up. "Be just a minute."

Hanna, wide-eyed, backed away from the front desk, wondering if she should run. Wasn't that what Maureen said, always be prepared to run? She casually turned and started for the entrance.

Scratched into the ribbed alabaster archway at knee-level, perhaps done with a pocketknife, was Hagar's water jug, the exposed gypsum in high contrast against the purple paint job. She would never have noticed it before, just mistaken it as vandalism, but now Hanna's keen eyes pinpointed the sign. Carved so low to the ground, she thought it possible the desk clerk didn't even know of its existence. Maureen warned her to watch for tricks, but the strength of the rotund jug reassured Hanna and gave her the confidence to wait.

A lanky, handsome young man in a UC Berkeley sweatshirt and jeans bounded down the stairs and into the lobby. He'd not shaven in days. He studied Hanna through wire-rimmed glasses, hands on his sides and chewing on his top lip. Then he went out to the sidewalk and looked both directions down Ellis Street. He returned to the lobby and motioned with his hand to the clerk.

The clerk slapped a key on the front desk's tiled top. The lanky man swiped it off with his palm and kept walking.

"Will you call Lenna for me?" he called back to the clerk. Then to Hanna: "Come on, then," moving toward the stairs, "let's go."

Hanna, confused by the man's abruptness, glanced to the clerk for a hint or a clue, but he'd already picked up the phone and was dialing. Hanna followed the lanky young man, hands clutching her backpack straps and wondering if she should have run after all.

Surprisingly, he took the stairs down, although he'd descended from an upper floor when he first entered the hotel lobby. A single bare bulb lit a steel door at the bottom of the stairwell. The man used the clerk's key to unlock it and they moved down a narrow dim hallway beyond. Slits of dingy brown glass ran along the top of the wall. Through them Hanna saw foot traffic: sneakers and hard-soled shoes and dog paws. They were underground, below the sidewalk, and they continued further underground.

They descended again to another steel door. The key unlocked this one as well.

Inside, the man threw a wall switch. "This is my theater." Two rows of fluorescent lights chained to the concrete ceiling shuddered on.

The lights revealed a concrete room with no windows, exposed pipes, and a fat iron boiler in the corner rumbling as though it had indigestion. For all the sound it made, it appeared to be nonoperational, as the room was quite cold. The room smelled stale as well, fetid and musty, much like the basement of Ma Cynthia's farmhouse where she stored her jarred preserves on open shelves like medical specimens.

Other than the boiler, the room appeared designed for no purpose other than storage. Paint cans and painting supplies were piled up beside the door. Along another wall, four wooden ladders lay on their sides, each in varying states of trustworthiness. A mystery pile in the far corner was covered with a paint-streaked tarp. Attached to the wall was the brownest, dankest, filthiest sink Hanna had ever laid eyes upon.

"There's the matter of the money," the man said.

Hanna, who'd been mesmerized by this little underground journey, snapped to and realized all of this might end right then and there. She offered Arch the money from her backpack pocket. He counted the bills with brisk efficiency, much like a bank teller, fronting and facing each bill as he went.

"How do you know why I'm here?" she asked.

"There's only one reason thirteen-year-old girls come looking for me," he said, still counting. He reached the end of the stack. "This isn't enough."

"I know," she said. "I can explain—"

"This isn't just about me," he said. "Miller upstairs, he's the owner. He gets fifty off the top. That buys his silence. I take five hundred. That's my fee."

Hanna's heart lightened. "Then I have enough."

"For me and Miller, yeah. What about for yourself?" He riffled the bills with the meat of his thumb, making the six hundred forty-five dollars seem as valuable as a deck of cards. "You need expense money. You're going to be on the run for a while. That's why I tell the girls to bring a thousand."

"I can get more," Hanna said.

"Are you an orphan?" he demanded. "A ward of the state?"

"What?" she said. "No."

"Where are you from?" When Hanna hesitated, he said, "Come on; let's hear it."

"Concord."

"*Concord,*" he murmured sarcastically. "You've got a long way to go before you're far enough away from *Concord.* From everyone in your life. Wherever you land, you can't know a single soul. One person recognizes you—" He snapped his fingers. The crack pierced the cold basement air and echoed off the concrete walls. "It's over."

Two sharp knocks sounded on the door. Arch called out it was open. A short woman stepped inside, platinum blond with high cheekbones and candle-wax skin. She wore a plain gray T-shirt and ragged blue jeans a size too large for her bony frame.

Behind her, out in the dark hall, the clerk stood with his hands in his pockets and his glasses atop his bald head. He was chewing gum. Arch counted six bills from the stack, making each snap when it separated from its brethren. He handed the clerk the fifty dollars and the borrowed key. The clerk's hand snaked out from its pocket, swallowed Arch's offering in one gulp, and slithered back to its hole. An instant later, the clerk was gone.

"If I don't have enough money," Hanna said, "why did you give him that?"

"That's nonrefundable," Arch said. "Miller gets his cut no matter what. That's the price of silence."

"She doesn't have the money?" the platinum blond woman said, her voice high-pitched and squeaky.

"She can cover our end," Arch said, "just not her own."

"Where are you going to go after this, honey?" the woman asked.

"Los Angeles," Hanna said.

"That's not far enough," Arch said.

"It could be." The woman approached Hanna. She put out a hand to warn Hanna of her intention to touch her. Her candle-wax fingers made gentle contact with Hanna's forearm, then moved up to her shoulder and neck. "What are your plans there?"

"I'm going to work at the flower market," Hanna said, uncomfortable at the woman's probing touch.

"Why flowers?" the woman asked, still probing.

"I love flowers," Hanna said. Then she said something she'd never said before, not even to herself. "They're my only real friends."

For all the discomfort the waxy woman instilled in Hanna, she found her hands surprisingly warm and nurturing. Her touch drew the poisonous anxiety out from Hanna's body.

"I'll pay you back," Hanna said to them. "I can work here in the city. I'll help you! I can help you until I've paid off what I owe."

"You can't stay here after this," Arch said. He snapped the stack of bills. "And like I said, you've got enough for us. You need money for yourself."

"Let me stay with you," she said to the woman. "I'll work and save and then I'll go. I'm good at a lot of things. I'm a hard worker."

"Oh, honey." The woman pressed a palm to Hanna's cheek. "You're so precious."

"How old are you?" Hanna asked without reservation.

"Thirty-one," the woman replied.

"Lenna beat the odds," Arch said. "I bet you've heard people say girls with bi-grafts can't live past thirty."

The new information took something out of Hanna. "No one's told me much of anything," she said.

Lenna patted Hanna's cheek and squeezed her shoulder. "I'll do this one for nothing," she announced to Arch.

"Why?" he said.

"This one's the first one not to beg for our money," she said. "She's a worker. And I like flowers too." She winked at Hanna.

Arch studied the stack of money in his hands. "She is different than the others." He removed bills from the stack one at a time, again making each snap as they left the group. "Since Lenna's dropping her fifty dollar fee, I'll lop fifty dollars off mine too." He offered the remaining money to Hanna, the bills folded in half and pinned between his fore and middle fingers, like a magician presenting the Ace of Spades. "One hundred forty-five dollars comes back to you," he said. "Diamond Jim Brady launched an empire from less than that."

"Is that enough for her?" Lenna asked.

"It'll have to be," he sighed.

Arch tossed the mystery tarp aside. Underneath was a collection of equipment Hanna did not recognize and a stack of flimsy cardboard boxes stained with oil. A white plastic case the shape of an oversized briefcase rested on top of the boxes. Arch unlatched it and in two quick motions extended it to a long surface with six legs clicked into place. It was a portable examination table with stirrups bolted to one end.

Stored in a cardboard box, along with other items, was a stack of white pressed sheets. He snapped the top one open and lay it on the floor, like a picnic blanket. He moved the examination table on top of it. Then he snapped open another sheet and draped it over the table.

Lenna started the sink in the corner. Soon hot water jetted from the tap. Steam smoked in the cold air and humidified the sealed room.

Arch said, "You've been seen by a gefyriatricist, right?" Hanna nodded. "Well, this is sort of like how your gefyriatricist examines you. I'll be doing some cutting, though. And there'll be some blood."

In all of Hanna's imaginings, she'd never considered blood as a part of the procedure. "Will it hurt?"

"This *is* a medical procedure," he said absently.

"You'll be sore for about forty-eight hours," Lenna said.

"What about anesthesia?"

He smirked and extended his arms to present the room *in toto*. "We're not a hospital."

"He'll do the absolute best he can, honey," Lenna said. "I'll be holding your hand the entire time."

Hanna, bitten by Arch's scoffs, shrank a bit. Maybe she didn't want to go through with this after all. But where else could she go? Who else could she see? He was right, after all. This was no hospital, there was no staff anesthesiologist; she would have to accept her circumstances and trust him to do his best.

She still wanted Arch to turn around while she undressed. She almost whispered the request to Lenna, her ally here, but Hanna thought twice. *What would Maureen do?* This was a doctor, Hanna reasoned, and the time to grow up was now. She shrugged off her backpack and pulled her sweater up over her head.

Lenna offered some privacy without her asking, however. She held the hospital gown wide open before Hanna and stood between her and Arch. While disrobing, Hanna peered over Lenna's shoulder. She saw Arch was entirely disinterested in her, focusing on assembling more equipment and tying on a surgeon's smock. So collected and businesslike, Hanna sensed Arch approached the bi-graft no differently than her father's mechanic repairing their car.

"Can I ask a question?" Hanna said.

"Ask all you need to," Arch said.

"What is a bi-graft?" Hanna asked.

"An intrauterine bi-graft," Arch announced, "freezes the gemellius' cortical functions, fastens its mass to the uterine wall, and cauterizes key vascular pathways. The gemellius' automated functions remain operational. Otherwise, its development is arrested."

"Do you understand?" Lenna asked. She was tying the back of Hanna's gown in place.

"It's like an abortion?" Hanna ventured.

"Not in the least," Arch announced again. "I am not an abortionist. Our government in its grand wisdom has made that procedure legal in all fifty states while keeping intrauterine bi-grafts punishable to the full extent of the law."

"Don't worry about all that," Lenna said to Hanna.

"What I will do," Arch continued, "is place your double in a coma. A persistent vegetative state. This sustains the symbiosis but terminates the progress of the fetus. It lives, you live."

"She stays inside me?"

"For the rest of your life," Lenna said.

"Some time in the next month or two, you'll suffer birthing contractions," Arch said. "Your body will attempt to fulfill its end of the bargain and expel the gemellius." He went to the sink, still spurting steaming hot water, and began soaping up his arms and hands. "A key step of the procedure is to affix the gemellius to your uterine lining. That prevents delivery."

The boiler in the corner, only grumbling up to this point, banged twice, just like the steam radiator had in Uncle Rick's and Aunt Azami's apartment when she spent the night.

"Affix?"

Arch, his back to Hanna, called out over the running water. "Surgical staples. They're permanent."

"Staples!"

"Under no condition can the gemellius exit your body."

"But what if she does? Do I call a doctor?"

"Don't go to doctors," Lenna said. "Doctors call the police."

"If it exits your body," Arched called from the sink, "it's all over."

Lenna helped barefoot Hanna to the folding table. The concrete floor was so cold, it made her soles burn. Hanna lay back while Lenna placed her feet in the stirrups.

"Are you being prescribed anything?" Arch called. "Any drug at all."

"Gefyridol," Hanna said. "I brought it with me, just in case."

Arch snatched up a white starchy towel and buried his hands in it. Lenna turned off the faucet. Drying his hairy, muscled forearms, he stood over Hanna.

"You just saved yourself a lot of money," he said. "You'll need to start taking gefyridol."

"When?"

"Today," Lenna said, "after the procedure. Then once a week."

"For how long?"

"The rest of your life," Lenna said.

Hanna sank her head to the surface of the folding table. "I don't have that much of it. Just one box."

"There's a low-dosage gefyridol tablet you can buy over-the-counter," Arch said. "But the acetaminophen in it is hard on the liver. Lenna can show you a way to separate the gefyridol."

"When you're older," she said, "you can try and get a prescription. That's a lot easier. But if you ever see the pharmacist dialing the phone, you get out of there."

"And in a hurry," Arch added.

"Don't even ask for the prescription back," Lenna said. "Just go."

"Who will give me a prescription?"

"Hagar's water jug." Lenna drew the symbol in the air. "Find women who can help. They'll get you gefyridol. Or a place to sleep. Or a job where they don't ask too many questions."

"And you need to start acting like an adult," Arch said. That bruised Hanna until he continued. "Start wearing makeup. Buy some grownup clothes at Goodwill. Talk like an adult. But don't overdo it. When someone looks at you funny, say your mother was small too."

"Tell them you're *Irish*," Lenna said, whispering *Irish* as though it was fatal.

"Eat well," Arch said. "Stay healthy. Your immune system will be compromised, so avoid hospitals. Hear that? Don't work at a hospital. Don't go to one unless it's an absolute emergency. You catch a cold, you get a fever, make yourself some chicken soup and sleep it off. Do not go to a hospital."

"And don't sell your *body*," Lenna said, whispering *body* the way she whispered *Irish*. "There's always a better option."

While Lenna washed her hands at the sink, Arch stood over Hanna on the table. Eyes on Lenna's back, he added, voice lowered, "And don't do heroin. Never."

Arch reached into an oil-stained cardboard box and produced a half-empty bottle of American vodka. He poured three *glugs* into a Pyrex beaker and drank it all in two swallows. The beaker shivered as it was pressed to his lips. Then he poured another two *glugs*, filling the beaker a quarter way up.

Lenna finished drying her hands. "You're smart, you'll learn." Lenna's waxy hands, gentle, wrapped around Hanna's right hand. "All of Hagar's sisters have to learn. You'll learn about medicine, about nutrition, about finding work and a place to sleep."

Is that what I'm to become? Hanna asked herself. *Hagar's sister?*

Arch said, "You still want to go through with this?"

"I don't want to die," she said.

"The whole world is waiting for you," Lenna said. "You deserve a chance to see it."

Arch plunked stainless steel medical instruments into the beaker of vodka: scalpels, calipers, forceps, and more. The boiler banged once and groaned.

"It's not fair," Hanna said, tearing up.

Arch positioned himself between Hanna's extended bare legs. He sat in a metal folding chair, the kind her parents would set out for a backyard party. He placed the beaker on the concrete floor beside his feet. The first instrument he drew was one Dr. Mayhew had used, a clamp that kept her privates open. Hanna gripped Lenna's frail, waxy hand. A moment later, the clamp locked in place. The cold of the room crept across Hanna's bare skin.

Lenna snapped on the lamp attached to Arch's forehead. He peered into Hanna's body, his unforgiving gloved hands on her legs and groin.

"You're well through *ponte amplio*," he said. "If you'd waited two more weeks, a bi-graft would be impossible. You'd have no choice but to commit to delivering the fetus."

"Is there really no way I can have the child and live?" Lying on her back, she felt she was talking to the concrete ceiling.

"Absolutely not," she heard Arch say. "That's how the ballgame's played."

"I can't have the baby and leave the cord in place?" she said up to the gray ceiling. "I know it sounds weird—"

"You're not the first to ask," she heard Arch say. "You want to have the baby attached to you like a leash."

"Is that wrong?"

"It's not possible. The *funiculus* occludes when withdrawn from the body, like picking a banana from a tree."

His hands continued to grip her thighs and probe her insides. He coughed. She hoped he was being sanitary about it. Then she heard a tinkling of metal against glass. He was taking another instrument from the Pyrex beaker.

"Why do I die?" she said to the ceiling. "Why doesn't it die?"

"Because God and Darwin got together in a room and agreed that was how things would be," Arch snapped.

"Arch," Lenna said softly. "Be nice."

"I don't mind answering medical questions," he said, "but don't ask me, of all people, why life is unfair."

The metal folding chair scraped on the concrete floor. Arch stood over Hanna again, his hands clad in powdered surgical gloves and a surgical mask over his mouth. Lenna tugged it down, making it a cloth chinstrap.

"Do you want this or not?" he said.

"I don't know…"

"I'm not here to sell you something you don't want," he said. "You say 'no,' I stop."

"Absolutely," Lenna said, stroking Hanna's cheek. "But you know what you want, don't you?"

"You say 'yes,' then let's go," Arch said. "We can't waffle around down here all day."

Hanna said softly, "My parents lied."

"Most do."

"They keep calling it their baby," Hanna said. "Like I borrowed it from them."

"It's *your* baby," Lenna said.

Arch forced a skeptical smile. "It's not your baby," he said. "Not genetically. But you never agreed to be your mother's surrogate either."

"My mother said she can't have any more babies. They cut out her womb."

"Her cervix?" Arch said. "Or her uterus?"

"I don't know," Hanna admitted. "But she said the doctors took me away from her. When I was born."

"Butchers." Arch shook his head dismissively. "The doctors back then, back in the sixties, they pumped pregnant women full of drugs they didn't need and then cut them up at the first sign of trouble."

"So you think she's telling the truth?"

"You have any younger bridge sisters? No? Then she's probably telling the truth."

"They're going to be alone after I'm gone," Hanna said.

"They can adopt," he said.

Arch was grim, his nostrils spread as though something foul was leaking into the air. Lenna offered Hanna warm, generous eyes and a soft smile. The boiler groaned and rattled, then went altogether silent.

"But if I give birth," Hanna said, "there's nothing little Hanna will remember about me?"

"Only in science fiction books," Arch said.

"Nothing about me survives in her?"

"Nothing."

Hanna, face hot and swelling with fresh anxiety, said, "Maybe my parents will take me back. I can do this and be their real daughter. Right?"

Arch said, "It never works out that way. All they care about is their baby inside you."

"Your baby," Lenna said again.

TWENTY-TWO

A SMALL BRASS BELL tied to the door announced Hanna's entrance with a tinny tinkle. Her jaw loosened at the sights within the store. Colored and patterned paper everywhere, some folded under glass, others sorted into reams on racks. Long shaggy sheets hung on wood poles like the newspapers at Concord's public library. Paper and craft goods went all the way to the rear of the store. In the center stood shelves of instructional books, some in English, some in Japanese, some in both languages.

A display case magnetically drew her close. Behind the glass stood origami the likes she'd never seen before or even imagined possible. A dragon twelve inches tall reared on its hind legs. A red-and-orange belch of paper flames emerged from its mouth. Beside it stood a knotty, arthritic tree, ancient looking, with a bushy green top and a whippoorwill resting on one ponderous branch. Smaller origami figures were displayed in the case as well, some with blue or red ribbons beneath indicating honors in origami competitions in the United States and Japan.

Taped to the case glass, in bold black ink:

NO CUTS, NO TEARS, NO GLUE

A woman behind the counter said, "Are you looking for

something in particular?"

Hanna, awestruck, turned and shook her head. "I just wanted to see."

"There's more in the back." The woman indicated the far end of the store.

"How do they do this?" Hanna turned again to the tree. It was huge, the size of the dollhouse her parents gave her when she was seven. "Is this really one piece of paper?"

"Not at all." The woman stepped through a small swinging gate between the counter and the shop floor. "That took three sheets of paper."

"*Three?*"

"One for the tree trunk," she said, "one for the leaves, and one for the bird."

Even the bird, not terribly larger than her cranes, seemed far too intricate to be composed purely of folds and creases.

"How do you fold the trunk like that?" she said. "Those knots look so real."

"Wet-folding," the woman said. "With the paper wet, you have a lot more control. When it dries, it holds its form. Wet-folding makes origami more like sculpting. Some purists look down on it," she confided.

"But did they really not use any glue?" Hanna tapped the glass near the dragon. "His eyes and nostrils, those holes; they weren't cut out of the paper?"

"Just folds," she said. "That would be cheating otherwise."

"I can do a crane," Hanna said. "But that's all."

"That's a good start." The woman led Hanna to the bookshelf. "There's so much more you can learn, though." She picked up a book and flipped to a random page. The color photographs demonstrated the steps for folding a sunflower.

"I'm trying to fold a thousand *tsuru* in one year," Hanna said. "I'm almost finished."

"Good for you," the woman said. "Have you started building your *senbazuru*?"

Hanna ducked her head. "I don't know what that means."

"It's a thousand cranes strung together." The woman located another book on the shelf and flipped it open. The center of the book was a photo montage of paper cranes strung by thread, dozens of lines hung in bunches and downpours of multicolored beaks and wings.

"I don't know about that," Hanna said. "I just want to get my wish." She confided, "I know wishing isn't real; it's just for fun." Hanna was inwardly surprised at the relief she enjoyed at the moment, being able to talk about origami and cranes and putting aside all that she'd been through the past two days.

"Well, that's how you get your wish," the woman said. "You take all thousand you've folded and string them into a *senbazuru*."

Hanna smiled sheepishly. "I gave a lot of mine away," she said. "Gifts for people. Although some of the people threw them away. But I'm okay with that."

The woman made an amused, almost confused look. "You don't get your wish if you give them away," she said. "You have to keep them and make a string."

Hanna's sheepish smile faded. "But I made them," she said. "I even numbered them." She stripped off her backpack and dug out the notebook. "See?"

The woman fingered through the notebook. "I've never seen someone so...organized. But you don't get your wish until you make the *senbazuru*." Sensing Hanna's dawning realization of wasted effort, she said, "It doesn't take that long. Every day, make some quiet time for yourself, sit down, and fold. If you do twenty-five a night, you'll be there in forty days. And, really, once you get going, you can do a lot more than twenty-five in a sitting."

"You don't understand," Hanna moaned, the weight of her situation returning to her. She pulled on the backpack and moped toward the exit. Eight months of work tossed away on the likes of Vivian Grimond and Liz Vannberg. "Thank you," she murmured.

Another paper structure under glass caught her eye. Puzzled, she approached and studied it. Constructed of blue paper, the miniature house had open windows and a front door ajar. The garage door was up. Inside stood a Ford Mustang and a lawn mower, of all things.

"They cheated!" she said, seeing the cuts in the paper.

Smiling, the woman took a key from her front pocket and approached. "That's *kirigami.*"

Taped to this case's glass, in bold black ink:

CUT FROM A SINGLE SHEET OF PAPER

The woman unlocked the case and swung the glass door open. With the edge of her finger, she carefully pushed at the bottom of the garage door. Hanna, stunned, watched it swing down, almost closed, then spring back up on its own. The woman touched the corner of the front door, demonstrating that it swung both directions.

"You can do a lot of things in *kirigami* that can't be done in *origami,*" she said.

"I've never heard of it before," Hanna said. "Is it new?"

"*Kirigami* is probably as old as *origami.* But, see, it has its own principles." She ran a painted fingernail along the crisp edges of the house, its chimney and Tudor roof and doghouse windows. "With *kirigami,* you can cut the paper, but it must be made from a single sheet. Even the garage door." She pointed out the hinge. "It looks like a separate piece glued on, but it's not. He carefully cut it from the master sheet, leaving it attached with a little bit of paper. He rubbed it with bone ivory to make it give and move without tearing."

"He?" Hanna said. "A man made this?"

"Sure. Another man made the dragon," she said, indicating the origami case.

"I thought only girls folded paper like this," Hanna said.

"In Japan, *origami* and *kirigami* are practiced by men and women. Even *ikebana,* flower arranging. Some of the *ikebana* masters are men."

Hanna couldn't imagine men wanting to arrange flowers, let alone appreciate them. Unless they were florists, like Mr. McReddy, but his arrangements were boring. Her father took little notice of the arrangements she left around the house. Valentine's Day, he griped about Mr. McReddy gouging him, swearing he'd be rich man if he'd planted rosebushes in the back yard ten years before. Even Uncle Rick treated flowers like auto parts, not the delicate works of art Hanna loved.

"I want to learn *kirigami*," she said, "and *ikebana*. And more *origami*."

"I'd start with one," the woman said with a smile.

"So with *origami*, the rule is no cutting," Hanna said. "And with *kirigami*, the rule is you can only use one piece of paper?"

"That's not how I would put it," the woman said. "They're ways of thinking. *Origami-do. Kirigami-do.*"

"*Origami-do*," Hanna repeated under her breath.

"*Do* means 'path' in Japanese," the woman explained. "*Origami-do* means 'the path of folding paper.' *Kirigami-do* is 'the path of cutting paper.' You choose a path and you follow it as far as it will take you."

"Is there such a thing as *ikebana-do*?"

"There is," she said, "but it's called *kadou*. 'The path of flowers.' Some of the masters, they spend a lifetime walking these paths."

"I wish I could go to Japan," Hanna breathed.

"Maybe some day you will," the woman said.

Hanna broke down then. Shaking her head, she apologized through the tears, mouth sopping wet. The woman, confused, took to one knee and lightly hugged her, telling her *Don't worry, it'll be okay*, whatever it may be.

Hanna had told Arch to stop, of course. She couldn't go through with the procedure, the twin purple pillars standing before her in her conscience. She couldn't bear to leave her parents childless, and she couldn't face the idea of becoming like Lenna, or even Maureen. She was not strong like them, she told herself. The idea of running away scared her deeply. Just running to San Francisco had exhausted her. How could she run to Los Angeles, or farther? How could she take care of herself with no house, no bedroom, no bed? She saw the people on Ellis Street sleeping on refrigerator box cardboard with only newspapers covering them for warmth, and knew she could not do that for a single night.

She would never make it to Japan, no matter how hard she wished, or even Los Angeles. It turned out, Hanna wouldn't make it any farther than the Santa Cruz redwoods.

TWENTY-THREE

THE WOOD SIGN over the gates was just as it appeared in the glossy brochure, "Susanna Glen" burned into the birch face with the Bible quote burned in below it. The sign topped a metal gate thirty feet tall, itself a part of a chain link fence with barbed wire plunging both directions into the dense forest of redwoods and ferns. Beyond the fence, a serene compound of wood cabins encircled an impressive fire pit of rough-hewn granite.

Hanna wondered what assurances the Susanna Glen people had communicated to her mother. She forbade even a Bible in the house, and now they were preparing to leave Hanna in the care of people who probably read from it thrice daily. The unremarkable Bible quote on the sign—"And the bridge provided"—was, for her mother, like a claim that the Earth was four thousand years old, or that God had deposited dinosaur bones in the ground to trick atheistic scientists.

Her father let the car idle before the gate a long while. He didn't know what else to do. Eventually, a bearded bushy-haired man in a faded denim jacket and faded denim trousers emerged from the largest cabin. He hurried across the dirt, a black loam flecked with the detritus of the countless redwoods and Douglas fir about the compound. He punched a code into a numeric keypad beside the gate and it gently parted, propelled by motorized arms.

Through her father's open window, the man introduced himself as Troy and directed where to park the car. Troy helped get the bags out of the trunk, then led them across the compound to Cabin Two, Hanna's new lodgings. The rules Susanna Glen had mailed to Hanna's parents stated each bridge daughter was allowed two suitcases and one personal carry bag for toiletries, effects, and so forth. Hanna had used her personal bag to bring a few books, as Susanna Glen had also informed them they had no library.

Hanna was assigned a spring bed along the cabin's rear wall. A window over the bed afforded a view down the fern-strewn hill to a brook running crystal-clear snowmelt. On the unmade bed were two crisp white sheets, a gray wool blanket, and a pillowcase as crisp and white as the sheets, all folded into squares. An uncovered pillow topped the linen pile.

Suitcases stashed, Troy led them on an impromptu tour of Susanna Glen. "We're just finishing up breakfast," he said as way of explaining why the common area between the cabins was devoid of people. "Would you care for a bite before we close the kitchen?"

Even though her father explained they'd stopped on the drive up for breakfast, Troy led them to the canteen, the largest cabin in the compound. Inside ran three rows of wood picnic tables painted the same chocolate-brown color as the exterior. Bridge daughters filled the hall, all of them big and pregnant, all clad in fusty bridge daughter dresses and soft shoes. They stacked trays, wiped down tables, and swept the wood plank floor. More worked hard in the kitchen, which was partially visible through the wide service window. The bridge daughters in the kitchen scrubbed and washed pans and dishes. Others wrapped leftovers to store in restaurant-sized refrigerators.

At the other end of the mess, an emergency exit stood wide open. The door was held fast by a metal canister ashtray pulled over to act as a stop. Two men stood outside in dirty kitchen whites with bandanas holding their hair back. Both were unshaven and chestnut tan, skin glistening from perspiration. One had greening tattoos down his right arm; otherwise, Hanna found them almost indistinguishable. They smoked cigarettes and murmured between themselves.

Every bridge daughter had a bow-tie ribbon pinned on her dress neckline. Troy pointed to the duty board on the far wall, a column of colored dots with responsibilities chalked in beside each.

"Green is on dishwashing duty today," Troy read from the duty board, "red mops, blue does countertops, and so on."

"What color am I?" Hanna asked.

"Hanna," her father warned, indicating she needed to ask permission before speaking.

Troy smiled. "Understand, here we don't follow that rule. As you might notice, not many adults here. It makes sense for everyone to speak up when necessary. But," he added, "we value respect of others and respect for *ourselves* above all else."

"How many adults are there?" Hanna's mother asked.

"Six," Troy said, and he counted them off: Troy himself, the staff doctor, two nurses, a camp mom, and Remy and Rex, the cooks smoking at the fire exit. "The nurses rotate on the weekend," Troy explained, "so there's only six adults here at any moment in time."

"What about..." Hanna's mother's voice trailed off, hoping Troy would gather what she was getting at. She finally was plain: "What about security? Only six adults?"

"We're plenty secure here," Troy said. "No one can get in past the fence. You saw it."

"What I mean," her mother said, "are you sure you can you can keep the girls *in*."

Troy leaned back and laughed. "They don't want to leave!"

Sleeping and bathing in a new place has its anxieties for any thirteen year-old, but sleeping and bathing in shared quarters for the first time is terrifying at that age. Hanna's personal mantra carried her through her first days in Susanna Glen. *What would Maureen do?*

Hanna forced herself to endure the reduced privacy she'd never faced at home. She took gang showers with the other bridge daughters, their bulging midsections as unique and individuated as their faces. She passed bowel movements with other girls seated in the stalls around her. At first, she sweated over emitting even the tiniest of bodily sounds. After a few days, she came to accept the noises as a function of nature. She stopped changing clothes under the bedsheets and began disrobing before the seventeen other bridges in Cabin Two. Now a Sister of Susanna, she learned to follow their lead. Trusting them allowed her to trust herself.

Troy assigned Hanna purple duties. The duty board changed daily, meaning one day she swept the mess hall floor and the next she loaded plates and cups and silverware in the industrial dishwasher. And there was more than one duty board at Susanna Glen. One beside the fire pit listed duties around the compound, site cleaning and maintenance. Another duty board mounted inside Cabin Two listed more hygienic chores: scrubbing toilets and washing mirrors and so on.

Hanna's mother's blend of traditional and new ways would have left her wholly unprepared for all the cleaning and kitchen duties here. Erica was right, she'd been brought up soft. Her mother's change to more traditional ways had, like an emergency exercise regimen, impressed on Hanna the basic skills she now needed.

One night in bed, exhausted from kitchen mopping duty, baby twisting inside her and lower back throbbing, she calculated she'd spent seven hours working that day, the same as every other day. The camp kept the Sisters of Susanna occupied, Hanna reasoned. *They're keeping us busy.*

Her mother had packed the Vannbergs' *wenschkind*. Miffed at her mother ignoring her disinterest in the doll, Hanna left the *wenschkind* in the suitcase under her bed.

Every night before bed, and sometimes in the mornings, Hanna watched the other bridges of Cabin Two with their own *wenschkinds*. They didn't play with them, serve them tea or move them like puppets, or make them talk in high-pitched voices. The girls cradled their *wenschkinds* in their arms, rocking them to sleep and jostling them in their arms as though they were crying. Sometimes they would press the doll's mouth to their bared breast as though feeding them, although none of the girls had developed, and would not due to their biology. The girls whispered reassuringly to their *wenschkinds* and hushed them to go to sleep.

The sight of aped motherhood made Hanna slightly ill. She trusted the other girls, she shared private quarters with them, but she could not respect them.

Hanna grew fascinated with the two swarthy men who were smoking outside the canteen her first morning there. Hanna didn't realize it, but most of the girls at Susanna Glen were fascinated with them too.

Hanna gathered that the men performed two recurring duties. They cooked massive meals in the kitchen, the efficient and humorless duo capable of feeding ninety-eight pregnant girls three times a day without fail. They worked in almost complete silence, one manning the grill and stove while the other ladled and spooned hot food onto sectional plates. When a serving tray was depleted, the server would drop it into the humongous sink with a *clang* while the other, in clockwork manner, slid another tray of the foodstuff across the metal prep table. Most days, no girls worked in the kitchen during mealtime. The men held complete authority until the last plate was served. Only after they'd vacated the kitchen to smoke their cigarettes did the bridge daughters dare enter and begin cleaning up.

The other task Remy and Rex performed was chopping wood and wheelbarrowing the cuttings to the compound's central fire pit. The California Conservation Corps delivered a felled tree in piece parts at the start of each month. Remy and Rex dissected it into serviceable chunks using axes and splitters. Stripped down to their undershirts, they produced a week's worth of firewood in a single morning, then wiped the grit and sweat and sawdust off themselves with rags before returning to the kitchen to prepare lunch.

Hanna had trouble telling them apart. Their faces were not identical, but with features so rugged and well worn, their individuality seemed to have been sanded down to the bare foundational matter that all males are built from. Hanna learned to distinguish them by the tattoos down Remy's right arm, crisscrossed rose vines with mermaids trapped in the fishhook thorns. When Remy served food at the window, she felt he'd tainted the food, as though he should wash the tattoos off before entering the kitchen. This unfair suspicion never suppressed her appetite.

The other major adult presence at Susanna Glen was the camp mother, Eloise, who watched over the girls throughout the day and spot-checked them at night. A matronly woman, Eloise had overly wide hips and kept her graying hair in a Danish roll atop her head. She roused sleepyheads from bed in the mornings and went from cabin to cabin to enforce a strict ten o'clock lights-out. She clapped her hands to capture the girls' attention and get them to do as they were told. She thumped the girls' earlobes when they dawdled. She was the subject of the cruelest gossip when not present.

Hanna wondered if Eloise was a kind of check-and-balance to Remy's and Rex's presence in the camp, a protective measure against these two coarse men. The men disturbed Hanna, their dour demeanors and the way they murmured to each other when smoking. Their manhandling of cookware and axes, the tattoos and their muscled backs, all indicated they were capable of so much violence. They could go anywhere in the camp, it seemed.

Then she wondered if she was supposed to be attracted to them. Some of the other bridge daughters insinuated they were smitten. Hanna sensed something new in herself when in their presence. Her gemellius was now consuming a portion of Hanna's natural gefyrogen and producing one part estrogen and two parts progesterone. Together, these foreign hormones introduced changes in Hanna.

Hanna's ruse to take back the sneakers she'd gifted Erica was not without justification. All the other girls had hiking shoes or boots in addition to the soft-soled bridge daughter shoes they wore around the compound. Some afternoons, Troy led a group of bridge daughters out into the redwoods to navigate one of the many footpaths meandering the property. This was their "duty" on the compound duty board. Never strenuous, the walks were just enough to get the blood pumping and fresh oxygen into the lungs' deepest branches. Troy asked for church-like silence as they traversed inclines and forded arroyos. Sweet-scented maples and commanding redwoods mutely observed the girls' movements.

On the walks, Hanna could not help but point out flora she recognized. Blue irises, violets, sword ferns, and azaleas she readily identified, to the surprise of the girls around her. They had to know how she could possibly name so many flowers from sight. She admitted trouble with other identifications, but did correctly name a cluster of trillium they encountered at the foot of a skyscraping redwood. It was with this Troy approached her.

"I love flowers," she explained to him. "I don't know trees, though." Troy, violating his own request for quiet, often named the trees' species as they passed by them, as though introducing lifelong friends.

"Who taught you?" Troy asked her.

"I like reading books about flowers," Hanna said. "And I learned from my uncle. He works at the Flower Mart in San

Francisco."

The girls stirred at this revelation. Troy, usually unaffected, was taken aback.

"It's not that big a deal," she said to them all. "He doesn't have a degree or anything. He just moves pallets and drives forklifts."

"I think everyone's surprised you read books," Troy said.

Hanna looked about, saw all the eyes on her, and shrank. She did not cotton to being evaluated so, even by other bridge daughters. Many of them could read, they would inform you, but only from absorption of common words encountered in their daily routines. They could read *sugar* and differentiate it from *flour* but not *The United States of America* printed across the face of a dollar bill, a slip of paper they had precious little contact with.

These walks would last ninety minutes or so. Each bridge daughter carried her own water canteen and a snack provided by Eloise, who brought up the rear of the expeditions. Hanna—a suburban girl lost in the trees—could not determine if they were walking in circles or straight lines, but she did note they never reached the far perimeter of Susanna Glen's thirty-foot fence. The organization's holdings must be enormous.

On another walk, she wondered if the fence truly circled the entire camp. Perhaps the gate and fence near the cabins was a facade, like the fronts of an Old West town, an illusion to assure the parents and their bridge daughters that escape was impossible. If she broke away from one of these paths and headed due west through the redwoods, perhaps she could make it to a highway, or a town, or the ocean. Southern California was a desert, she'd read once. Maybe she could make it to the desert.

The night after a nature walk, one of the girls of Cabin Two meekly approached Hanna. Her name was Bridget. She wanted to know more about flowers and flower arranging. Delighted, Hanna spread her books across the bed and invited Bridget to look through them. Together they pored over the exquisite hand-tinted Victorian prints in *The Symphony of Flowers*, the book Aunt Azami had gifted her months before.

"Are you excited?" Bridget asked Hanna.

"No," Hanna said, knowing full well what Bridget was alluding to.

"You aren't excited that you're going to give your mom and dad a new little baby?"

Bridget's wide, eager eyes told Hanna she saw her finality as a kind of Christmas morning, and the child inside her was the present.

One morning soon after, the girls of Cabin Two awoke and discovered Bridget's bed empty: sheets stripped, pillow missing, the suitcases stored beneath the bed now gone.

Two days later, a new bridge daughter arrived by car. Eloise assigned her Bridget's spring bed. The new girl changed clothes beneath the covers, covered her genitals and breasts with her hands while showering, and cried herself to sleep. Hanna, only ten days in camp, felt like an old-timer compared to this fresh, fragile flower.

TWENTY-FOUR

EVERY WEDNESDAY AND SATURDAY, Hanna was called to the camp clinic and administered a shot of gefyridol for her Hoff's Syndrome. Through these ministrations, Hanna met the rotating nurses. Nurse Robyns was the younger of the two, bright blond and soft-voiced, and more tender with the needle. Nurse Halper, also blond but a bit older, made the injection feel like her personal inconvenience. Nurse Halper's breath sometimes smelled of whiskey, a familiar odor to Hanna after a brief lifetime around Uncle Rick's alcoholism.

Soft-spoken Nurse Robyns worked Friday to Sunday. Monday mornings, her boyfriend picked her up. He sported five o'clock shadow, feathered hair, dusty jeans, and a leather jacket of buckles and snaps. His red Pontiac Firebird announced itself to the camp with a throaty growl. He pulled it up to the clinic and pumped the engine twice before killing it. When Nurse Robyns kissed him in her nurse's uniform, one leg up and one hand holding her white cap in place, the girls on the cabin porches swooned and gasped. Hanna's knees also quivered at the sight of Nurse Robyns' boyfriend. He made her feel funny below her belly, as though she had to urinate badly, but in a good way.

Behind Cabin Two, Rex and Remy sharpened their axes. It was

Monday morning, wood-chopping day. While the girls swooned, the men broke down a quarter-cord of wood, backs rippling with each heave, each split cracking like a bullwhip through the fresh misty air.

One morning, Eloise woke Hanna early for breakfast service duty. Hanna, surprised, whispered, *Me?*

There was precedent. Twice since she arrived at Susanna Glen, Hanna had noticed a bridge behind the serving window. Both times the girl worked the breakfast shift, not the later meal services. Both times she toiled with a frazzled, bewildered expression, indicating either the terror of serving breakfast to ninety-seven impatient girls or the terror of being confined to the kitchen with one of the coarse men. The other was not there, for some unexplained reason. It was never explained to Hanna why the girls worked those two mornings.

Rex was mixing batter when Hanna arrived. Remy was nowhere to be seen. In curt language, yelling over the restaurant-grade mixer, Rex explained the system. He worked the griddle. Hanna dished up and served plates through the window. When she emptied a serving tray, she was to put it in the sink and call out what she'd run out of. Rex slid trays of hot replenishments across the metal prep table to her. If she needed more of something cold—in this morning's case, peach slices in syrup—she was expected to pull another jar from the refrigerator. *Lift with your legs, not your back,* Rex yelled over the mixer, and, *For godssake, don't burn yourself on a tray.*

Hanna did her best to keep up with the gaggle of girls filing into the canteen, each groggy or cranky or demanding in their own way. They sassed her. They talked back to her. They never talked like this to the men. Some complained about the size of their portions or Hanna's presentation. Some asked for eggs done differently, although Hanna knew nothing was to-order in Rex's and Remy's kitchen. She spooned peach slices into melamine dishes and spooned syrup on top for good measure. Hurrying to assemble plates while standing over trays of steaming-hot food, sweat accumulated on her forehead and under her armpits. She came to appreciate the frazzled and bewildered look on the other girls' faces when it had been their turn to serve breakfast.

"Flapjacks!" Hanna yelled, dropping the empty tray into the stainless steel sink with a roaring *clang*.

Flapjacks! Rex yelled in return, sliding a tray of silver-dollar-sized cakes across the prep table.

"Eggs!" Hanna yelled. *Clang*.

Scrambles! Rex yelled back. Hanna made a mental note to use his lingo next time, and she did, hoping for his approval. He seemed not to notice, which disappointed her.

He relieved her at ten minutes to nine. *Good job,* he said with a hoarse voice and a slight nod of his unshaven jaw. He dished a plate of flapjacks and scrambled eggs, added a melamine bowl of peaches-in-syrup to the tray, and told her, *Eat up.*

Famished, devouring the hearty and well-deserved breakfast by the mouthful while the others cleaned, she listened in on two girls at the end of the table lingering over their meals. Someone from Cabin Four was missing that morning. Bed empty, sheets stripped, luggage gone. "She was due," one of them said to the other. "She said she could tell it was coming any day now."

Now Hanna remembered. The last time a bridge had served breakfast, Bridget had disappeared and, for some reason, Rex was unavailable to work kitchen duty. Or was it Remy?

Every night after dinner, the girls pulled on layers of warm clothes and dragged Indian blankets out from a common closet. They sat side-by-side on the granite blocks around the fire pit sharing the blankets and consolidating body heat. Shivering, they watched Troy, Rex, and Remy build a massive fire in the dusk light. When the fire was alive and radiating, Rex and Remy would retire to the staff cabin while Troy led the girls in a nightly talk. Eloise walked the outer edge of the granite block circle in a bulky ski jacket and a wool cap, flicking earlobes to silence gossip and chitchat.

Troy started with campfire songs. Then he invited the girls to speak up one at a time, to share their feelings and fears and desires. Some admitted to hoarding their parents' money and planning to run away from home. Hanna kept quiet during these exchanges, waiting for someone to admit to actually escaping only to be caught, but no one did. No one broached the subject of intrauterine bi-grafts.

When a girl from Cabin Three admitted she was afraid of passing away, Troy told them, "We don't use words like 'pass away' here. We never use the word 'finality.' You'll never hear that from me, or Eloise, or from Dr. Wynn. That is our promise to you." Troy spoke from the inner hub of the granite circle, close to the fire. "When you all give birth, you will die." It was the first time Hanna had heard an adult use the word *die* in reference to her fate. "But you will also be giving life. That is your role in this world, your responsibility."

Another evening, one of the girls started crying and complained it was unfair. Without rebuke, Troy said, "The only fair thing in this world is to learn how unfair the world is."

Troy peppered all his talks with the words *interlocked* and *correlated*. He emphasized *the universe and the world*, he taught them about *future generations*, he emphasized how change occurred *slowly but surely*.

"Hagar ran away to live with God and to find solace in Nature," Troy told them one evening. "She was very brave to do that. All of you are. The tragedy is, you'll never know just how brave you all will be when the time comes."

Hanna used her precious spare time to complete her *senbazuru*. The rotating duty board sometimes included free hours. Most of the girls took advantage of them in the rec room, which had a black-and-white television set with rabbit ears. Hanna folded origami. Nighttime too, Hanna could get in forty-five minutes between showering and Eloise's mandatory lights-out.

The *tsuru* her mother had bagged and stored in the garage had been packed in her suitcase. Although slightly crushed on the ride up the mountains, they counted toward her one thousand. Taking a census of them on her bed, Hanna accounted for seven hundred and six cranes. She'd given away almost three hundred of them. How many of them were tossed out? she wondered. How many had she wasted on other people?

Her program of folding cranes at Susanna Glen was far more productive than at home. No television to distract her, no mother interrupting her to start cooking or to vacuum the house. Regimented time at Susanna Glen meant true progress toward her string of one thousand paper cranes.

The girls of Cabin Two took a natural interest in Hanna's project. Some of them had heard of Hiroshima. All of them knew of the atom bomb. None had heard of Sadako Sasaki. Hanna explained to them the legend of a thousand paper cranes.

"What are you going to wish for?" one of the bridge daughters asked.

"It's just for fun," Hanna said. "You don't really get your wish."

"Then why do you do it?"

Hanna shrugged and said, "Because maybe I will get my wish. Maybe."

"When I blew out my birthday candles," another said, "I always wished for money."

"My own room," another one said.

"I wanted to sit at the table when we ate," another said. "But I never got a birthday cake." So, no candles to blow out, no wish to make.

One of the girls shied away. Hanna said, "What would you wish for?"

The girl shook her head. The other girls persisted until she said, "To read," as though embarrassed by it. Then, opening up,

"I always wanted to read Judy Blume books." And the other girls went quiet.

The first girl asked Hanna again for her wish. "It doesn't matter," Hanna insisted.

Before folding each crane, Hanna would turn to her notebook. The numbered lines with no name; she could account for those cranes. They were in the grocery bag, smooshed. The numbered lines with names, the ones she'd given away, she crossed out the name for each crane she folded on her spring bed. She crossed off Mrs. Vannberg and Cheryl Vannberg. Erica Grimond, Viv Grimond, The Grimonds as a family; she lined through their names. Dr. Mayhew, Mr. Cullers, all the neighbors Hanna visited with *tsuru* gifts. Her mother, her father, even Maureen. She ran a heavy line of ink through their names until they'd all been crossed out and replaced by a new paper crane.

Troy abruptly halted the line of bridge daughters before the broad trunk of a staunch redwood. He crouched to the springy black soil and spread his hands. Speckles of alabaster-colored chippings were scattered underfoot.

"These are seashells." He picked up three shards and set them in his open palm for the girls to gather around and see. "Millions of years ago, this area was underwater. These shells are the fossils of ancient sea creatures."

Some of the girls bent to pick up a bit of shell, holding their backs or cradling their bellies while doing so.

"These shells are not only the past, they are the present and the future," Troy said. "Slowly but surely, change is happening all around you. Millions of years ago, we would be standing on the bottom of the Pacific Ocean. Today, we're at four thousand foot elevation and four and a half miles from the ocean."

Troy windmilled his arm to shape a giant letter O in the air. "The universe is interlocked. All of life is connected. The redwoods make oxygen for us to breathe. We make carbon dioxide for the redwoods. The redwoods shed their dead leaves and branches. Insects and slugs convert that dead material into compost, which in turn becomes the nutrients the trees need to grow." He wiped the broken shells from his hands. "The past is interlocked with the present. The choices we make today decide our world's future."

Hanna slipped one of the shards into the pocket of her bridge daughter dress as a souvenir.

"You can't take that, honey," Troy said to her. Frightened at being singled out, she dropped it to the ground. "Take nothing, leave nothing behind," he told them all.

On the walk back, Hanna, flush with embarrassment, avoided eye contact with the other bridge daughters. *You can't take that, honey,* she aped Troy's words in her mind. *You're all so brave. Think of your responsibility. There is nothing unfair in this world.*

Of course we're to take nothing and leave nothing behind, she thought. *If we did, they might have to think of us as people and not just the soil for planting their seeds.*

One day after lunch, Hanna finished stacking trays early. The fire exit door was propped open by the ashtray, but the two men were not to be seen. Hanna poured a glass of ice water for herself and wandered outside to enjoy it in the sun. Redwoods stood in an erect row behind the canteen. Idle, bored, Hanna trailed along the edge of the building. She came to another building, one she'd not noticed before, tucked behind the canteen and the clinic.

It was a garage, taller and wider than the garage at her home in Concord. A pale violet delivery van was parked halfway out of the garage with blocks under its wheels to prevent it from rolling. One of the men stood on the front fender with his head down in the engine block. The other lay on a mechanic's creeper under the van, only his legs showing. Both wore dark blue coveralls. With their arms covered and faces obscured, she couldn't tell Rex and Remy apart.

Hanna had never noticed the delivery van before, although she'd been at Susanna Glen for over two weeks now. It bore no markings, not even the camp's swirly logo. On closer inspection, the van resembled a small hunchbacked garbage truck, right down to the rear hydraulic lifter stowed against the back doors. Through the van's side window, she saw steel racks inside.

The man on the creeper rolled out from under the van. It was Rex. He sat up and looked straight into Hanna. *What's this?* he mumbled.

After that one morning with Rex—"Flapjacks!"— she'd been thinking of him a great deal. She had started searching for him through the serving window as she passed with her tray. Rex and Remy switched places in the kitchen with each meal. When Rex served, she was shy and voiceless, his captive, as she accepted a sectioned plate of food from him. Now so close to him, the funny feeling returned to her belly, like she had to urinate, but in a good way.

Hanna stepped forward and offered him the glass of ice water. Puzzled, still seated on the creeper, he accepted it with an offset grin and a nod. For a moment, they held the glass together. The auto oil and tobacco smoke and his body odor—he smelled delicious.

Laughter erupted behind her. Hanna spun around, startled. Standing on the fender and leaning around the hood, Remy said, *You got an admirer, I think.* Rex laughed with him. Hanna, purple with shame, heard their laughter all the way back to the fire exit, waddling side to side from the weight she carried.

All the girls went to the clinic once a week for checkups. It was listed on the compound board as a duty, like anything else. Hanna and the other girls wearing purple bows swung their legs in the waiting room chairs until their name was announced.

Dr. Wynn was paunchy and balding, with a meager web of gray hair combed over the bare spot. He made no idle conversation with Hanna. The vomiting sensation had left Hanna months earlier, and she'd not had a fainting spell since her birthday party. Dr. Wynn seemed to neither approve nor disapprove when she informed him of this. The gemellius kicked often, but Hanna had grown used to it, almost tired of it. *Alright, alright,* she told it, *you'll be out of there soon enough.* Again, Dr. Wynn seemed indifferent.

On her fourth visit, Dr. Wynn told her, "It'll happen in the coming week."

"It feels like she wants to leave," Hanna said.

"You'll be assigned lighter work chores from here on," he said. "No more walks in the trees. Keep off your feet, plenty of rest, don't exert yourself. Understood?"

Hanna nodded. She loved walking among the trees and regretted losing that duty—a privilege, in her mind.

"You need to start taking these." Dr. Wynn handed her an orange prescription bottle. "One with each meal. You'll run out before I see you again."

Hanna recognized the name of the drug, gefyraprogestagen. *More drugs.* "Will this make me fat?" she said, recalling the last time she saw Cheryl Vannberg.

"You'll gain weight," Dr. Wynn said.

"What are they for?"

"All the girls take them when it's time," he said. "One with each meal."

Hanna, sour, placed them in the pocket of her bridge daughter dress. *At least tell me what they're for,* she thought.

"Some of the girls here," Dr. Wynn said absently, "they like to write letters to their loved ones. Or draw pictures if they can't write. Can you write? Well, I suggest you start tonight, then. If you're inclined."

"Who should I write to?" Hanna asked.

"Who you want to say goodbye to," he said. "Your parents. You have friends at home?"

Nurse Halper smelled of whiskey again, the way some people smell of mouthwash. "Tell her about writing to the baby," she said to Dr. Wynn.

"Right," Dr. Wynn said. "Some of the girls here write to their gemellius. They call it 'writing a letter to yourself.' Of course, it's not. You share nothing with the gemellius other than biology."

"Your baby won't remember you or anything you've done," Nurse Halper said. "It's not like in the movies."

Hanna sat on her bed with a writing pad and a ballpoint pen. She started three different letters to her parents, all unsatisfactory, all accusing in tone. Hanna decided the time for grinding axes had passed.

She tried writing a letter to her father, but did not feel particularly drawn to tell him anything but "I love you," and even that statement felt forced. She wanted to know why he stood behind her for so long in the kitchen that one night. She wondered if he wanted to say or do something to Hanna but couldn't bear to carry through with it.

She addressed one letter to her mother. Her words of love were flaccid and forced too, and she grew accusatory in just a few sentences. *You worked so hard to avoid growing attached to me*, she wrote. *You forgot I was your child too.*

She abandoned it and wrote a new letter to her mother. *I could have had a bi-graft. I'm doing this for you and Dad. I would have hated myself either way. So here. You win.*

Her letter to herself, her letter to the gemellius within her, she stared at the blank page for a minute before scribbling, *This is all your fault.*

Around her, bridge daughters comforted their *wenschkinds* and rocked them asleep. Hanna pulled her suitcase out from under her bed. Her *wenschkind* was folded up inside like a ventriloquist's dummy. Hanna cradled it, rocked it in her arms, pressed it to her chest. Nothing. Annoyed, she yanked down the top of her nightgown. She pressed the ready mouth of the *wenschkind* to her right nipple and mashed its head to make it suckle. Nothing. How foolish. Little Hanna—big Hanna. She felt nothing and she felt everything, and she felt it all at once.

Eloise shook her awake. Through the window, Hanna saw it was well before dawn.

"It's time," Eloise whispered to her.

"Kitchen again?" Hanna said, groggy.

"Your parents are outside," Eloise whispered. "Don't worry about your things. I'll take care of everything."

Hanna, belly swollen like never before, swung her feet around to sit up in bed. Still in her nightclothes, she slipped on her bridge daughter shoes and, with Eloise's assistance, rose to her feet. The predicted weight gain had set in. The added pounds on her neck and thighs made navigating in and out of bed that much more difficult. From under her pillow, Hanna took a paper crane. She slipped it in a small pocket of her nightdress. The girls of Cabin Two slumbered on.

"You have letters?" Eloise whispered.

Hanna shook her head. The night before, alone and the camp songs long over, she'd tossed all her false starts in the pit's dying fire. *Take nothing, leave nothing behind.* The letters curled in the flames to gray char.

TWENTY-FIVE

IN THE COLD DARK of the compound's central area stood Hanna's parents, Uncle Rick, and Aunt Azami. All were bundled up, the women hugging themselves to stay warm. They beamed as Hanna emerged from the cabin, but Eloise prevented a joyful greeting with a shush and a warning not to awaken the other girls. Hanna's mother had brought a long wool coat, lavender with square yellow buttons. She put it over Hanna's nightgown. It smelled of Ma Cynthia, her farmhouse beet pies and the fruit preserves on shelves in the moldy basement. The smell recalled the crescent-bladed knife mounted on the wall over the kitchen table, and the horseflies hovering over the garden compost pile like vultures.

"This was your grandmother's," Hanna's mother whispered. "I thought you might like to wear it."

"Fits well," Aunt Azami added, tugging at the collar to straighten it out.

"I'm fat now," Hanna whispered.

"You look fine," her father said.

The group walked across the compound toward the clinic. Eloise led the way with a sweeping flashlight.

The interior of the clinic was flooded with fluorescent light.

The adults stripped off their jackets. Hanna kept hers on. Eloise told them to wait for the nurse and wandered back into the nighttime.

"Hey, squirt," Uncle Rick said, now free to talk without whispering. He rubbed her hair. She fell into him and hugged him deeply. "Missed you too," he said.

"We've all missed you," her father said.

"Have you?" Hanna said.

"How are you feeling?" her mother said.

Hanna shrugged. "Nothing to report." Her mother seemed hurt when Hanna said it. That surprised her, but she felt no need to apologize or ask what she'd done.

Nurse Halper met them wearing a crisp white nurse's uniform and a white smock. "We're ready for you now." She led them to an empty waiting room. Hanna had not seen this wing of the clinic before. All her examinations took place on the far side of the building. Two windowless doors were on the waiting room's far wall, one marked *A*, the other *B*.

"Dr. Wynn will be with you in about twenty minutes," Nurse Halper said, and she left through door A.

"I thought they were ready for us," Hanna's father said.

"I think there's another girl," Aunt Azami said, nodding toward room A. "I saw her and her family walk in when we were parking the car."

That must be Kendall, Hanna thought, a green-ribbon girl from Cabin One also on the pills Dr. Wynn prescribed. Hanna noticed her taking them with her meals.

Hanna sat in a chair, almost motionless. She was surprised at how tranquil she felt. Aunt Azami couldn't stop looking at Hanna, one hand tightly clutching Uncle Rick's. Hanna's father remained standing, as was his wont, hands thrust deep in his trouser pockets.

Hanna's mother started straightening Hanna's hair with her fingers. She'd not combed it since rising from bed. She asked Hanna how camp was going so far, as though she was only halfway through her time at Susanna Glen.

"Lot of walks in the woods," Hanna said. "Every night we have campfire songs."

"Kumbaya and granola?" Uncle Rick said jokingly.

"Did you make any friends?" Hanna's mother said.

"Two," Hanna said. "No, wait. Three. But they're dead now."

Uncle Rick winced at that. Aunt Azami's eyes widened. Hanna's mother seemed unaffected.

"They make you pray?" Hanna's mother said.

"Just campfire songs," Hanna said.

"Make you read the Bible?" Uncle Rick asked.

"Just campfire songs."

"What did they teach you?" Hanna's mother asked.

Hanna jerked her head from her mother. She was tugging her fingers through a snag. "I'll fix it," Hanna said, and she went to the bathroom out in the hallway.

It was cramped, a toilet and a square sink and a mirror. She cupped water from the tap and poured water into her hair. Unevenly wet, she combed her fingers through it until the cowlicks were tamed and the amber bangs hung more or less down. She tugged two paper towels from the dispenser and patted her hands and face dry.

The bathroom's sole window was narrow and frosted. It opened with a hand crank and had been cracked to let in air. Through the slit, Hanna could see the rear of the clinic. Although far from sunrise, wispy morning light was filtering through the Pacific mist. The pale violet delivery van was there, the van that looked oddly like a small garbage truck. It was parked backwards with its double doors toward the clinic. Rex leaned against the hood of the van, his back to Hanna. He smoked and drank steaming coffee from a ceramic mug, reveling in the valley below of kingly redwoods standing like giant chess pieces.

Aunt Azami hugged Hanna when she returned. "Your mother said you personally wanted me and Rick here," she said. "Thank you."

Hanna had demanded it. Although she had little bargaining power when she returned home from her second escape to San Francisco, she insisted Uncle Rick and Aunt Azami be invited to her finality. When her mother refused—convinced Azami had seeded the idea of a bi-graft in Hanna's mind—Hanna insinuated that she could do damage to herself and the gemellius, even at a controlled environment like Susanna Glen. Hanna's mother didn't believe the threat at first, but Hanna's bitter seriousness made her accede.

Hanna held out the paper crane she'd taken from under her pillow. "I finished the last of them here at camp." Hanna turned it over, showing Azami the number *1000* inked on its underside.

"I knew you could do it," Aunt Azami said.

"Do what?" Hanna's father said.

"Did you make your wish?" Aunt Azami said.

"Yes, and I got it," she said. "I wished for you and Uncle Rick to be here."

Aunt Azami, shaking her head and eyes watering, hugged Hanna again. Uncle Rick reached over from his chair and squeezed the back of Hanna's neck. His eyes were veiny and red too.

Outside, a truck engine turned over and coughed to life. Metal began grinding and hydraulics began churning. If the adults heard it, they took no note.

Nurse Halper emerged from door A. "It's time."

What would Maureen do? Maureen would bravely power forward. Hanna had committed to finishing this. Now it was time.

But something about the motor and the churning piqued her. "I have to go to the bathroom," she said, rising from her chair.

"We'll be right here," Nurse Halper said. She didn't smell like whiskey this morning.

In the bathroom, door locked, Hanna peeked through the slit of the open window. Rex was gone now. The van's rear doors were open. From its rattling exhaust pipe, she knew its engine was running and the churning told her the rear lift was being operated. Hanna tugged on the frosted window's hand crank to widen her view, but it was stuck. She pushed hard, putting her weight into it, even setting a foot against the toilet seat, but it would not budge.

Time running out, she scrambled around the bathroom for a lever or degreaser—anything that would give her an advantage over the damned crank. She considered pounding the crank with the butt of her hand but feared the noise would bring the adults. She had to see what was going on back there.

Hanna ran hot water in the sink. Cupped hand burning, she poured handfuls on the crank, hoping the water would seep into its workings and loosen them. Success—a moment later, she had the window open as wide as it would go. Standing on the toilet seat, she could've squeezed through the aperture and out to the great redwood pillars, then plunged headlong into the mist and lush growth. Four and a half miles to the ocean. She could make it.

The hunchbacked van was backed up to a loading door marked *A*. Rex operated the hydraulic lift with one hand, cigarette in his mouth. His other hand guided into the van a hospital gurney draped end to end with a lumpy white sheet.

Kendall, Hanna thought. *The only fair thing in the world is to learn how unfair it really is.*

Lying on a gurney of her own, staring up at the ceiling of delivery room B, feet in stirrups once more, Hanna took deep breaths while Dr. Wynn searched the surface of her swollen belly with the metal button of his stethoscope. Hanna's parents hovered in the rear of the delivery room, Hanna's mother's arm hooked around her father's midsection. Uncle Rick and Aunt Azami stood apart from them and not as tightly embraced. Not too long before, Hanna would have been aghast at the idea of her father and Uncle Rick seeing her privates. Today, it seemed unremarkable. Hanna had learned to abandon shame.

Aunt Azami murmured to Uncle Rick she had forgotten

something in the car. She hurried from the delivery room. Soon she returned with a bouquet of asters and African violets, a bold purple wash of colors exploding like fireworks. The stems were neatly tied with a purple ribbon. She placed them in a small glass vase she'd also brought from the car. With Dr. Wynn's permission, she set them on the table beside Hanna. When Hanna craned her neck, she could admire them, but only from afar.

"Everything is exactly as hoped for," Dr. Wynn announced. He produced a hypodermic with a frighteningly long needle, tube already loaded with a liquid, and without warning, injected it into Hanna's side. Trussed up, her egg-shaped belly slathered with disinfecting gel, Hanna felt like a turkey being basted by Dr. Wynn.

"I'm not having contractions," Hanna called up to the ceiling. She remembered that detail from *Mother & Baby*. Its chalk drawings depicted the father holding the mother's hand in the delivery room. He breathed and counted along with her while her womb convulsed out their bridge daughter. "When do they start?"

"Hanna," Dr. Wynn said from between her legs, peering over his horn-rimmed glasses, "we haven't done a natural *pons* childbirth since Truman lost China. This will be a cesarean."

"I don't know what that means," Hanna said to the ceiling.

Hanna's face began to feel rubbery, then her neck and arms. Lolling her head about, the room spun and blurred. She took a deep breath to regain herself. She wanted clarity all the way to the end. She wanted to know what was happening each step of the way.

"We're ready," she heard Dr. Wynn say. A burning line seared under her navel. She instinctively reached for it. Nurse Halper had restrained her wrists and arms to the gurney with straps made of the same material as car safety belts. She gasped but could not hear her voice. *What would Maureen do?* She couldn't answer that question now.

"And I see her," she heard Dr. Wynn say. "Healthy and sound." Hanna craned her head to look. Dr. Wynn's hands were plunged inside her body as though searching a tightly packed suitcase. She so wanted to see the gemellius she'd carried within her for almost fourteen years now, but it remained hidden.

A slap sounded and the baby began crying. "Nurse, if you would," she heard Dr. Wynn say. Hanna scanned the ceiling for any clue. "And now, the *funicular cerebrum*—"

Uncle Rick turned his back. Aunt Azami hugged him tightly.

Everything went black. Too dark for an electrical outage. Emptiness, a void.

"I can't see," Hanna heard herself say.

"That's the severing of the *funicular*," she heard Dr. Wynn say. "It's perfectly normal."

Over the infant's crying, she heard her parents saying *She's so beautiful* and *Isn't she precious?* and baby-talk. Steel medical instruments were set on trays with clangs and tinkles. Carts of equipment were wheeled way. A hard clamping fist pinched together the flaps of her deflated belly. Due to the massive local Dr. Wynn had pumped into her abdomen, Hanna could not feel his final medical duties, a quick run of sutures stitched across her gaping belly. They sealed Hanna's innards and prevented them from slopping out while her corpse was in transit down the mountain. "We're done here," she heard Dr. Wynn say.

Hanna writhed against the straps. The nurse pushed the gurney headfirst through swinging double doors and out of the delivery room, leaving the doting parents with their new baby daughter. In the finality room, Nurse Halper locked the gurney's wheels and disconnected the IV from Hanna's arm. "Only a minute or two now," she said to Hanna who, mouth gaping and blank eyes searching for light, thrashed and tossed about.

Dr. Wynn washed up at the hands-free sink in the corner. Hanna's parents cooed and cradled the swaddled infant. The nurse emerged from the finality room to rejoin the others. Before the swinging doors behind her could close, Uncle Rick stepped in her path. He held a clipboard and pen.

"I'm supposed to be witnessing this," he said. "I'm kind of lost with the paperwork." Rick used his height and girth as a barrier between the nurse and Azami behind him. "I was hoping you could help me fill out this section?"

The nurse leaned in to assist Rick. On lithe feet, Azami slipped unseen around his mass and through the swinging doors before they shut.

In the dim finality room, Azami crept to the gurney and leaned to Hanna's ear. "These are for you," she whispered. She pushed the bouquet to Hanna's nose.

The feathery butterflies of the flower petals danced against her cheeks and lips. Their strong, overpowering perfume filled Hanna's nostrils and sang to her. She inhaled and inhaled, determined for their fragrant symphony to be her final aspiration.

Heady and joyous, Hanna relented. The thousandth *tsuru*, crushed, dropped from her now-limp hand. It rolled headlong across the floor and under a cabinet, where it came to live among the dust there.

Jim Nelson's books include *A Concordance of One's Life, Everywhere Man,* and *Edward Teller Dreams of Barbecuing People*. He lives in San Francisco.

Made in the USA
Monee, IL
01 May 2021